The Golden Hour

Janna Miller

Contents

Dedication

For My Dad,
Richard Effland
A man who could fix anything.
Even if that broken thing was me.
I miss you dad, everyday

Chapter 1

Alice lay awake, staring at the ceiling.

Go check on her, the thought whispered.

No—you already did that, twice. But that was hours ago. What if something had changed?

More than once, she had slipped into Rowan's room, rocking in the same chair where she'd soothed her as a baby, watching her chest rise and fall. Rowan was sixteen now, too old to need her mother's constant watch. But Alice couldn't stop. Not when each breath felt like a fragile promise, not when one missed heartbeat could mean life or death.

Beside her, Jonathan slept deeply. Alice envied his calm as she pulled the comforter back over him before slipping into her robe. She paused outside Rowan's door, hand on the knob, listening to the silence. *Just a quick peek*, her mind urged. Alice hovered a moment longer then forced herself to let go.

Downstairs, she started the coffee, the quiet pressing in. Fear followed her everywhere, even into the kitchen. Alice was putting breakfast on the table when Ian bound in, a whirlwind of soccer gear.

"What's cooking? I'm starving."

Alice raised an eyebrow. "You're always starving," Alice replied. "Honestly, I don't know where you put it all. I have made scrambled eggs, pancakes, and bacon."

"Yes please," he said.

"Yes what? Which do you want?" Alice asked.

"All the above" Ian shot back.

Alice brought out the food and watched as Ian loaded up his plate and then drowned all of it, eggs and bacon included, in maple syrup, and tucked in. Something about watching your kid woof down food is so comforting.

"Did you happen to see if your sister was up and about?"

"I heard some stupid boy band music playing from the upstairs bathroom, so yes, her Royal Highness is up, dressing for the ball. Dad had talk radio going on in your bathroom, so that was out. I was lucky you weren't in the bathroom downstairs, or I would have had to piss outside and shower with the hose."

"Ian, language please." Alice scolded, though she turned away to hide her smile. Her son had a knack for making her laugh—it was his superpower. Though it is fleeting, even a few seconds away from the doom and gloom she constantly walked around with was a welcome distraction.

Jonathan entered next, juggling his work bag and an avalanche of blueprints. After rescuing them from rolling across the floor, he gave Alice a quick kiss on the cheek.

She relayed the breakfast menu, and, like Ian, he requested everything. Rowan was the last to enter impeccably dressed and smelling of floral body spray.

"Good morning, princess," Alice greeted her with a teasing smile. "How is Her Royal Highness today?"

Rowan sighed dramatically. "Oh, you know, the hassle of it all, making myself presentable for the commoners."

Ian looked up and said "Oh, good you're done in the bathroom after an hour and a half. I had to take a bird bath in the downstairs powder room using that foam peach soap and sinking balls deep in that furry rug moms got in there."

"Ian Miller, language...again! I'm telling you, last warning or Pastor Carl with have you scrubbing the church bathrooms all weekend." Alice said.

She looked over at Jonathan for support, but he was concentrating very hard on his food, barely able to contain himself with laughter. He looked up and saw Alice glaring at him. He cleared his throat and said to Ian, "Ok, dude, let's keep it clean."

Ian said "I AM trying to keep "it" clean, using air quotes. Do you know how hard it is to wash your di..."

Alice cut in fast...lightly swatting him on the head "Don't you dare!" knowing what he was about to say.

Rowan looked at her brother as she sat down and said, "You are so totally gross, I can't even believe we are related."

Alice picked up a plate and said to Rowan, "Would you like eggs or pancakes or both?"

"Just juice." She said.

Alice's smile faltered. "You need something to eat. Taking your medications on an empty stomach never ends well." Alice said as she scooped some eggs onto Rowan's plate.

"I said, I'm not hungry," Rowan said flatly.

Alice's glare stayed firm on her daughter.

Rowan stared at the plate and then slammed her hands on the table. "For God's sakes mother, I am not going to force feed myself if I'm not hungry!"

The room froze. Jonathan and Ian stared, forks midair.

Alice continued eye contact on her daughter's defiant stare, sadness rising like a tide. Such a small thing—skipping breakfast—could unravel everything. Every minute of every day is made up of these moments. These ordinary decisions Rowan must navigate.

Rowan looked down, eyes closed tight and said in a soft whisper, "Maybe a peach with the juice."

Wordlessly, Alice placed the juice, peach and then a small paper cup of pills, in front of her, watching as Rowan swallowed them two at a time. Alice saw her tears welling up. Angry..her daughter was so very angry. All day, every day. Jonathan reached across the table, silent but steady, and gave Rowan's arm a squeeze.

After Rowan took the pills, Alice exhaled, but the fear never left. Not when every morning felt like a battle against time. Either time to heal, or time to lose it all. They all lived with that dark cloud over them. Any deviance from the regimen could cause a relapse and that is not an option.

Alice went to the laundry room and brought out a freshly laundered cheer uniform just as Rowan was asking if it was ready to go. As Rowan kissed her cheek before leaving, Alice caught the word she longed for: "Thanks, momma." Alice gave a smile was glad the morning ended in "momma" and not "mother."

Alice stopped doing the morning "bag check" as that never went over well. Rowan resented the implication that she does not know how to take care of herself.

Instead, she had started to slip into Rowan's room at night when she was in the shower to make sure all her equipment and medication were in her bag and charged. pulse ox, BP cuff, nitro, salt pills, and extra water. Lastly, she would check the top handle of her backpack to make sure Rowan's medical alert necklace was attached. If it was on her bag, she would remember to put it on before she left. Alice knew she should trust Rowan, but she just could not let go of those reins. Teenage rebellion for Rowan could have deadly consequences.

The end of the morning battle soothed her for a moment. But as the door slammed three times, Alice's heart clenched. She mentally started counting the hours before Rowan would be back home under her watchful eye. She said a quick prayer that all would be well for the day. One day at a time now was the only way Alice could function. The clock was always ticking.

Chapter 2

After finishing the breakfast cleanup, Alice heads up to her study, hoping to get in a few hours of writing. She is now in the third week of writer's block. Before she can begin, she first checks her email and MyChart for Rowan. Managing Rowan's medical needs has become a full-time job—one that Alice agreed to take on when Jonathan's firm really took off. He used to help with everything—the emails from doctors' offices, the medical reports on MyChart—but Alice always found herself double-checking things. It wasn't that she thought Jonathan was incapable; she knew he was. But if she wasn't in the driver's seat, it made her an anxiety-ridden mess. Eventually, Jonathan let go of the reins, content to receive updates as needed.

Each side of Alice's desk has a set of bookends. On one side, there's a dictionary, a thesaurus, and various bound and spiral notebooks. She has notebooks scattered throughout the house—one in the car, one in her purse. She has lost count of how many times she has reached for a notebook in the grocery store, at a doctor's appointment, or even during a hair appointment. She even keeps one next to her bed because sometimes, she wakes up in the middle of the night with an idea that will disappear just as quickly if she doesn't write it down. On the other side of the desk, another set of bookends holds various medical books and publications, as well as a binder containing all of Rowan's visit summaries and test results from her various doctors and specialists. Alice maintains a detailed spreadsheet of all of Rowan's medications—what has worked, what hasn't, and what worked until it didn't. It's tedious, but Alice believes it's imperative to be fluent in Rowan's conditions so she can advocate for her daughter. Rowan's doctors have many credentials, but they aren't her mother, and no doctor, *no doctor*, no matter how qualified, knows Rowan like Alice does.

Alice picks up her coffee and gazes out at the lake, her mind drifting back to that Tuesday two years ago when Rowan was in ninth grade. The day had started out like any other getting everyone up, fed, and out the door. Looking back, Alice realizes that was the moment their lives became divided into "before" and "after." The "after" has sent them on a journey that continues to this day. There had been warning signs, but no one expects their fourteen-year-old to have a heart and blood pressure condition. At first, she had attributed Rowan's pale skin, lack of appetite, low energy, and poor stamina to typical teenage habits—staying up too late, stressing over school drama, and general moodiness.

Then came the first call. There would be many more to come, but she would never forget the first one. The school nurse had called to inform Alice that Rowan had passed out in cheerleading practice. Though she had regained consciousness, they had called an ambulance as a precaution. Alice had been momentarily paralyzed with fear before her maternal instincts kicked in. She ran out the door, dropping her purse twice on the way to the car. She called Jonathan, furious that his assistant didn't immediately recognize the urgency in her voice. When he finally picked up, she sobbed through the explanation. Driving to the hospital in a frenzy, she honked and flashed her lights at anyone in her way.

At the ER, a bored-looking attendant asked for Rowan's name and date of birth. Alice provided the information, watching as the woman slowly typed on her computer.

"She came by ambulance," Alice said, receiving no immediate response.

"She's only fourteen," Alice added, hoping to convey the urgency. The attendant finally glanced up.

"She's in room twelve," she said, pressing the button that opened the ER doors.

Alice rushed through, scanning the signs for room twelve, momentarily disoriented as she struggled to distinguish left from right. Finally, she found it. Rowan lay there, pale as a sheet, an oxygen mask over her face, an IV in her arm. A nurse's aide sat beside her. The aide introduced herself, but Alice barely registered it and started firing off a barrage of questions.

"I'm a nursing assistant and I have no information about your daughter, I'm just here because she is a minor." the woman said, holding up a hand. "Let me get your daughter's doctor."

Jonathan arrived just as Rowan stirred.

"Hey there, punkins'. What's all this about?" he asked gently. Rowan gave a small shrug before closing her eyes again. Only then did Jonathan seem to register Alice's presence.

"What happened?" he asked.

"I don't know yet," Alice said, never taking her eyes off Rowan.

She took Rowan's hand, squeezing it. Rowan opened her eyes briefly, smiled faintly, then closed them again.

"Momma's here, punkins'. I'm right here, and so is Daddy."

Alice was on the verge of hysteria when the doctor walked in. Her first thought was that he looked incredibly young. Way too young.

"Hello, I'm Dr. Gregory," he said, washing his hands before shaking theirs. Alice remembers that her first thought was that this kid graduated medical school sometime in the last month. He was so young. Appearing to be barely out of his twenties, and yet *this* was our doctor. Alice immediately launched into questions. To his credit, Dr. Gregory let her finish before responding.

"Since you gave the school nurse permission to treat Rowan, I started with some blood tests. She's stable. Her results show dehydration, which could explain everything, especially if she was exerting herself in cheer practice. Her heart enzymes were slightly off, but that's common with dehydration. It can make the heartbeat faster than normal. Her oxygen was a bit low, which is why she has the mask, but as you can see here,"—he pointed to the monitor—"she's back to normal. He moved closer and gently removed the mask. "Most of the time, with kids, this can be very scary, and they tend to hyperventilate due to the fear, which can make oxygen saturation low. The combination of dehydration and stress is likely what made her lethargic."

9

"So, she's okay? Just dehydrated?" Alice asked.

Dr. Gregory nodded. "Yes. I'd like to keep her until the saline drip finishes. After that, I'll check her vitals again and release her. She should stay home and rest for a few days and I will provide you with a note for school. I also recommend a follow-up with her pediatrician."

"That would be Dr. McMillian," Alice said.

"I know Dr. McMillian well. I'll send him all my notes and test results. He may want to run additional tests."

Alice tensed.

Dr. Gregory raised a hand reassuringly. "Sorry, I didn't mean to alarm you. I doubt he'll see the need, but it's good to keep him informed."

Rowan stirred and looked around, her gaze settling on Dr. Gregory. "What happened?" she asked.

He explained it in simple terms. "You were dehydrated, which means your body was thirsty and needed more water. When you are at cheer practice, you have to drink plenty of fluids. If you do, this shouldn't happen again. I want you to rest for the next few days. Nothing strenuous."

Rowan's eyes widened and said, "So I can't cheer at the Friday night football game? I have to cheer; I'm the captain and..." Rowan looked down a slight blush on her face. Alice knew she was thinking of Corey, the star quarterback. They had been "talking" as the kids say, but both dancing around one another, too shy to "*make a move*." "Sorry kiddo, I'm going to have to bench you, for that game at least." Dr. Frederick said

10

Rowan crossed her arms across her chest and just nodded. When she looked up at Dr. Frederick again she had a hopeful look on her face. "I don't have to miss church do I?"

Alice knew this question would be confusing to Dr. Frederick, so she chimed in. "Did you ever hear of a "*hand raising church*"? Half our worship is up on our feet singing and dancing to Christian rock." Alice looked pointedly at Rowan and said, "so it is more *strenuous* than say a Catholic service." Alice knew that Rowan was strong in her faith, but she had another reason for not wanting to miss church. Corey and his family went there as well. Dividing his time between playing the guitar and sitting in the youth group section with all the other teenagers.

"Ah, ok I understand. Well, my answer is the same. You can certainly go to church, but no rocking it out. However, I will clear you to resume normal activities the next week, Ok?

Rowan huffed and then nodded. "Can I at least have something to drink and eat? I missed lunch."

Dr. Gregory smiled. "That, I can do. I'll have the aide bring you some ginger ale and graham crackers. How would that be?" Rowan nodded yes with a smile. "Good. So, when the IV finishes, press the button for the nurse. I'll check on you before you leave."

Rowan nodded again.

Dr. Gregory gave a final smile and wave as he left. Alice didn't know it then, but this was only the beginning of a very, very long journey.

Chapter 3

I n the weeks that followed, life seemed to return to normal—at least for everyone else. But Alice, ever the "hover mother" (or "helicopter mom," as Ian teasingly called her), was monitoring Rowan's every move. If she sensed Rowan hadn't been drinking enough, a bottle of water would magically appear in front of her. Needless to say, Rowan was not amused.

"I'm not a baby, Mother. I know how to drink. It was a one-off, so just drop it, okay?" Rowan had said about two weeks after the "episode," as they had begun calling it.

Jonathan, always ready to play the role of "daddy's little girl's" rescuer, finally intervened. Finding Alice in the laundry room, he shut the door and addressed her.

"Alice, I think you need to back off a bit. She was running around too much in cheer practice and got dehydrated. That can happen to anyone. Sometimes, when I'm on the golf course, I feel a little dehydrated too. Now I make sure to grab two bottles of water at the clubhouse, so I have enough by the time I reach the smaller clubhouse on the back nine."

That was Jonathan for you—practical, logical, always putting things in perspective. It infuriated Alice because it was a skill she had never mastered. She reacted first, then thought things through. However, in times of true emergency, it was Jonathan who froze up, leaving Alice to take charge. This time, however, she wasn't budging.

"She passed out! What if she collapses at cheer practice? What if she falls on the hard gym floor? Or worse, what if she's mid-routine, and she drops another girl because she loses consciousness first?"

Jonathan cut in. "Yes, all those things could happen. Or she could get hit by a meteor. Or struck by lightning. Or a deranged panda bear could escape from the zoo and attack her."

Alice glared. "So, this is funny to you?"

"No," Jonathan replied. "Rowan passing out and going to the hospital is in no way funny. But it's been two weeks, and she's fine. You're sending her to school with an extra lunchbox just for bottled water. Look, you are by far the world's best mother," he said, pulling her into a hug, "but you tend to be a little... overbearing. She's fourteen. Would you have wanted your mom to show up at your cheer practice to make sure you were drinking enough?"

Alice sighed. "I only did that once! I just wanted to make sure Lauren knew what was going on." Lauren, the cheer coach, had a reputation for being strict about breaks. But she was also an excellent coach, and the team had won many competitions under her leadership.

Jonathan continued, "And I get that. But a phone call would have sufficed. And as it turned out, not even that was necessary, because...?"

Alice exhaled. "Because Rowan had already told her, and Lauren was giving her extra breaks when she needed them."

Jonathan turned her around to face him. "So, it seems Rowan has it under control. Try to hold back a little, okay? I know it's hard for you, but I agree with her—this was a one-time thing. At most, she just needs to be more conscious about hydration."

Alice was quiet for a few seconds, then nodded. "Okay, I'll try."

What she didn't tell Jonathan, however, was that she still planned to watch Rowan like a hawk. That was a "momma thing," and he just wouldn't understand.

As more time passed, Alice relaxed, slowly coming around to the idea that it really had been a one-time event. Rowan resumed her normal routine at home and school, and her first cheer practice after the incident came and went without issue. The reprieve, however, was short-lived.

A few weeks later, as Alice sat in her study, finally getting some writing done, her phone rang. It was Lauren.

"Alice, it's happening again. Rowan passed out at practice."

Alice nearly dropped the phone. "What! What happened?"

"She wasn't even doing anything. All the girls were sitting on the bleachers while I explained the cheers for Friday's game. She was drinking her water, just sitting there. When it was time to stand up and start, she got up and then just collapsed. Blake caught her before she hit the ground, thank God. She came around after about thirty seconds, but she was really out of it. The nurse is with her now, and we've called an ambulance."

Alice was already grabbing her purse and shoving her feet into her shoes. "I'm on my way."

Lauren stopped her. "The ambulance just pulled in. You're better off meeting her at the ER than trying to get here before they leave."

Alice changed course and headed straight for the ER, calling Jonathan as she sped down the road.

"She went down again at practice! She wasn't even moving this time! Do you still think I'm overreacting?"

Jonathan's voice was calm but firm. "Slow down, Alice. I can hear how fast you're going. I'm heading to the ER now."

Alice hung up without saying another word. Usually, every call ended with a quick "love you," but not this time. Jonathan had been dismissive before. Now, though, she suspected he was rethinking that stance.

When she arrived at the ER, the same receptionist was at the desk. This time, she didn't even need to ask.

"She's in room nine, down the hall to the right."

Alice reached the room just as two nurses were setting up an IV and attaching sticky pads and wires to Rowan's chest. Alice fought the urge to push past them, instead settling near the top of the bed.

She gently rubbed Rowan's head. "I'm here, sweetheart."

Rowan barely stirred, her pale face even whiter than before. Oxygen was being administered again.

Alice turned to the nurses. "What are those stickers for? What's going on? Has she seen a doctor yet?"

One of the nurses, barely looking up, replied, "Dr. Gregory has already been in. He's running tests. We're setting up an EKG to monitor her heart activity."

Alice felt a wave of panic. "Her heart? What's wrong with her heart? I want to speak to Dr. Gregory now."

The nurse barely reacted. "He's busy with other patients. He'll update you when the test results come back."

The other nurse, sensing Alice's distress, intervened. "I know the results aren't back yet, but I understand this is scary. Let me see if I can get him in here just to put you at ease."

Jonathan arrived just as the nurses left. He rushed to Rowan's bedside, his face full of concern. She looked so small and fragile, and when Alice touched her hand, it was ice cold.

Alice was in a daze but managed to indicate that one of the nurses was going to inform him they were there. They both pulled their chairs up to the bed—Alice continued clutching Rowan's hand, while Jonathan gently rubbed Rowan's leg as if trying to warm her up.

Alice tried to reassure herself that Rowan was so cold because the room was cold. But the thought offered little consolation, especially when she realized she was barely chilly herself, yet her daughter felt like a block of ice.

She glanced around the room, really taking it in for the first time. A chilling thought crept into her mind—how many people had died in this very room? How many had gone about their day, unaware that they would end up here, never to leave alive?

With growing unease, she studied the medical equipment that took up half the space—machines she had only seen on TV shows like *ER* or *Chicago Med*. These were the machines that brought people back to life. But how often did they fail? How many times a day, a week, or even a month were they used in a losing battle?

Alice shuddered. A wave of dizziness washed over her, making her feel just as pale and weak as Rowan. She forced herself to push the thoughts away. *Rowan isn't in that category. If she were, she'd be surrounded by doctors, with those very machines beeping and flashing in a desperate attempt to save her.* The logic helped—a little. But not much.

Jonathan was uncharacteristically quiet this time. Maybe he felt guilty for not taking things more seriously before. Maybe he was contrite, ashamed at having told Alice to "chill out" about the whole situation. Or maybe, she realized, he was now just as terrified as she was.

Jonathan had always been levelheaded, but even he had his limits. When things truly became overwhelming, he had a tendency to freeze—like a deer caught in headlights.

The little tiffs and past admonishments no longer mattered. Alice reached over and took Jonathan's hand, giving it a firm squeeze. He squeezed back.

That small gesture carried so much weight— apologies, understanding, unspoken fears—but most importantly, it meant they were on the same team again.

And whatever happened next, they would face it together.

Chapter 4

They waited for what felt like an eternity for the test results. Rowan slept most of the time, waking only briefly and that was to check if Corey had texted her, which he had multiple times. It's one of the only normal teenage things she's able to have right now and Alice was grateful for that. Finally, Dr. Gregory entered the room. Though he smiled, it wasn't as reassuring as before, immediately putting Alice and Jonathan on edge. Alice stood, ready to speak, but Dr. Gregory began first.

"I know you both have a lot of questions. This situation," he gestured to Rowan and the monitoring machines, "is a bit different from the last time she was here. She was dehydrated then, and that is again the case today…"

Alice cut in, "That can't be possible! She drinks at least six to eight bottles of water a day. I've made sure of it."

Dr. Gregory held up a hand. "I understand, and I believe she's been following my hydration directive. However, while she is dehydrated, it's not as severe as last time. What concerns me is that despite her increased fluid intake, her bloodwork still indicates dehydration. Her heart rate was elevated last time as well, which I initially attributed to the anxiety of passing out. But now, after being here for over thirty minutes, mostly asleep, her resting heart rate is still 115 bpm. That's tachycardia—anything over 100 bpm is considered elevated. Given that, I ordered an EKG, which is why she has the leads on. The results were unremarkable, meaning no abnormalities were detected at the time of the test."

Jonathan spoke next. "What do you mean, 'at the time of the test'? Does that mean there could be an abnormality you didn't catch?"

"Yes," Dr. Gregory admitted. "Unfortunately, unless a cardiac event is happening during the test, it won't show up. However, let's focus on the fact that right now, her EKG is normal. As with last time, her heart rate has started to regulate itself with IV fluids. When she arrived, it was 135 bpm, but it's coming down naturally as she rehydrates. Her bloodwork also showed low sodium levels, which could be related to her fluid intake. The body needs sodium for normal muscle and nerve function, and it helps balance body fluids. Excess fluid intake can dilute sodium in the blood, causing cells to swell— a condition called 'water intoxication,' which can be serious. But Rowan's six to eight bottles per day wouldn't cause that. That amount is standard for everyone, so I don't believe overhydration is the cause."

Alice felt overwhelmed by the medical jargon. She needed him to get to the point.

She tightened her grip on Rowan's hand and asked, "So, what does this all mean? What's wrong with her?"

Dr. Gregory sighed, his smile now completely gone. "The short answer is, I don't know. And I know that's not what you want to hear. As an ER doctor, there's only so much I can do. I'm beginning to feel like this is beyond my expertise. I'd like to refer Rowan to a cardiologist, Dr. Frederick Mason. He's highly regarded, particularly with pediatric patients."

Alice felt the blood drain from her face. Jonathan squeezed her hand, signaling that he was just as shaken. Dr. Gregory continued, clearly noticing their reaction.

"I'm not saying there's something wrong with Rowan's heart. This could be a hematology issue, and the tachycardia might be a secondary symptom. Hematology deals with blood disorders. My bigger concern is the persistent dehydration and low sodium levels. The paramedics noted that Rowan had been sitting for fifteen minutes before she passed out at cheer practice, which makes it odd that her heart rate spiked without exertion. It could still be dehydration, but I want Dr. Mason to take a look. He has multiple specialists within his practice and takes a holistic approach. Think of it as a one-stop shop."

Jonathan and Alice exchanged glances before looking at Rowan, still asleep. Alice was grateful she wouldn't have to hear this right now. She and Jonathan needed to process everything before explaining it to her.

Dr. Gregory continued, "You're free to find your own specialist, but I trust Dr. Mason. If there's something deeper going on, he's the one to find it."

Jonathan turned to Alice, who nodded slightly. "No, we'll go with Dr. Mason if you think he's the best option."

"I do," Dr. Gregory confirmed. "I can call his office and get her scheduled. ER referrals can often get patients in faster."

Alice exhaled in relief at the thought of seeing a specialist sooner rather than later. "Yes, please set up the appointment as soon as possible."

Dr. Gregory nodded. "It's still early in the day. I'll call now. I also want Rowan to stay for another IV bag before discharge. If she wakes up hungry or thirsty, you can call the nurse or grab her something from the cafeteria." He offered a small smile. "I'm also sending you home with a prescription for salt pills—one per day until Dr. Mason advises otherwise. We don't want to overdo it, but we need to address the sodium deficiency."

Alice and Jonathan nodded, fear making it difficult to form words.

Dr. Gregory moved toward the door, then turned back. "You're going to worry—I get that. But keep in mind, this is likely something manageable. It's just beyond what an ER doctor can handle."

Alice could only nod. Dr. Gregory seemed to understand their silence, recognizing it for what it was—sheer fear.

Chapter 5

D r. Gregory certainly worked some "doctor magic" because, within a week, Alice and Rowan were sitting in the waiting room of Dr. Mason's office. This was the first time Rowan had been out of the house since her ER visit. Dr. Gregory had said she could return to school in a few days, but Alice wasn't comfortable with that. She contacted Rowan's teachers, letting them know she would be out until after her appointment with Dr. Mason. The teachers were understanding and prepared a week's worth of schoolwork for Alice to pick up. Rowan wasn't thrilled about missing cheer practice, but Alice reassured her that, after speaking with Coach Lauren, her spot on the team was secure. What Alice didn't mention was that the coach had said Rowan wouldn't be allowed back without full medical clearance. Rowan was already upset enough; she didn't need to hear that too.

Dr. Mason's medical office occupied an entire floor of the building. It truly was a one-stop shop, just as Dr. Gregory had described. The facility had rooms for sonograms, ultrasounds, tilt-table tests (whatever that was), stress tests, EKGs, EEGs, and even a cardiac catheterization procedure room. Several specialists were also on staff—a neurologist, a hematologist, an immunologist, a cardiac surgeon, and, of course, Dr. Mason himself. Alice felt like they were wrapped in a medical safety net. Surely, with all these resources, they would figure out what was wrong with her daughter.

Even though it was early—only 8:00 a.m.—the waiting room was already crowded. Alice noticed that many people had been there before they arrived, making her wonder if she had got the time wrong. She asked the receptionist just to be sure.

"No, you're right on time," the woman assured her. "We have many doctors and testing rooms. Some people are here just for a doctor's visit, some for follow-up tests, and some for both. We ask patients to set aside at least five hours per visit. In Rowan's case, she's here for a full workup, so you'll be here most of the day."

Rowan groaned, but Alice was relieved. She was willing to stay all night if it meant getting answers.

The waiting room was comfortable, with cushioned chairs and couches. The walls were painted in calming shades of light green and muted gray. There were vending machines for drinks and snacks and even a coffee bar, which Alice gratefully took advantage of. Rowan, as usual, had her earbuds in. The music was so loud that Alice could hear every word, though she couldn't understand how anyone could stand listening at that volume. Rowan was also scrolling through Instagram, occasionally chuckling at something. Alice didn't mind being shut out; she knew this was how her daughter coped. She buried herself in social media and music, escaping into someone else's world, even if only for a little while.

Alice glanced around the room. Some kids were younger than Rowan, some older. A few were on oxygen. Others were in wheelchairs. Some had medical ports visible under their shirts. Alice took a deep breath and tried to focus on the book she had brought, but she found herself rereading

24

the same paragraph three times. *Why are we here?"* she thought. *This happens to other people, not us.*

It was a selfish thought, and she knew it, but she couldn't help herself.

The night before, Laura—her best friend since Rowan and her son, Dylan, were in kindergarten—had called from Hawaii to check in. Alice filled her in on everything she knew so far, including the upcoming appointment with Dr. Mason.

"Everything will be fine," Laura had reassured her. "It sounds like she's in good hands. I bet it's just something minor—maybe a vitamin deficiency or something easily managed."

Alice appreciated her friend's optimism, but when she hung up, she felt worse. Not just because she was worried about Rowan but because Laura was on vacation, enjoying time with her healthy family in a beautiful place. Alice hated the wave of jealousy that washed over her. She vowed to text Laura later—not just to give an update, but to tell her to enjoy her vacation and have fun. *She deserves that,* Alice thought. *And I miss her.*

After an hour, they were called back, expecting to see Dr. Mason. Instead, they were greeted by his medical case manager, a young woman with a warm smile. She entered the room, extending her hand before she had even fully stepped inside. She was petite, with long, curly blonde hair loosely braided. Her scrub top was covered in emoji designs, which immediately caught Rowan's attention.

"So, my name is Abby, and I'm Dr. Mason's medical case manager," she introduced herself. "I also help the other doctors when needed, but I primarily work with Dr. Mason's patients. I'm a nurse, but my role is more administrative."

Abby explained that she handled new patient profiles, scheduled tests, and coordinated appointments with other specialists within the practice. She emphasized that they took a team-based approach, meaning Dr. Mason worked closely with the other doctors to ensure every aspect of a patient's care was addressed. Alice immediately felt at ease. Glancing at Rowan, she could tell her daughter felt a sense of relief as well. Dr. Gregory had made the right call.

Abby sat down and opened a folder. "I've reviewed Rowan's medical records from the hospital, and Dr. Mason has too. The ER visit gave us a good starting point, but we'll be running a lot of tests today." She paused, seeing the concern on Alice's face. "I don't say that to scare you. Dr. Mason is extremely thorough—he leaves no stone unturned."

She then turned to Rowan. "Let's start from the beginning. Take me through everything, day one to now."

Alice began recounting the events leading up to Rowan's hospital visits, but Abby gently interrupted. "I already know the medical details," she said, smiling. "What I want to know is how *you* have been feeling, Rowan. Were you feeling off before the incidents? Any changes in your appetite, sleep patterns, stress levels? Have you noticed anything different—maybe dizziness, irregular heartbeats, fatigue? Anything at all?"

Alice was grateful Abby directed these questions at Rowan. She had asked similar things before but had only gotten vague answers. Rowan had been trying to downplay everything from the beginning. But now, perhaps because she was being asked by someone new, she finally opened up.

"I've been feeling really tired all the time," Rowan admitted. "I get worn out in school, and it's hard to concentrate or stay awake. Walking up and down the stairs between classes makes me feel out of breath. The first time I passed out, I felt lightheaded. But the second time, I don't remember anything—I just kind of... melted to the floor."

Then she giggled. "Well, I *melted* into my friend Blake, who basically caught me. Which is funny because I'm a foot taller than her and outweigh her by like twenty pounds."

Alice sat in stunned silence. Rowan had never mentioned any of this before—to her, Jonathan, or Dr. Gregory. She looked at her daughter, realizing just how much she had kept inside.

Rowan sighed and looked at her. "I'm sorry, Momma. I just thought I was stressed from school and cheer practice. And, um... I was struggling with my grades because I was too tired to study. I didn't want you to know I was resting instead of doing schoolwork. I thought I could fix it before report cards came out."

Alice looked away, taking a deep breath. A whirlwind of emotions ran through her—frustration, guilt, sadness. But before she could respond, Abby spoke up.

"That's pretty normal," Abby said with a chuckle. "When I was fourteen, my standard answers to my mom were 'it's fine', 'nothing", and her personal favorite, "whatever."

Alice smiled weakly. She had done the same thing at Rowan's age. But deep down, she knew—this wasn't *nothing*.

It was *something*. Every maternal instinct screamed that this was far from *fine*. And whether the doctors realized it yet or not, Alice was certain of one thing: something was wrong with her daughter. *Terribly, unmistakably wrong.*

Chapter 6

T hey spent the remainder of the appointment moving from one room to the next, undergoing a battery of tests. Before each one, Abby explained its purpose and procedure. It was a lot of information to take in, but Alice did her best to jot down notes in her journal so she could research them later. Eleven vials of blood, a tilt table test, a stress test, an EKG, an EEG, an orthostatic test, a head CT, and finally, an ultrasound. Rowan handled everything like a trooper, but after several hours, the exhaustion was evident on her face. Alice, despite not undergoing any tests herself, felt drained.

Jonathan had called several times throughout the day, and each time Alice provided what little updates she could. She explained which test Rowan was currently undergoing but admitted that much of it blurred together. She reassured him they would go over everything together and have a long research session once they got home. She knew he felt guilty for not being there, but his client presentation was critical for his firm. Alice had even reassured him earlier that having both of them present might make Rowan more anxious, reinforcing the idea that something was seriously wrong.

Alice had spent much of the day mindlessly scrolling through Facebook or staring at her book without truly reading. She knew that Rowan took her emotional cues from her, so she made a conscious effort to appear calm and unfazed. If she remained steady, Rowan wouldn't be as stressed.

By the time Dr. Mason entered the exam room, Rowan was fast asleep on the exam table. Alice instinctively moved to wake her, but Dr. Mason raised a hand.

"I've put her through a lot today. Let's talk for a few minutes before we wake her."

Dr. Mason appeared to be in his mid-fifties, his hair beginning to turn salt and pepper. He was tall, with the lean build of an avid jogger. If not for the white doctor's coat and stethoscope around his neck, you wouldn't know he was a doctor. He wore a soft grey suit, complete with vest, and a crisp white shirt. Alice could see a gold chain which, she presumed, was tethered to a pocket watch. His handshake was warm and reassuring, much like his smile. When he spoke, his voice had a smooth candence..dignified, just like the outfit suggested. Alice felt herself relax slightly. She could see why he worked well with children.

Checking the time, Alice realized Jonathan's presentation should be over.

"Can I call my husband and put him on speakerphone? He wanted to be here, but he couldn't get away."

Dr. Mason nodded. "Of course."

Alice quickly dialed Jonathan via FaceTime so he could both hear and see Dr. Mason.

"I'm sure you both have plenty of questions, and I'll do my best to answer them," Dr. Mason began. "These initial appointments take time, but future visits will be shorter. Some tests will be repeated regularly, while others only every few months. We try to consolidate as much as possible so parents don't have to take off work for frequent individual tests."

Alice smiled wearily, her eyes welling with tears. "I work from home as a writer, but as of about five days ago, my full-time job is taking care of my daughter. Since you're talking about future visits, does that mean you know what's wrong?"

Dr. Mason nodded, not in confirmation, as if he had anticipated that question.

"I've run a significant number of tests on her today, so let's go through them. One of the key tests was the tilt table test, which helps determine the cause of syncope—what we call fainting. It monitors changes in blood pressure and heart rate as the patient moves from lying to standing. We also did an orthostatic test, which is similar but performed in a standing position, measuring blood pressure at intervals while she moved from lying down to walking. Both tests gave me the same result."

Alice recalled that test but had only been told it was a blood pressure assessment.

Dr. Mason continued, "I also ordered extensive bloodwork, particularly because her hydration and sodium levels were low during both ER visits. Those results remain concerning—her sodium levels are still low, and she is slightly dehydrated. Not as severely as before, but Abby mentioned that you've been making sure she drinks plenty of water, yet she remains dehydrated. That's unusual. I also see from Dr. Gregory's notes that he prescribed sodium tablets. Has she been taking them?"

Alice's throat felt dry. She simply nodded, confirming she had followed instructions precisely. A creeping sense of unease filled her.

Dr. Mason's expression remained neutral as he continued. "I am fairly certain that Rowan has POTS— Postural Orthostatic Tachycardia Syndrome."

Alice felt her mind search for recognition of the term and came up blank.

Jonathan spoke first. "What is that? I've never heard of it."

Alice could hear him typing rapidly, undoubtedly on Google, searching for answers online.

"POTS is a syndrome, not a disease," Dr. Mason explained. "It's characterized by a heart rate increase of at least thirty beats per minute within ten minutes of standing. In Rowan's case, she failed both the orthostatic and tilt table tests, meaning her heart rate spiked significantly. This rapid heart rate, or tachycardia, often causes dizziness, fatigue, and fainting. The root issue is a dysfunction of the autonomic nervous system, known as dysautonomia. Essentially, her body struggles to regulate blood flow and pressure when she moves between positions."

Alice nodded slowly, absorbing every word. Jonathan had gone silent.

"These episodes can lead to syncope, or fainting, because the brain isn't receiving enough oxygenated blood quickly enough. Think of it like a computer freezing up. When your screen stops responding, you hold the power button down until it reboots. That's what's happening with Rowan— her brain essentially 'reboots' when it isn't getting the proper signals."

Alice swallowed hard. "So, is this a blood pressure issue? Not her heart?"

"Yes and no," Dr. Mason said gently. "The syndrome causes the tachycardia, which impacts the heart. Prolonged episodes of extreme tachycardia can cause heart damage over time. However, it's a symptom of POTS, not a heart disease itself."

Alice exhaled in partial relief—until Dr. Mason added, "That said, Rowan does have mild mitral valve prolapse, or MVP—a minor heart murmur. This means the valve flaps don't close properly, but in her case, there's no regurgitation of blood. It's not a major concern, but with her tachycardia, we will monitor it."

Alice's mind reeled. The word *heart* clung to her, tightening her chest. She felt exhausted, both physically and emotionally. She wanted to go home, crawl into bed, and cry.

Sensing her distress, Dr. Mason placed a reassuring hand over hers. "Let me give you some good news. While POTS has no cure, it's manageable. Most children grow out of it. With proper treatment, Rowan can live a normal life."

Jonathan cleared his throat. "So... this could go away?"

"At this stage, I can't guarantee that," Dr. Mason admitted. "But many children see significant improvement over time."

Rowan stirred, and Alice quickly composed herself, forcing a smile. Rowan looked at Alice and then at Dr. Mason. Dr. Mason stood up and moved toward her and proceeded to explain everything to her, including the medications she would be starting. Dr. Mason also informed her that whereas ramen noodles were frowned upon, primarily due to high sodium content, they were practically essential to POTS patients. This garnered a smile from Rowan as Alice was one of those parents who rarely allowed that indulgence. Alice marveled at how well he was able to communicate with her by getting down to her level. Some doctors just talk way above a child's head leaving it to the parents to break it down for them. Rowan listened patiently and asked the first question Alice knew was coming.

"So, since I am on these medications, I can cheer, yes?" The hopeful look on her face broke Alice's heart because she already knew the answer.

"Well, I am afraid, for the time being, that is not going to be a good idea. We really need to get a handle on this, and that kind of physical activity is just not a good idea right now."

Rowan did not take this well and tears rolled down her face and she looked away, staring out the window. Dr. Mason glanced at Alice and said, "Perhaps, you can still participate in other ways? Perhaps the coach could have you doing other things for cheer that don't involve you actually cheering?"

Alice rubbed Rowan's back when she did not respond. "I am sure that Coach Lauren would love to have an assistant coach again." Coach Lauren's assistant coach, Macy, who was also the art teacher, had gone off on maternity leave for the rest of the school year and they have yet to find someone to replace her.

"Yeah, maybe," Rowan said quietly. All Alice wished at that moment was that she could take this burden away from Rowan, and trade places with her. That not being an option, she instead held tightly to Dr. Mason's reassuring words— *manageable, normal life, possible improvement.* For now, she would put the unknowns on the back burner. She would not fall apart in front of her daughter. Alice held onto hope. The road ahead would be tough, but at least now, they had a map.

Chapter 7

F inally, the appointment is over. Not surprisingly, Rowan asks for ramen noodles for dinner, and soon they find themselves in the store buying both chicken and beef flavors.

"So, these are for me, right? Ian doesn't get any?" Rowan asks, her tone teasing yet serious.

Alice can see the battle ahead, but Rowan needs this win today. So, she informs her that Ian will not be eating any of her noodles. Alice can already feel Rowan's excitement at getting home to rub it in as much as possible. They drop the prescriptions off and head home. Alice plans to get Rowan settled—noodles in hand—while she makes roast beef and potatoes for the rest of them. Then, she'll head back out to pick up the medications. After that, she intends to spend the next few days glued to her laptop, researching everything she can about POTS, MVP, and all the medications Rowan will be taking. She vows to immerse herself completely until she knows more than even Dr. Mason. They will tackle this head-on and face it together as a family.

"It will be okay," she told herself. And so far, it had been.

It took time to find the right medications, and adjusting to the necessary lifestyle changes wasn't easy. Now, two years later, Rowan is mostly stable. She hasn't grown out of it yet, but she has more good days than bad. She no longer faints, though she still experiences occasional tachycardia and lightheadedness when she moves too fast. After much trial and error, they found the "magic" cocktail of medications. With careful attention to her body's signals, Rowan has managed to lead a mostly normal teenage life—except for the medical equipment she carries daily and the journal she records her vitals in.

Rowan has handled it all with resilience. That's not to say she hasn't resented it—who could blame her? Missing out on cheer for the rest of ninth grade had been the hardest. Even though she embraced her role as assistant coach, Alice could see, from her seat in the stands, that a small piece of Rowan's heart was missing. But now, in eleventh grade, Rowan has been cheering all year. There have been no major incidents. The few minor ones have only required her to take a break, sit on the bleachers, and drink some water.

Alice pulls herself from her thoughts. A familiar twinge at the back of her neck signals the onset of a migraine. When she gets a regular headache, it begins and ends in her forehead. A migraine, however, starts at the base of her neck and works its way up. She has no idea what causes them but suspects stress is to blame. Her family doctor agrees. With Rowan's health struggles and her own bouts of writer's block, stress and anxiety seem the likely culprits. He prescribed Imitrex for as-needed use. So far, it has worked well. If she takes even half a dose at the onset, she can avoid a full-blown migraine or, at worst, have only a mild headache.

After swallowing a pill, Alice opens her laptop, determined to get some serious writing done.

The day unfolds just as she hoped. She completes an entire chapter and makes significant progress on the outline for the next. The book's ending is already written. Alice always writes endings first—that's just how her mind works. An idea for an ending will come to her, and she will craft the beginning and middle around it. This process frustrates Cheryl to no end.

"Do you have any idea how annoying it is to read an amazing ending without knowing what came before it?" Cheryl complained during a recent call.

Alice laughed. "Sorry, but my mad skills are 'take them as you get them.' It's just how my brain works. I've redecorated entire rooms in my house because I saw a decorative pillow in Target."

"Well," Cheryl conceded, "whatever works. Are you still on schedule for another chapter by the end of the month? How's Rowan doing?"

Alice knows Cheryl genuinely cares about Rowan, but she also knows that Rowan will always come before her writing. So, Cheryl's question is both out of concern for Alice's daughter *and* concern for the book's publishing status.

"The timeline for the chapters is still on track, and Rowan is stable," Alice assures her. "She has minor episodes here and there, but nothing serious."

Alice hears Cheryl exhale, relieved. "Great! Great about both things, I mean—the book and Rowan. That's really good news, Alice."

"Yes," Alice agrees. "It is great news, and we're all praying it stays that way."

Wanting to get off the phone before her thoughts slip away, Alice quickly reassures Cheryl, again, that everything is on schedule. Alice adores Cheryl, but the people *she* answers to are relentless. If she can give Cheryl a little extra peace of mind, she might be spared another "progress call" for a few weeks.

She ends her workday by jotting down a few lines in a separate document—ideas she likes but hasn't yet found a place for. Feeling accomplished, she rises from her desk. A productive writing day lifts her spirits. Writer's block can be the death of a writer, but today, it has been successfully beaten back.

Alice heads downstairs to start dinner. It's a rare night when everyone will be home at the same time. The marking period just ended, meaning the kids had only half a day of school. Technically, they had a half day of *instruction*—soccer practice for Ian and cheer practice for Rowan carried on as usual. Jonathan, meanwhile, is having a relatively quiet week at work. He has presentations coming up, but for now, he's at his architect's desk, doing what he loves best: drawing and creating. Alice often tells him their shared love of creativity is what brought them together, but in true Jonathan form, with a twinkle in his eye, he always responds, "No, it was the tight jeans and high heels you were wearing when we met."

The kids groan at this exchange every time. "C'mon, Dad, she's *my mom*... it's just gross," Ian will say, while Rowan will roll her eyes and mutter, "Ugh... get a room."

Alice decides on something easy for dinner. The kids love it when she takes a break from healthy meals, so cheeseburgers on the grill it is—*with* French fries, fried in actual grease rather than baked in the oven. Since she finished writing early, she even earns extra brownie points by whipping up a yellow cake with chocolate frosting. Not that it takes much effort—it's a boxed mix with canned icing—but it's the thought that counts. About an hour later, she hears the front door open and slam twice. She long ago gave up trying to get them to close it gently. Without looking, she knows the first slam is Ian—his soccer gear lands piece by piece on the floor as he heads upstairs for a shower. He refuses to shower at school. "I hang with the guys in class, at lunch, and on the field," he once explained. "I really don't need to see them *naked*, too." Rowan follows close behind. She, unlike Ian, showers at school immediately after practice—she *refuses* to walk around sweaty. Normally, she would pop into the kitchen for a small bottle of juice and to share the "girl drama" from school. It's Alice's favorite part of the day. Even at sixteen, Rowan still wants to talk to her momma. Most of Alice's friends complain that their teenagers barely say a word to them. Alice treasures the fact that both her kids still share— Ian in brief, general terms; Rowan in full-on detail, depending on the day's drama. But tonight, Rowan doesn't come to the kitchen. Instead, Alice gets a text: *When's dinner?* Alice frowns. *Why is she texting me?* Immediately, she goes on high alert.

She sets her phone down and quickly heads upstairs. A small kernel of panic blooms in her stomach. When Rowan's routine is even slightly off, Alice's instincts kick in. She knocks softly, but when there's no response, she opens the door.

Rowan is lying on her bed, already in pajamas, her arm draped over her eyes.

Alice sits beside her. "Hey, Punkins. What's going on? Are you having an episode?"

She automatically reaches for Rowan's wrist. She could take her daughter's pulse in her sleep.

Rowan sighs. "Kind of. Not really right now. I just felt off a few times today, and now I'm really tired. Coach told me I could sit out today and just call cheers."

There was no resentment in her voice, which is odd. If Coach Lauren feels Rowan looks pale or a bit run down, she will bench her.

"So, coach saw you not looking so hot and made you sit out?" Alice asked.

"No," Rowan responded, "I just told her I was feeling off and asked if I could just sit out and then if I felt better, I could call cheers."

Alice tried to ignore the feeling of dread in her stomach. Rowan had "*asked*" to sit out?

"Ok, so what does "off" mean?" Alice asked.

"Momma let's not make a big deal of it. I just had some lightheadedness and a few minutes of tachycardia today. I feel fine now. You know if that happens too much in one day it really wears me out, so I am just tired. I just want to eat and lay in bed."

There are now bells going off in Alice's head and she sees this as the double-edged sword for what it is. It's great

41

that Rowan has not had a bad day like this for almost two years. On the other hand, by the same token, Rowan has not had a bad day in school for almost two years, so Alice is wondering what is going on and gets a sinking feeling in her stomach. The momma bear vibe is kicking in because her daughter has never asked to sit out of cheer practice, let alone want to eat dinner and lay around in bed on a Friday night. It was clear that Rowan did not want her to make a big deal about it, and outwardly she wouldn't, but she gave up any notion of being able to blow this off.

"How about I bring you your dinner up here on a tray. You could put something on Netflix and just have a "veg" night. I thought we would have a fun dinner tonight. Burgers and fries with chocolate cake for dessert. So, it's a very unhealthy dinner and packed with salt, which may be exactly what you need, a bit more salt in you." Alice said, with what she hoped was a big smile that conveyed "big deal, bad day, no worries."

Rowan nodded and gave a smile to the plan Alice laid out to her. Rowan had not even seemed to notice that her mother had taken her pulse, which was ninety-one. Not tachycardic, but just a bit high given that she has been laying there for about twenty-minutes. Alice got up and walked over to the door when Rowan spoke.

"Maybe after dinner, we can watch a chick flick, like together?" Bells, bells, bells getting louder and louder, now, "movie with momma" on a Friday night? Alice thinks to herself.

"That sounds like fun! Absolutely, and since I am so bad at it, you pick the movie. Ok, right, so let me get dinner done and then it's cake and a movie."

Alice walked out of the room and closed her daughter's door, but held onto the doorknob, squeezing it so hard her knuckles were white. Alice tried to slow her breathing, but she knew her girl. Every inch of her inside and out. Rowan downplayed everything that had happened that day and yet she wanted to be near her momma, and Alice just knew, something was not right. Back in the kitchen, she was picking up the pace with getting dinner done, when she heard the third, and final slam of the door for the day. She heard Jonathan throw his keys and wallet in the ceramic bowl by the door and hang his bag up on the coat rack. He came into the kitchen and immediately took an exaggerated sniff of the air.

"Wow...are we having burgers and, oh what do I see here, French fries to be cooked in grease? Whoa, is that a cake cooling on the counter?" Just as he mentioned the cake, Ian comes bounding in the kitchen and takes in the food situation.

"Cool eats...who died?" Alice was not in the mood.

"Ian, can you put the burgers on the grill and watch them for a few minutes. DO NOT turn the grill up to cook them faster, you get the same result every time you try that. I will come out and finish cooking them in a few minutes while you set the table."

"Why do I have to do all that, where is her royal highness at?"

Alice gave Ian a look and then said, "She is not feeling well, so just give me a break ok"? Ian may be a boy, in all the

43

annoying ways a boy could be a boy, but he loved his sister, even if he didn't show it. Ian nodded and then picked up the platter of burgers. When he got to the sliding door he turned,

"So, like, what's the deal? Is she ok"? Alice knew she had been sharp with him, and she walked over and ruffled his hair, which he hated, but seemed to almost crave the affectionate touch at that moment.

"She just had a few bad spells today and it has been quite some time since she has had any at all, let alone several in one day. It could be something as simple as not enough salt over the last couple of days and if that is the case than my idea of having this very unhealthy dinner should fix her right up." Alice said with a smile she hoped conveyed, again, "no biggie." Ian furrowed his brow, but nodded in ascent, and took the burgers outside. Jonathan walked up behind Alice and put his arms around her waist. Alice leaned into him, loving his arms around her, his tall and broad body, encasing her within him. It made her feel safe and warm, like nothing bad could get to her.

"So, you going to fill me in... what's going on"?

Alice put her hands on his hands and pulled him tighter to her. "She came home and went right to her room. She sent me a text about dinner, *a text*. As in, she was too worn out to come down to talk to me. I don't know the nitty gritty specifics yet, but she had a bad day that involved a couple of episodes. She also requested to sit out of cheer today."

At that Jonathan turned her around and looked at her. "She *willingly* sat out of cheer?" he repeated incredulously.

Alice nodded yes and then said "I am going to take her dinner up to her and then she asked me to watch a Netflix movie with her. It's Friday night by the way."

Jonathan nodded yes, indicating that his daughter, being the major social butterfly that she was, staying in on a Friday night to hang with her mother, was out of character. Alice picked up the can of icing and began to ice the cake she had made.

"I think I might call Dr. Mason's service and see, even though it's after hours, if he will call me back." Alice said.

"Well, how is she right now?" Jonathan asked. "I mean if she is stable right now, I doubt he does anything tonight." Jonathan said.

Alice loved her husband, but again, his good logic and practical thinking sometimes really got on her nerves. Jonathan sensed the shift in Alices' demeanor.

"Then again, I did not see her when she first got home, so I think you should do whatever you feel we need to do." Alice just nodded her head, but did not turn around, but kept on with the cake.

Jonathan kissed her on the top of her head and then said, "I'm going up to change and then peek in on her, be back down in a few minutes." Sensing she was not going to acknowledge him a second time, he walked out of the kitchen, without a parting glance.

Chapter 8

"Knock, knock…your royal highness, can your old man come in?" Jonathan heard his daughter chuckle and then say, "Yes, you may enter."

Jonathan walked in and performed an exaggerated bow with a flourish. "I hear that Her Majesty will be dining in her room while being entertained with Netflix this evening. It must be nice. I, on the other hand, must sit at the kitchen table with all the other peasants." He sat down next to her. "So, Mom tells me you had kind of a rough day. What's up, bub? What's the tea, sis?"

Rowan laughed as Jonathan hung his head in mock shame. "Daddy, please don't try to be cool. And even bigger please—do not try to be a cool girl. And the biggest please of all," she said, trying to catch her breath, "please do not try to talk like a cool girl in front of other girls."

Jonathan smiled and shrugged. "Just trying to keep it for reals, ya know?"

Rowan laughed again and gave her dad a playful push. "Don't worry, Dad. We'll work on it." As the laughter died down, she sighed.

"Yeah," she admitted, "I had a bad day today, but I feel better now. I'm just really tired. I might be extra tired because I was lightheaded earlier, which made me nauseous, so I didn't eat lunch."

Jonathan's expression grew serious. "Did you tell your mom about not eating lunch? Even though you didn't eat, did you at least drink anything?"

Rowan's eyes widened. "No, I forgot to tell her about lunch. And since I was nauseous, I didn't take my salt pill either. Oh man, she's going to lose it on me."

Jonathan waved the thought away. "Nah, I'll give her the heads-up. I mean, you were zonked out when you got home, right?"

Rowan nodded and smiled, knowing her dad was about to take the heat for her.

"So," Jonathan continued, "it seems like there's a simple explanation. But you haven't had any episodes in quite a while, so let's be sure to keep an eye on it. It might not be a bad idea—just for a week or so—to start tracking episodes in your journal again. Just to be safe, okay?"

"Okay," Rowan agreed, but her expression turned somber as she looked down.

Jonathan lifted her chin gently, raising his eyebrows in question.

"So, today's not the only bad day?"

Rowan hesitated before answering. "I've had a couple of bad days over the last week. Not as bad as today, but more often lately. I didn't want Momma to freak out and roll me in bubble wrap before sticking me in the corner of my room."

Jonathan took her hand. "I get that, I really do. But hiding these episodes can be dangerous, honey. If this is getting worse again, we need to know. Dr. Mason needs to know."

Rowan nodded. "I know. But they were really small episodes. Until today, I wasn't even worried about them. Honestly, Daddy, they only lasted a few minutes, and then they went away."

Jonathan studied her for a moment before nodding. "Okay. If they were that minor, I'll totally downplay it to your mom—but only if you promise that, no matter how small the episode, you'll tell us. Deal?"

Rowan smiled. "Got it. I promise."

Jonathan kissed her forehead. "I'm sure your mom will be thrilled that *you* suggested keeping the journal again."

He winked, signaling that it would be their little secret. Rowan leaned forward, hugged Jonathan, and whispered, "Thanks, Daddy."

Jonathan felt the familiar surge of love for his sixteen-year-old daughter—the same little girl who still called him Daddy. As far as he was concerned, she could call him that forever.

Standing, he gave her a mock salute. "Of course, my lady. Now, I must go check on the burgers. Your brother is cooking them, and I'd rather not eat a charred meatball. I'll send the royal cook up with your meal." He backed out of the room, bowing dramatically.

"How was she when you went in?" Alice asked as Jonathan stepped into the kitchen.

"First things first," he said, sniffing the air dramatically. "Have you checked the burgers? I promised Rowan we wouldn't be having charred meatballs with melted cheese on them."

"They're fine. I took over, and now they're in the warmer." She crossed her arms. "So?"

Jonathan sat down at the table. "Okay, so don't freak out... or get... how you get."

Alice opened her mouth to speak, but Jonathan held up his hand. "Rowan had a bad day, but there were a few things she left out—not on purpose. She was just really out of it when she got home. Yes, she felt lightheaded most of the day, which made her nauseous. So, she drank a little at lunch but didn't eat and didn't take her salt pill because she was afraid she'd throw it back up. So, it's likely a hydration and salt issue. Let's keep a close eye on her over the weekend and see how she's feeling by Monday." He paused before adding, "Rowan also thinks she should start journaling these episodes again."

Alice's eyes widened. "Episodes? As in plural?"

"Okay, again—stay calm. She told me about it because she knew you would overreact."

Alice's patience was wearing thin. "Are we going to play charades, or are you going to tell me the big secret you two have?"

Jonathan sighed. "This is exactly what I mean. She admitted she's had more episodes lately—nothing major, just more frequent. They only last a few minutes, so she didn't think much of it until today."

Alice stood up, but Jonathan gently placed a hand on her shoulder. "Listen to me. She knows she should have told us. And she decided—on her own—to start tracking the episodes again. That shows maturity. She's taking this seriously."

Alice sank back into her chair, feeling defeated. "Am I so bad that she doesn't feel comfortable telling me these things? I'm not trying to smother her, but I am her mother. She fights me on everything, but I'm just trying to do what's best for her. Sometimes, it feels like I'm always the heavy, and you're the superhero. Sometimes, I don't feel... needed."

Jonathan pulled her into a hug. "Of course she needs you. But maybe it's time to trust her more. Maybe ease up on the morning backpack checks. Instead of showing her that her salt pills are in her lunchbox, just put them there and trust that she'll take them." He paused before adding, "She's sixteen now. She may never grow out of this. She has to learn to manage it on her own. What's your plan—bunk with her at college?"

Alice sighed. "I just want to take care of her. Sometimes, I feel like she doesn't want me to."

Jonathan smiled. "Well, she never talks to me about the soap opera that is West Lake High School, or the cheer drama, boy updates, or the new eyeshadow packet at Ultra, or..."

Alice cut in, "Ulta, the makeup store is Ulta not Ultra and it's eyeshadow pallet not packet."

He smiled, "See, Ulta or Ultra...pallet, packet or whatever, she's not talking to me about any of that. I also did not get a Friday night invite to the Netflix chick flick marathon."

Alice laughed. "Fine, I will ease up and not make a federal case out of it, but I am calling Dr. Mason on Monday." She then assembled all the food on a tray, grabbed two forks, and went upstairs to hang out with her daughter.

Chapter 9

F irst thing Monday, Alice made good on her promise to call Dr. Mason. She thoroughly relayed the events regarding Rowan to the receptionist, who read everything back to ensure accuracy and promised that Abby, Dr. Mason's nurse case manager, would be in touch. Alice would have preferred to speak directly with Dr. Mason, but she knew that most doctors didn't take calls from patients—hence the reason for a nurse case manager. Her anxiety grew by the minute while waiting for a response, and she told herself she would call again if necessary, determined to speak to either Abby or Dr. Mason before the end of the day. She carried her phone everywhere, even into the bathroom, unwilling to risk missing the call.

She checked on Rowan intermittently, finding her sleeping on and off throughout the day. With each passing hour, Alice grew more on edge. Finally, just before four in the afternoon—just as she was about to call again and lose her cool—her phone rang. The screen displayed Dr. Mason's office.

She answered, expecting Abby, but was surprised to hear Dr. Mason himself. "Hello, Alice, it's Dr. Mason. I got your message and wanted to call you back personally."

"Oh," Alice said, caught off guard. "Dr. Mason, hello. I expected to hear from Abby but thank you for calling."

"Yes, well," Dr. Mason explained, "normally that would be the case, but when I read the message, I decided I wanted to speak with you directly."

Alice remained silent, so he continued. "I read through everything but go ahead and give me a play-by-play of what's been going on over the last week or so."

Alice recounted the details of Friday and the days leading up to it, including Rowan's reluctance to share what had been happening. She felt a pang of guilt, as if she were betraying her daughter, but quickly reminded herself that this was different. As a teenager, Alice had hidden things from her own mother—but sneaking a few drinks at a sleepover or trying marijuana once was nowhere near the same as withholding information about a potentially life-threatening condition. Rowan might be upset with her, but that was a risk Alice had to take.

"Well," Dr. Mason said, "it's very important that Rowan communicates these things. That's something I'll be discussing with her as well—gently, of course."

Alice nodded, even though he couldn't see her. "I know she has an appointment in just under a month, but I felt I needed to check in, even if it was just for reassurance that flare-ups were bound to happen and that waiting for her next scheduled visit was still the best course of action."

"No, it's good you called," he assured her. "But, actually, I don't want this to wait. My weekly schedule always includes time blocks for emergent visits."

A chill ran down Alice's spine, and she gripped the phone tighter. "Emergent?" she croaked.

Dr. Mason was quick to clarify. "That's just what we call those time blocks. It allows me to see patients who are having issues I don't want to postpone until their next scheduled appointment. It doesn't necessarily mean there's an emergency. I like to be proactive—if something new develops or an existing condition worsens, I prefer to get ahead of it. I checked with scheduling—can you bring her in at one o'clock tomorrow? I won't see her until about two, though, because I want her to have bloodwork done first so we can review the results during the appointment. Sound good?"

Alice closed her eyes, took a deep breath, and said, "We'll be there. One o'clock on the nose."

After ending the call, she immediately phoned Jonathan and relayed the plan.

"Okay," he said, "I'll move some things around so I can go."

"I know you want to be there, and I get that," Alice said, "but if we *both* go, it might scare Rowan. We don't know if this is anything serious, but if we both drop everything, she'll assume something is really wrong. It might be best if I take her alone."

Jonathan hesitated before saying, "Okay, then maybe put me on speaker when you see Dr. Mason—like we did last time. If it turns out this *isn't* just a flare-up, I want to hear everything firsthand."

Alice could hear the tension in his voice, which put her further on edge. He was always so easygoing; the *everything will be alright* kind of guy.

"Yes," she agreed, "let's do that. But again, this could just be a flare-up."

After ending the call, Alice leaned back in her chair and stared out at the lake. She wasn't sure who she was trying to reassure—Jonathan or herself. But one thing was certain: *something* was wrong. Something was being missed. Dr. Mason might have a slew of degrees and letters after his name, but *she* was Rowan's mother. She knew her better than anyone. She had known every facial expression, every shift in body language, since the day she was born.

Alice had always known what Rowan needed—what each type of cry meant as an infant, whether she was hungry, tired, cold, or just wanted to be held. There had been a particular cry that meant something was wrong—like when she had an ear infection or a virus coming on. Jonathan had always marveled at that ability. To him, a cry was simply a cry—a sign that something was amiss, but he had never been able to *hear* what it meant. Alice had. It was more than just maternal intuition; it was instinctual. Primal.

She shook herself from her thoughts and stood to check on Rowan. As she headed for the stairs, her resolve hardened. She wasn't leaving that doctor's office tomorrow without answers.

As predicted, Rowan grew quiet when Alice told her about the appointment.

"Momma, I'm sorry I didn't tell you what was going on," Rowan admitted. "At first, it was nothing—just little things here and there. But when it started getting worse, I didn't tell you because I *knew* you'd be mad that I hadn't told you sooner. I guess I was just hoping it would go away again."

Alice's heart clenched. "Again?" she repeated. "What do you mean *again*?"

Rowan winced, and Alice immediately picked up on it. This past week hadn't been the *first* week things had gone bad. Fear twisted in her gut, but she forced herself to stay calm. She needed all the information. If she reacted too strongly now, Rowan would downplay everything—or worse, shut down completely. Dr. Mason had said they would talk to her about this, so Alice decided to let him be the *heavy*.

"Okay," Alice said gently, "it's best that you tell me or Daddy when something is going on. Keeping track in your journal also helps Dr. Mason see the full picture. But I *do* understand—you just want to be a normal teenager. I get that. Still, we need to keep the lines of communication open. So why don't you tell me what's been happening? That way, when we see Dr. Mason tomorrow, we'll all be on the same page."

Rowan sighed in relief, some of the stress lifting from her face. Alice knew she had taken the right approach.

As Rowan pulled herself into a sitting position, Alice saw the small tic in her daughter's expression—just *sitting up* had made her dizzy. She filed that piece of information away for the doctor.

Rowan took a steadying breath. "It really started about three weeks ago..."

Chapter 10

T he next day was gray and overcast, with sprinkles of rain here and there. Alice hadn't slept well the night before and expected to wake up exhausted. She had suffered another bad migraine. She had dealt with migraines her whole life, but lately, they have become more frequent. She tried to avoid taking the Imitrex her doctor prescribed, as it was a controlled substance, limited to nine pills at a time. Instead, she attempted other methods—warm baths, Tylenol, rocking in her recliner with an ice pack on her neck. But last night, when all else failed, she took the pill. It didn't completely alleviate the pain, but it dulled it enough to allow her to sleep—a little, at least.

Every muscle in her body was strung tight, like a guitar string, and the anxiety she felt gnawed away at whatever fatigue she might have had. It was ten o'clock in the morning, and Rowan was still asleep. Alice had checked on her at least ten times, quietly stepping into her room to watch her sleep. She wouldn't admit it to herself, but she was watching the rise and fall of her daughter's chest. Every inhale and exhale helped to slow Alice's own breathing.

After another glance at the clock, Alice closed Rowan's door once more and went back downstairs, her mind heavy with worry. Normally, Rowan never slept this late—not even on weekends. No, this was yet another symptom getting worse. Alice knew they both had a long day ahead, so she decided to let her daughter sleep a bit longer before bringing up a bowl of the fruit salad she had made the night before along with some orange juice. Rowan loved fruit, and even if she wasn't hungry, Alice hoped she'd eat at least some of it. Right now, she would take whatever she could get.

Without Rowan as part of the family's morning routine, the house had felt subdued, the weight of her absence pressing on Alice's heart. Jonathan sat at the table with only a cup of coffee, reading the newspaper—normally, he'd be playfully bantering with the kids. As Alice packed Ian's lunch, she stole glances at her husband and noticed that he hadn't once turned a page. It dawned on her that he wasn't really reading; he was just trying to create an illusion of normalcy. Whether that was for himself, for her, or for Ian, she wasn't sure. But the altered routine wasn't lost on Ian either. He was perceptive, able to read between the lines with ease. Of course, his concern for Rowan always came out in sarcastic remarks—it was his defense mechanism. If he didn't treat something like a big deal, then it wouldn't *be* a big deal. Alice envied that mindset, but mothers didn't have that luxury.

"So, what's up with the queen? Is she not slumming it with the commoners today? Did anyone put out a press release? The people have a right to know," Ian quipped.

Alice knew he was covering his worry with humor. The night before, he had gone into Rowan's room, making a dramatic fuss about having to bring home her schoolwork for her, though he could have easily left it on the kitchen table. She knew he had wanted an excuse to check in on her. Not wanting to intrude but needing to hear if Rowan would tell Ian anything she hadn't told her, Alice had crept up the stairs, stopping just below Rowan's room. She wasn't trying to pry for the sake of it—she just needed to know if there was something else going on.

She heard Ian's voice soften. "So, what's up? Mom said you haven't been feeling well."

"Just a flare-up," Rowan had responded. "I don't think it's a big deal. Don't worry about it."

Even now, Rowan was protecting her little brother. They acted as though they couldn't stand each other, but it was all for show.

Ian had scoffed. "Yeah, I'm not worried. It's probably all bullshit anyway to get out of school."

Alice had covered her mouth to stifle a laugh. Ian had heard what he needed to hear—Rowan's reassurance—and so it was back to business as usual.

"Well, get on the horn and let your groupies know the deal," he had added. "I'm sick of all these squeaky, high-strung cheerleaders hassling me about where you are."

Rowan had sighed. "Yeah, sorry. I had my phone off because it kept waking me up."

Ian had softened for a moment before snapping back to his usual self. "Well, I'm not your social director, you know. I've got an image to protect. I can't have all these airheaded, lip-glossed, pom-pom-wielding weirdos crawling all over me."

Alice had smiled, shaking her head as she carefully retreated down the stairs.

***

Upon arriving at Dr. Mason's office, Rowan was sent directly to the lab. The technician was having a tough time finding a vein. If Rowan were even the slightest bit dehydrated, her veins would "roll," making her incredibly hard to stick. At this point, Rowan knew how to draw blood as well as the phlebotomist did. She raised her arm over her head, silently counted to ten, then let it hang straight down and wiggled it. Keeping it lowered, she slapped her forearm a few times until a vein appeared.

Rowan just smiled, like it was the coolest thing ever, and said, "In patients with POTS, the blood will pool to the lowest point momentarily because their blood pressure cannot regulate itself instantaneously. So, you better hurry if you want to catch that vein."

The technician looked down and, in one swift movement, swiped the area with an alcohol pad and stuck her. Sure enough, the blood began to flow into the tube. Then the technician grabbed another tube, then another, and yet another after that. Once the draw was complete, they headed to the waiting room. Alice could tell Rowan was already getting tired. Within minutes of settling onto one of the couches, she had slumped down with her head resting on the armrest. She was asleep in minutes.

A little while later, a woman walked over with a throw pillow from the only couch that had pillows.

"If you don't think it will wake her up, you could put this under her head. She may have a sore neck when she wakes up still on the arm of that chair."

Alice looked up and smiled as she took the pillow, gently tucking it under Rowan's head.

The woman stretched out her hand. "Hi, my name is Audrey, and I am a fellow POTS mom."

She had a warm smile but also the telltale signs of a parent caring for a chronically sick child—the sunken cheeks, dark-rimmed eyes, and a to-go cup of coffee at two o'clock in the afternoon to push through exhaustion. Audrey indicated to the empty seat next to Alice, who motioned for her to sit.

Audrey glanced at Rowan. "I've seen her before. She's beautiful. How old is she?"

Alice smiled. "She's sixteen. Young—too young to have to deal with this when her friends' biggest worry is which lip gloss goes best with their Friday night movie outfit."

Audrey shook her head knowingly and said, "My daughter, Mari—she's only fourteen. We've been dealing with POTS, hers classified as severe, since she was nine. She has no idea what normal teenage life is supposed to look like. I'm not sure if that's a good thing or a bad thing. On one hand, if she had some experience, even on a limited level, she'd at least know what it meant to be a normal teenage girl. But on the other hand, she has no idea what she's missing. She's been homeschooled for the past five years. So, I ask myself… is it better to know and not be able to have it, or is it better to have never experienced it at all—so you don't have to mourn something you never had?"

At first, Alice could only look at her in silence. And then said, "I don't really have an answer for you," Alice admitted. "Until last week, Rowan's symptoms had been drastically reduced for almost two years, and Dr. Mason thought she was growing out of it. But now… whatever was getting better is getting worse." Alice thought to herself about how thankful she was that this was *Mari's* reality and not *Rowan's.* And then, just as quickly, she was overcome with self-loathing for even thinking that—*for thanking God that someone else's child was worse off than her own.*

But she had to say *something,* so she chose honesty.

She let out a breath, trying to organize her thoughts. "I can tell you that Rowan is devastated about missing school— not the work, obviously."

Audrey gave a knowing smile and nodded.

"But she misses her friends," Alice continued, "the boy drama, the girl drama, and most of all, cheerleading. You know, *all* the things that are *tremendously* important to a sixteen-year-old girl. I can't imagine her never experiencing any of it, but at the same time… maybe it's easier not to long for something you've never had." Alice sighed. "I'm sorry. That's probably not very helpful."

Audrey smiled warmly. "You're just being honest. Most people can't answer that question anyway. Maybe I don't even need an answer. Maybe I just need someone to listen."

Alice couldn't help it—her eyes instinctively flicked to the woman's left hand, searching for a wedding ring.

Audrey let out a small laugh. "You know, everyone does that."

Alice looked down, embarrassed, but Audrey reached over and placed her hand on hers.

"It's okay," she reassured her. "It's the obvious question." She exhaled softly before continuing, "No, I'm no longer married. He couldn't handle it anymore. *Or*—more accurately—we couldn't handle it together anymore.

"David is still very much in Mari's life, but we fought constantly—over money, treatment options, changing doctors, public school versus homeschool. It was never-ending. And eventually, we realized… we weren't really there for *her* anymore. We were too wrapped up in ourselves.

"We work better apart. I'm more hands-on, but I don't have to work—he fully supports us financially. So, Mari and I downsized *a lot.* I didn't mind. Our apartment is all we need. Of course, *she* thinks it's all her fault." Audrey's voice grew softer. "We both reassure her that if our marriage had been strong enough, it would have survived *anything.* Odds are, we wouldn't have made it anyway. POTS or not, it would've just been *something else* that came between us."

Alice's throat tightened. All she could manage was a quiet, "I'm sorry."

For *what,* she wasn't sure. But she knew she wasn't about to sit there and praise Jonathan for the *Best Husband of the Century* award. *Talk about salt in a wound.*

Instead, she asked, "How do you do this on your own? For me, this is physically and emotionally draining—and I *have* help."

Audrey simply shrugged. "Because my little girl is sick," she said. "I do it because I have no choice. When David—who's working two jobs—can help, he does. Otherwise, it's just her and me against the POTS."

Alice hesitated, then asked, "Does she *just* have POTS, or is there something else?"

Audrey nodded grimly. "Her POTS is severe, but she also has Lupus SLE and a seizure disorder."

Alice just stared. She couldn't even *fathom* Rowan dealing with *all* of that. She was barely holding it together with Rowan having *mild to moderate* POTS.

Audrey shrugged again. "She's stable *for now*. If she stays where she is, she might be able to go back to school next year." She paused. "I mean... she'd be in a wheelchair. On oxygen. But at this point, I don't think she even *cares*. She's just so *tired* of being alone.

"I mean, she has *me,*" Audrey clarified, "but... she's a teenager. She's *teenager* lonely."

Alice knew exactly what she meant.

Rowan had only been out of school for a few days, and already, she was desperate to go back. She missed her friends. She missed cheer.

Alice said a silent prayer that this was *just* a medication issue—that Rowan's body was changing and needed a new dosage. That was all.

Right then, a nurse stepped out from the exam room doors and called Mari's name.

Audrey stood up and glanced down at Alice. "It was really nice to meet you. Fellow POTS warrior and all. Thanks for listening."

As she started to walk away, Alice called after her. "Wait."

She tore a piece of paper from one of her journals and scribbled her number on the back. Then she got up and handed it to Audrey.

"I'd love for us to stay in touch," Alice said. "Us POTS warriors have to stick together."

Audrey took the slip of paper, then pulled Alice into a hug. When she pulled back, she smiled. "I'd really like that," she admitted. "Mari isn't the *only* one who's lonely for a friend.

The nurse then looked at Alice. "I'll have a room for Rowan in about twenty minutes."

Twenty minutes, Alice thought. Twenty minutes away from finding out what was behind door number two. With Rowan still asleep, she finally gave herself permission to let the tears come.

Chapter 11

Within twenty-five minutes, a nurse called Rowan's name. They followed her back to exam room number twenty. Alice realized they had now been in every exam room in the office. Given the sheer size of it, it was a stark reminder of just how many times they had been here, just how sick her child really was.

Rowan was put through the usual gamut: orthostatic blood pressure test, EKG on the portable machine, oxygen saturation, and heart rate check. She was so used to all of it. Alice smiled as she remembered the time Rowan had corrected a technician, pointing out that one of the sticky nodes had been placed in the wrong spot. Confidently, Rowan had explained the proper placement, reinforcing just how familiar she was with the procedure. "Don't worry," Rowan had said, "I have to help the phlebotomist get a vein to stick. I'm just complicated, but most royalty is." Alice had looked at the technician and said, "It's easier to just go with it."

Once the vitals were recorded, Rowan lay on the table and popped in her earbuds while Alice settled in. Just because they were in a room didn't mean they would see Dr. Mason anytime soon. He likely had a full patient load, and Alice assumed they would be taken for Rowan's stress test before he came in. She also wanted another ultrasound done today.

About thirty minutes later, Dr. Mason stuck his head into the room. "Didn't want you to think I forgot about you folks. I'm just waiting on a few more lab results, and Abby is trying to get the stress test room free so Rowan can hop on the bike while we wait for the last labs."

"Okay," Alice said, "but I also want her to have an ultrasound today."

Dr. Mason grabbed Rowan's chart and flipped through it. "She had an ultrasound at her last visit, and her mitral valve prolapse was unchanged. We only do ultrasounds every other visit unless there's a significant change. Insurance won't cover another one when she just had one a month ago."

Alice hesitated. Was she overreacting? Dr. Mason had patients flying in from other states to see him—who was she to question him? She had no medical training and was running purely on intuition. But she couldn't shake the feeling. With every fiber of her being, she knew something was *off*.

"I don't care if insurance won't cover it," Alice said firmly. "We'll pay out of pocket. I'll pay you today if necessary. Something is wrong with Rowan. Something *other* than the POTS, and I want an ultrasound today."

Dr. Mason looked confused. "Something other than POTS? Have you seen another physician or had an ER visit since we last spoke?"

Alice moved closer, her voice unwavering. "No, but I have a *feeling*. I'm not trying to undermine your expertise, but I *am* her mother. And I'm telling you—there is something happening that you aren't seeing."

Dr. Mason seemed taken aback but quickly recovered. "I have a packed schedule today. All the ultrasound rooms are booked, and even if I shifted things around, I'm not sure I'd have a technician available."

Alice squared her shoulders, her jaw tightening as the air in the room grew thick with tension. *She couldn't back down—not now. Every instinct screamed that something was wrong, and she wasn't about to ignore it.* "I'm *not* leaving here without an ultrasound." I don't care how long we have to wait or if you have to do it yourself. Her symptoms have worsened since the last ultrasound. Maybe her valve has gotten worse, or *something* else is going on. I base this on absolutely no medical training. The only qualification I have is that I am her mother, and my "momma" instincts are telling me that something *else* is wrong.

Alice glanced at Rowan, who remained oblivious, lying on the table, swaying her feet to a beat Alice couldn't hear.

Dr. Mason sighed, frustration evident. "Mrs. Miller, I understand this is scary, but I *assure* you that her valve hasn't worsened in such a short time. I'll schedule an ultrasound at her next—"

"No," Alice interrupted. "*Not* next time. *Now.* I'll wait all night if I have to, but we are doing this *today*."

Dr. Mason studied her for a long moment before exhaling sharply. "I'll have Abby check the schedule and see if we can move things around. But be prepared to wait— possibly for hours."

Alice smiled victorious. "I've got nowhere else to be."

Dr. Mason nodded and left. Alice settled in, prepared for however long it would take. She *knew* she was right, and if she had to eat crow later, she'd gladly devour it. She would eat a five-course meal of crow if it meant that everything that could be checked was checked. She knew what she knew, and she felt what she felt; this ultrasound was happening. They waited a little over two hours. Whether that was just how long it took or if Dr. Mason was making a point, she didn't care. Just before they were taken to the ultrasound room, she called Jonathan.

"So, you basically told Dr. Mason how to do his job? How is that supposed to help us?" Jonathan's frustration made Alice's blood boil.

"I am *advocating* for our daughter. Something is happening that they *aren't* catching."

"I see," he said sarcastically. "And you base this on how many years of medical school?"

Alice clenched her jaw. She had never hung up on Jonathan before, but she was close. Then she thought of Audrey and her ex-husband. *Is this how it starts?*

Jonathan sighed. "Look, I'm sorry. I feel helpless. I've felt like a crap dad all day for not being there, even though I know it's best for Rowan that I'm not."

Alice softened. "That was my fault. I can't imagine being the one stuck at home, waiting for news. I'm sorry, Jonathan. I wasn't thinking about you." Jonathan exhaled. "That's exactly what I *want* you to do. Put *her* first. Don't listen to me—I'm being a butthead right now." Alice chuckled despite herself. In the background, Ian's voice rang out. "Right now? Hate to break it to you, Dad, but you're *always* a butthead." Jonathan laughed. "Well, *that's* just plain rude." Then, in a lower voice, "Right, babe? It's not true. Say it's not true." Alice smiled, her anger melting. "Sorry, but it's true.

69

You're a *total* butthead. But you're *my* butthead, and I love you."

"I love you too. Call me with an update."

***

Shortly thereafter, a nurse came in and led her and Rowan into the ultrasound room. "We are rearranging staff so we can free up a technician. Just have a seat, and I will get someone in here as soon as possible."

The nurse ripped off the paper covering the bed from the last patient and pulled out a fresh sheet from the roll at the head of the table. Rowan crawled up onto it and immediately pulled her hoodie down over her eyes. It was as if she had fallen asleep the moment her head hit the table.

The nurse gave her a second look and said, "Bless her heart, she is exhausted."

Alice nodded. "We've been here since one o'clock. Though, that's my fault. We would have been gone by now if I hadn't insisted on the ultrasound."

She looked down, feeling a bit embarrassed. It was already four o'clock—was this nurse going to have to stay late because of her insistence? Was the technician now scrambling to find extended daycare for a child because a *neurotic mother* was demanding a test the doctor had said wasn't necessary?

Was it wrong that Alice was asking herself these questions but didn't *really* care about the answers?

Noticing Alice's anxiety, the nurse reassured her. "We have to stay late all the time, and we take turns doing it. Dr. Mason gives us comp time for that, so no worries."

Alice nodded again as the nurse left the room.

Rowan was already fast asleep, so Alice leaned her head back against the wall and closed her eyes. She had no idea how long they would have to wait, but if this was a game of chicken, she was prepared to win.

About an hour later, the door opened, and a woman walked in. She was short, with shoulder-length curly brown hair that looked permed rather than natural. Dressed in plain-colored scrubs and black nursing clogs, she had a no-nonsense demeanor. She didn't speak, only offering a weak smile as she walked over to Rowan, who remained asleep.

Alice assumed she would wake her, but instead, the technician simply opened the front of Rowan's gown and squeezed a gel-like lubricant onto the ultrasound wand. Rowan stirred and opened her eyes.

The technician smiled at her. "You can just stay relaxed. This won't take long."

Rowan didn't need any convincing—her eyes fluttered closed again.

Alice had thought that by now, she would understand what she was looking at on the ultrasound screen. But to her, it was still just a grainy black-and-white blur. She leaned her head back again but kept her eyes open, watching the test take place.

She sat up, however, when she noticed the technician furrow her brow.

The woman paused, then placed a small pulse oximeter on Rowan's right hand.

71

Alice sat up straighter when she saw the technician furrow her brow again.

"What's wrong? What are you seeing?"

The technician dodged the question. "I am recording everything, and Dr. Mason will review it."

Alice had expected this answer before she even asked. The people who performed these tests never revealed anything, and whenever she pressed, she got the same response.

Still, Alice was now on high alert, watching the technician closely. If she noticed anything else concerning, she gave nothing away. She was probably already chastising herself for letting her expression slip earlier.

When the test was finished, the technician grabbed some paper towels and wiped the gel off Rowan's chest. Looking at Alice, she reiterated, "Dr. Mason will review the scan."

"In the meantime," she continued, "I'm supposed to take you down the hall for the stress test. I'm sorry it's so late in the day—I know you're both exhausted and anxious to leave. But since we had to rearrange things for the ultrasound, the stress test room is only now open for a new patient."

Alice and Rowan followed her down the hall to the stress testing room, where Rowan would get on a stationary bike. Leads would be connected to both her and the bike, with a blood pressure cuff on her arm and a pulse oximeter on her finger. Every vital function of her body would be monitored during the test.

A fully successful test required her to stay on the bike for seven minutes. But so far, Rowan had only managed to last four and a half.

At that point, her hands and feet would go numb. Her breathing would become labored. Her heart rate would skyrocket to dangerous levels.

This was the test that frustrated Rowan the most.

Each failure was another bitter reminder that her dreams of cheering full-time were slipping further and further away.

Alice had seen the determination in Rowan's face every time, as if sheer willpower could force her body to cooperate.

And every time, Alice's heart broke a little more at the resigned expression on her daughter's face when she fell woefully short of the goal.

Alice hoped that since Rowan had been resting most of the day, she might last a little longer this time. Even an extra thirty seconds would be a victory.

Baby steps. If that was all they could get, they would take it.

Once Rowan was completely wired and hooked up, two technicians stood on either side of her, ready to catch her if she passed out.

She began to pedal.

As expected, Alice saw Rowan's face set in determination. She said a silent prayer that this time, *this time,* Rowan would get a win.

Even a small one.

She had only been on the bike for a little over two minutes when the door to the room swung open.

A nurse rushed in, pushing a wheelchair.

"Get her off the bike. Now."

Alice's pulse spiked. "She's only at two minutes. She can do better—"

The nurse raised her voice, prompting the two technicians to get Rowan off the bike and into the wheelchair.

"Mrs. Miller, Dr. Mason will go over everything. Just follow me back to the exam room."

Rowan looked at Alice, her eyes wide as saucers as she grabbed her mother's hand. Alice felt weightless, floating above the floor. Only Rowan's hand in hers kept her grounded. *How did we get here?* she wondered. *How did things escalate so quickly when Rowan has been stable for just almost two years?* The fear settled deep in her stomach, but she gripped Rowan's hand tighter, as if holding on to her could somehow keep everything from spiraling further.

Twenty minutes later, Dr. Mason hurriedly entered the exam room, clutching Rowan's chart. Rowan had again fallen asleep on the table. Alice moved to wake Rowan, but he shook his head.

"Let's talk first."

Alice held up her phone, signaling him to pause, and called Jonathan to ensure he heard the diagnosis firsthand, reinforcing the urgency of the situation. "Jonathan, I'm putting you on speaker."

Dr. Mason's voice was grim, and he got right to the point. "There is, in fact, something else wrong." Alice gave him a pointed look, conveying, "I told you so." He continued, "Rowan has IST, which is

Inappropriate Sinus Tachycardia. It is a condition where for no reason—no physical activity at all—the heart becomes tachycardic. The fact that you insisted on the ultrasound today, combined with Rowan having to lie there so long waiting for the test to begin, is, ironically enough, the only way we found the IST. This is an exceedingly rare condition, even more so in children, and very difficult to detect. What we had here today was a series of events that created the perfect storm." Dr. Mason looked pointedly at Alice and said, "It was a very lucky catch and one we may not have caught had it not been for you, Mrs. Miller."

Jonathan chimed in, his voice edged with alarm. "A lucky catch? What could have happened if you hadn't caught it?"

Dr. Mason looked at Alice and then down at the phone, "Well," Dr. Mason said, "If left undetected, Rowan's heart, at any time, could have reached 180 bpm, at which time, if cardioversion, which is stopping her heart and then restarting it, had not been done, there would have been a possibility she would have gone into cardiac arrest. In other words, her heart could have stopped beating. The good news is, we can fix it."

The room went silent for a few seconds; Alice, numb since she heard the words "*her heart could have stopped beating*" said, "How?"

"The sinus node needs to be ablated by at least sixty percent. An ablation means we will burn away part of her sinus node so that it no longer has the capacity to beat harder than normal. We would use a laser and go in through a vein in her neck. Once we get to the sinus node, the laser will burn off the amount that needs to go. It is a very delicate procedure and will take about three to five hours. However, it is not very invasive and carries negligible risk."

Jonathan's voice was shaky. "Are you saying Rowan has to undergo heart surgery?"

"Yes," Dr. Mason said. "That is exactly what I am saying."

Alice could only whisper, "When?"

Dr. Mason met her eyes. "Now. An ambulance will be here in ten minutes."

Chapter 12

A lice had heard the expression 'paralyzed with fear' before, but she had never truly understood its reality—until now. Within seconds, she felt nothing but cold. A cold that went deep into the bones. She had to force herself to breathe, managing only small, shallow gasps. Mostly, she was having trouble making herself move. Her brain was screaming at her body to "get it together," but her body remained frozen. It was only the sound of Jonathan's voice that brought her around.

"Alice! Alice, are you there?" Jonathan screamed through the phone. Alice slowly turned her head toward the noise and saw her cell phone lying at her feet. She must have dropped it. Then, as fast as the fear had overcome her, it was gone, and Alice went into high gear. She picked up the cell phone and, as she always did with emergencies, took control and gave orders.

"Is Ian still home?" she asked.

"No, Nate's dad came and picked him up about an hour ago. They have a Rec game tonight at Logan Park." Jonathan said.

Ian was on both a school soccer team and a community recreational league where they played against other recreational leagues in the surrounding counties through the Parks and Recreation Department. Logan Park was about two hours away, so she knew that Ian had another hour to go before getting there.

Jonathan had not yet said another word. Alice knew this was on her, and he was waiting to be told what to do.

"Ok, there is no need to freak him out, and there is absolutely no reason he should turn around and sit at the hospital for three to five hours. So here is how we are going to play this. Call Ian and let him know that Rowan must go to the hospital and have a procedure done. Do not tell him it's a surgery. Tell him you are only calling him so he knows where we are if he gets home and we are not there. He will ask questions...I want you to downplay everything. It's no big deal, or it's routine, and they happened to have a slot open. Say things like that. He will buy it as long as you talk to him on the phone."

Alice knew that neither of them could pull it off in person—Ian would see right through them like an open book. Alice continued.

"The game is two hours away, the game itself over an hour, and then a two-hour car ride back, so the surgery should be done by then, and Rowan should be in a room. Of course, I will stay there with her, and you will go home to Ian. If, for some reason, Rowan is still in surgery, we can ask Nate's dad to drop him off at the hospital."

Jonathan said, "Ok, but he's only an hour out. I'm sure James will turn around and meet me. I can run and get him..."

Alice broke in. "No, Jonathan, this is happening now. She is not going to be put in a room or even go to triage. She is going right into surgery, and Rowan will want you at the hospital. She will want to see you before if there is time. Ian is already too far away; he would never make it to the hospital before she goes in."

Alice knew she sounded cold and authoritative, but she knew her husband, and this was what he needed. He worked better in emergent situations if he simply did as she instructed.

Jonathan knew this, so instead of ever being annoyed by it, he welcomed it.

Alice continued, "I will ride with Rowan in the ambulance to the hospital and meet you there." She heard the slam of the car door and the roar of the engine as it started. She could hear through the phone that Jonathan was pulling out like a bat out of hell. She knew he was scared and felt even worse he was not here with her and Rowan; however, wrapping his car around a tree would help no one.

"Jonathan, slow down; the ambulance is not even here yet. You may actually get to the hospital before we do." There was no response. "Jonathan...are you there? Jonathan?" She said again, a bit louder. Then she could hear, plainly, his sharp intake of breath and the shudder of the exhalation. Alice closed her eyes tight against the tears she did not want Rowan to see when she was made to wake up. Jonathan was alone— terrified—and so overwhelmed with emotion that he could barely speak.

"It's going to be ok." She said to him. "Just get to the hospital safely. I promise it will be ok." He mumbled something that resembled a shaky "ok" and then ended the call. As Alice stood up to wake Rowan, she took a few deep breaths, in through her nose and out through her mouth. She walked over to the exam table, and as she was shaking Rowan to wake her up, she summoned every ounce of energy she had and put a huge smile on her face.

"Hey, punkins… teenagers are so impressive with their napping skills." Rowan began to sit up, but Alice gently placed a hand on her shoulder to keep her down.

"Are we done; can we go home now? What happened to the bike? Was it broken or something? Why did they make me get off?"

Alice took Rowan's hand and said, "Well, the thing is that when you had your ultrasound, they found something that was not right and the reason why your heart was beginning to beat too fast even though you weren't really doing much. So, they need to fix it, and they must do it right away, so an ambulance is on the way. Rowan's eyes got big as saucers, and she latched on to Alice's hand like an icy vice grip.

"Are you saying I have to have surgery on my heart?" Are they doing it today because it is an emergency? Where is daddy?" Alice was crumbling into little pieces on the inside, but on the outside, she was dismissive and unphased.

"Well, yes, it is best to have it done right away, and well…well, they happened to have an open surgical room, so Dr. Mason said, "No time like the present." Alice continued to smile and said, "It's really not that big of a deal. It's more a procedure than an actual surgery. They are going to insert a tiny little laser and burn off a small part of your heart that is beating too fast when it shouldn't be. They only need to do it in an operating room because you need to be under anesthesia. You will be in and out in no time."

Rowan looked down for a few seconds, and Alice could see she was trying to take all this in. Alice remained smiling, and when Rowan looked back up.

"So, I'm going to be, ok? Will I see daddy before I go in... Ian?"

Alice was way ahead of this question and knew the perfect answer because, as usual, Rowan took her cues from her momma. "Daddy is meeting us at the hospital, but Ian has an away game. Since this really is a simple procedure, we didn't feel the need for Ian to miss his game."

Alice watched as Rowan's shoulders relaxed and the stiffness of her face melted away. If Ian was still able to go to his game, clearly, in her mind, this was no big deal and exactly what Alice wanted her to think.

"Will I have to stay in the hospital after?"

Alice furrowed her brows and said, "You know, I'm not sure. Dr. Mason did not say. But if you do, it probably won't be for more than a night. Of course, I would stay with you, and we would send daddy on a knight's errand to get us Starbucks and pizza. Hospital or not, your royal highness must be kept up to the standards to which you are accustomed."

Just as Alice finished, Dr. Mason came in. Before he could say a word, Alice looked pointedly at him and said, "I have already explained everything to her. She understands that this is more of a procedure and not an operation. Not an uncommon procedure for someone with POTS, and it's all very simple."

Alice couldn't tell whether Dr. Mason was annoyed by her downplaying the situation or relieved that he didn't have to break the news himself. She didn't much care. Rowan was calm and no longer seemed scared, and that was all that mattered to Alice.

"Will I have to stay in the hospital overnight?" Rowan asked.

Dr. Mason looked at Alice as if he had no idea what she did or did not say about this very question. Alice looked at Dr. Mason and said, "I was not sure how to answer that one, but I should think that at least one night would be needed, given how late in the day it is."

Alice saw his face relax a bit, probably because Alice gave him the answer to the question. Dr. Mason smiled, getting on board with Alice. "Yes, it is quite late in the day. So, yes, I would like at least one night so that we can monitor your recovery. I shouldn't think more than one night should be needed."

"Momma said afterward, we can get Starbucks and pizza. Will I be allowed to have that? I mean, as a treat, you know, for having to have this procedure and all."

Dr. Mason gives a faux expression of pondering this question. "What kind of pizza?" he asks.

"I want pepperoni and sausage with extra cheese from Angelo's," she says.

He gives a big smile. "Angelo's, you say? I think we can do that. But we are getting large, and I'm buying. That is if you're willing to share?"

Rowan laughs and says, "Well, yeah, sure!"

The ambulance crew arrives, and Dr. Mason pats Rowan on the knee and says, "Ok then, it's a deal, kiddo...see you soon."

***

Since Rowan's surgery was being done on an emergency basis, the ambulance was a flurry of activity. The crew did their best to answer all of Alice's "what's that? and what are?" questions. They were prepping Rowan for the surgery, as much as they could, in the ambulance. As Alice watched them, she was quite impressed. By the time they had reached the hospital, they had already started an IV drip, placed all the leads for the heart monitor on her, and gave her a mild sedative to calm her nerves. Alice was glad they did that, as she could see that Rowan was getting nervous again despite the reassuring smile that never left Alice's face. It's quite simple. If Rowan is nervous, just like anyone else, her heartrate will speed up, and where that is normal for most people, it can be a very detrimental response for Rowan, who is about to go into surgery. So, the sedative, she was told, was to keep her body calm prior to going into surgery. Jonathan pulled into the emergency room just in time to see them getting Rowan out of the ambulance. He parks quickly, not even sure he is in one parking spot or taking up two. He meets the gurney as the doors of the ER slide open, and he sidles up to the side of her the best he can. Rowan is not asleep but in more of a relaxed twilight stage. Jonathan looks to Alice for answers to the questions and as usual, Alice does not need Jonathan to verbalize those questions.

"They prepped her in the ambulance, so she is going right into surgery." Jonathan went white and grabbed his daughter's hand, bringing it up to his lips for a soft kiss, all while trying to keep up with the gurney as it took fast turns down the hallways leading his sixteen-year-old daughter into heart surgery. As they go along, more medical personnel are joining in the rush to the operating room. They made one last turn when a nurse looked at both Jonathan and

Alice and said, "Ok, mom and dad, this is a far as you go. There is a surgical waiting room down the hall. The surgery should take anywhere from three to five hours, depending. We do our best to call the waiting room to give people updates on surgical procedures, but please do not worry if you get no updates. That in no way means something is wrong. Rowan's surgeon is Dr. Effland, and she will come out after the surgery to provide you an update."

Alice and Jonathan looked at each other, and then Alice said, "Dr. Mason is not performing the surgery?"

"No," the nurse says, "he is a cardiologist, but he is not a surgeon. Please be assured that he has been in partnership with Dr. Effland for a very long time and is rated one of the top pediatric cardiac surgeons in the country. I promise, your daughter is in good hands, and with that, we need to get Rowan in the OR."

Jonathan gave Rowan a kiss on the forehead and said, "I'll be right here when you wake up, punkins... ready to run the neighborhood gauntlet for all the normal comfort foods you women seem to prefer."

Rowan managed a faint smile and murmured, 'Pizza...chocolate...st...' before drifting into a light doze. Alice leaned down and kissed her daughter, and finished her sentence. "And Starbucks, of course. You've got this honey...it's a simple fix, and so I will see you soon, punkins; momma will be right here waiting."

As the gurney disappeared through the OR doors, Alice held on for those last fleeting seconds until Rowan was completely out of sight. Then she fell back against the wall, slid to the floor, covered her face with her hands, and let go of her emotions, sobbing until she had no more tears left to cry.

Chapter 13

The waiting room was fairly large and nearly empty as Alice and Jonathan entered. There were only three other people in the room. One was an older gentleman who had his head back against the wall, sound asleep and snoring lightly. The other two were a man and a woman, clearly together. Alice estimated them to be about ten years older than her and Jonathan, respectively. They looked up as she and Jonathan entered but said nothing, returning to their hushed conversation.

A TV high up on the wall was tuned to the news, though no one was watching. It seemed to serve merely as background noise, a distraction from fear. It may have been working for the others, but it did nothing for Alice. Terror gripped her, and she had to remind herself to breathe in and out. She was also chilled to the bone and feared she was going into shock. She had read about that—how people who experience trauma, whether physical or emotional, can go into shock. It was just one of the hundreds of medical research topics she had poured over since Rowan became ill.

Alice rallied, forcing herself to pull it together. She was "the leader" and "the fixer." Jonathan and Ian had always followed her example. Since Ian was not there, she took a deep breath and turned her focus to Jonathan. With any luck, she could have him reeled in before Ian arrived from his game so they could support him together. A united front was always best for Ian. If there was dissension in the ranks or if he sensed an emotion that contradicted their words, he had no problem calling them out on it. Vulgar jokes aside, her son was highly intelligent and perceptive.

Alice turned to Jonathan and inhaled sharply. He was pale as a ghost, and unlike her, he didn't seem to be holding it together enough to even regulate his breathing. His breaths were short and shallow—hyperventilating. She took his hand and turned to face him fully.

"Jonathan, calm down... you've got to slow your breathing... look at me."

Jonathan didn't move, not even to turn his head toward her. He just kept staring downward, his breaths coming faster.

"Jonathan," she said more firmly, gently taking hold of his chin and guiding his gaze to hers. "You need to calm down. Listen to me and watch me. Big breath in through your nose... big breath out through your mouth. Just do it with me, okay? In through your nose, out through your mouth."

Slowly, Jonathan began matching his breathing to Alice's, and his body became less tense.

"That's it... just keep doing it... in and out. Okay, a few more times, in and out."

When Jonathan started breathing on his own without her coaching, Alice stopped speaking, ready to praise him for regaining control. They balanced each other this way—when one faltered, the other stepped in. Once he was steadier, she massaged the back of her neck. A migraine was coming.

Alice rummaged in her purse and took one of her migraine pills. She knew it was stress-induced and that stress wasn't going away anytime soon. She hoped the pill would work, but if necessary, she'd take another. She had to be fully functional—not just for Rowan, but for the whole family. Jonathan noticed her rubbing her neck and reached over, placing his hand on hers. Then he began massaging the tense muscles, allowing her to lean back against the wall and take deeper breaths.

"That one came on pretty fast," Jonathan said.

"It's just stress; it won't last long," Alice replied.

"Maybe when things calm down, you should make an appointment. See if they can give you something stronger."

Alice rested her head on Jonathan's shoulder. "I will, I promise. But I just can't focus on that now."

Jonathan said nothing, only nodding and continuing to rub her neck. The current situation demanded center stage. Her migraines were pushed to the back burner—if they were even on the stove at all.

The waiting room had a vending machine stocked with sodas and snacks. There was also a Keurig with a basket of assorted coffee and tea. Alice squeezed Jonathan's hand in her lap.

"How about something to drink? Maybe a snack?" she suggested.

"Yeah, sure. Anything. It doesn't matter. Whatever you're getting," he murmured.

Alice wasn't hungry or thirsty, and she knew Jonathan wasn't either. But it was about having something to do—something tangible to focus on. She got up, made them each a coffee, and bought a small pack of mini donuts from the snack machine.

Jonathan accepted the offering gratefully. "How long has she been in there? I kind of went off the grid for a few minutes. Sorry about that."

"No need to apologize. You pulled it together within a minute or two." Alice stretched the truth a bit—he likely had no memory of how long he had been out of it. "I have no idea how long I sat in the hallway crying, so I don't know how long you had to stand there waiting for me to pull myself together. We're even."

Alice glanced at the clock on the wall and was shocked to realize that Rowan had already been in surgery for half an hour. She needed to do a better job of keeping track of time. Jonathan, as always, read her mind.

"You're not made of steel, you know," Jonathan said, taking her hand. "It's okay to fall apart for longer than sixty seconds. I promise I won't time it." Then he smiled and whispered, "I will say nothing... no one will ever know."

Alice smiled at him. Whenever she went off the rails— whether about dirty dishes, muddy shoes, backpacks left on the stairs, or towels piled high in the bathroom—he could bring her back down with humor. They grounded each other, and those two halves made a whole.

I called Pastor Carl on the way over here and told him what was going on. He told me to keep him in the loop and he would provide updates to church members in a group chat. He thought it better than us being bombarded with individual texts." Jonathan said.

Alice nodded to him and said, "Good, that was a good idea. I am not really up to that right now anyway but I would have felt bad ignoring the texts." Alice smiled to herself as she pictured her front porch covered in every conceivable form of casserole and baked goods.

No more than ten minutes later, Alice's phone began to ring, and she saw it was their Pastors' wife Wendi. Alice considered letting it go to voicemail, but Jonathan was deep in thought and pacing—a sign he was coping. With hours to go before Rowan would be out of surgery, Alice answered the call.

"Alice! my friend, my sister, my giiiirrrrrlll, talk to me. What do you need me to do?"

"Not much you can do right now but pray," Alice said to her.

Wendi gave a small laugh. "Girl, that's all we've been doing over here—praying. Then we pray for our prayers to be answered, and then we pray the first prayers all over again."

"What do you mean *over here*?" Alice asked. "Where are you?"

"We're at the church. The prayer warriors doubled in size, and then they started showing up at our front door. We were going to have to start stacking people on top of each other, so Carl hopped up on a kitchen chair and said, 'We're regrouping at the church before you break my house.'"

Alice laughed despite herself. It wasn't hard to picture Pastor Carl doing just that.

Wendi continued, "By the time I got myself and the kids out the door, the warriors had already been hard at work at the church—making coffee and food. Half of that food is now on your porch. You know us God-fearing Christians... strong prayer and a casserole can fix anything."

Alice smiled, knowing she had been right about her porch being full of food.

"So, do you have an update yet?" Wendi asked.

"No," Alice said. "Not yet. They've only been in there just shy of an hour. They said it would take three to five hours and not to get too worked up if we didn't get an update during surgery."

She went on, "And Ian, where is he? Do you need me to help get him around?"

Wendi's son, Luke, as well as Ian were youth pastors in training. They both do activities with the younger kids, mostly involving sports or any outdoor game or activity. They acted like it was such a chore, but Alice had seen both in action and knew they both ate it up when the younger kids looked at them like they were rock stars.

"We are good with Ian; Nate's dad is dropping him off after his game either here or at the house, depending. We just told him that Rowan had to have a very "minor procedure" done and blew it off as no big deal. We saw no need to worry him. By the time this all went down, he was already over an hour away for a game."

"Good, that's perfect. If you seemed aloof about it, he would go with that...until he sees your face anyway...then you're cooked. Ian is very perceptive."

91

It didn't faze Alice in the least that she could pick up on Ian's perceptiveness; nothing much gets by her.

"Ok, so more people are storming the gates...there's a whole lotta love going around this building. I need to work on crowd control. Call or text me or Carl when you know something. I'm going to announce that you two are not doing the private messaging thing and that updates are to come through us. You've got enough going on...is that a good idea?"

"That is perfect, and I think Jonathan already talked with Carl about that," Alice said.

Wendi snickered and said, "Oh, well, of course he did. Why should I know about that since I'm only his wife...geez, men can't live with'em and can't drop them off with the Catholics. Can I get an amen?"

Alice laughed fully and properly, then eliciting a glance from Jonathan. "Wendi, your parents are Catholic!" Alice said through laughter mixed with tears.

Wendi laughed and said, "Yeah, I know, but you can't pick your parents, right?"

Alice giggled and said, "You are terrible."

"Guilty as charged," Wendi said, "but I'm joking, and you know that. No matter the religion, when the going gets tough, we all end up down on our knees praying to a God who loves all. Things were a bit too much, and we needed to ease the tension even for just a minute; it's good for the soul. I cannot imagine what you are going through, but keep your head up. I don't just mean to keep your head in the game. I mean, lift your head up and pray and keep on praying, and you will gain strength from that. He sees you, and he hears you.

Now, I'm telling you that's good pastoral advice. Alice got quiet. "Alice? You still there?"

Alice gave a shuttering sigh and said, "Yeah, I'm still here, and I so appreciate your guidance, but does He? Hear me and see me, I mean, because I'm not sure He does. I just don't understand. I am just so lost. I am scared, frustrated, and so incredibly angry."

Wendi asked, "Angry with God, do you mean?"

Alice took a ragged breath, and all her emotions started to seep out at once. "Yes, I am! I will own that. I am truly angry at God. Why her Wendi? Why is God allowing murderers and rapists to run amok and be alive and well, while Rowan is suffering so? I've been praying a lot. Praying for answers, praying for Him to make her better, praying for Him to take this burden from her and give it to me. That is all I do is pray. But I don't think He is listening, for He has answered nothing, and Rowan is getting worse. You know me. You know how steeped in our faith I am and that all my family is.

So, I ask you again, is He really there, because I don't see it, or feel it. If He is there, as you say, then why is he not answering? I don't know what else to do, but minute by minute, hour by hour, and day by day, my faith is dwindling, and trying to hold onto it has become exhausting."

Wendi gave Alice a few seconds to calm herself and a few seconds of reflection and then said, "Faith is not always easy, Alice. Faith will be strong when all is going well, but faith can easily falter when things are going wrong, yet that is when you need it the most. Faith is a powerful emotion, and once it is lost, it is hard to get back. As I said, it is not particularly easy to have to begin with. You are being tested, and keeping your faith is the only way you will pass the test and make it out on the other side. For example, how do you open a door?"

Alice sighed again and said, "Wendi, really, I appreciate the support, but I'm not in the mood for a parable or a scripture lesson."

"It's not either of those," Wendi said. "I am literally asking you, how do you open a door?"

Alice rolled her eyes and said in exasperation, "You turn the knob and open the door. I'm sorry, but I don't get your point."

"The point is," Wendi said, "is that you know the doorknob will work. You have the knowledge, tangible proof, that the doorknob will open that door. You know, because you can see it, you can feel it when you put your hand on it, and you can hear the mechanism inside when you turn it, which allows you to open the door. Faith and knowledge are two vastly different things. Having faith is believing in what you cannot see, touch, or hear. There is no scientific evidence that God exists, and yet we walk in faith daily because we believe it to be so. That is why having faith in God is hard. If it were easy, everyone would have it. God does not give you your faith. You get and give your faith to Him and through Him. A good number of people cannot or choose not to see it. They lack faith in Him. For instance, look at the rainbow. The Bible tells us that as the waters receded, Noah came up on deck and saw a rainbow. God told him that this was an outward sign, a solid covenant, that he would never again flood the earth or punish us, regardless of how we choose to live our lives. That His "judgment" for everyone would be a "to be determined" later, so to speak. I've seen a rainbow. You have seen a rainbow. We of faith do not think it is just a coincidence that you see that rainbow directly following a rainstorm, just as it did in the bible. The explanation for it was written thousands of years ago before science came about and scientifically explained it as being like a prism. That water molecules lingering in the air or reflected off the ground when the sun immediately comes back out. Yet, some people totally discount the explanation in the bible and instead go all in on the science because science is easier to believe and, to them, much more likely. I'm not judging anyone. I have the utmost respect for those who take science over God because that is *their* belief system."

Wendi continued, "I am not one to force my God on anyone, and I appreciate it when friends do not try to force their science on me. They walk in the knowledge of it, and we walk in the faith of it. God gave us free will, and with that comes happiness and good times, but it also comes with tragedy and sorrow. Terrible things will happen to good people, and when that happens, more than ever, you need to lean on your faith, not doubt it. There can be no good without evil, and vice versa. That is just the "free will," the natural order of things, *here*. But being here is our temporary home. When it is all said and done, the light pushes through the darkness. God answers all prayers, every single one of them. However, the answer is not always yes. Sometimes, it is "maybe" or "not yet," and sometimes, Alice, the answer is no and without any explanation for it. I do not have the answer to that, but God does. Faith that He has a plan is all we have, so we must make it enough, *for now*. The answer will come. In time, the answer will make itself known. I guarantee it. He does not want or expect you to go through this alone, but only faith will bring Him to your aid. Ultimately aid you in what, I don't know, but *He* does know. Is this making sense to you?"

Alice responded, "Yes, and I don't know how you do it, but no matter what is happening, even just a regular Sunday service, you or Pastor Carl always know what to say, to say exactly what I need to hear. You both are truly gifted Pastors."

Wendi said, "Well, I don't know about all that, but my daddy always used to tell me that every now and then, even a blind squirrel finds a nut."

Alice couldn't help but smile. "Thanks, Wendi. I didn't realize how much I needed a faith power-up."

Alice ended the call and said a quick prayer that God would shoot her a bolt of faith. However, she ended that prayer by telling God that Rowan must be ok and pleaded with Him to understand. Because the alternative was not only unacceptable, but it was also unthinkable, whatever his plan. As far as her faith was concerned, that was the best she could do for now, but she promised herself she would work on it.

Chapter 14

T he surgery ended up taking just over five hours. Rowan's blood pressure wasn't fully cooperating, and they had to stop several times to let it stabilize. Now, Alice and Jonathan sat on either side of her in the recovery room. It had been about thirty minutes, and she still hadn't come out of anesthesia.

Alice wasn't too worried—yet. When Rowan had her tonsils removed at six years old, she had been the first child on the surgical roster that day but the last to wake up. Alice had grown nervous back then, watching other children who had gone in after Rowan woke up and left while she remained asleep.

"Some people just come out of anesthesia slower than others, and she happens to be one of them. Her vitals are fine, so she should wake up soon," the anesthesiologist had reassured her.

Alice could tell Jonathan was getting anxious, and normally, she would have been able to talk him down. But tonight, he was having none of it.

"What's taking so long?" he asked, his voice edged with panic. "Should we have someone check on her again?"

Alice reached for his hand and gave it a reassuring squeeze. "Let's give her another fifteen minutes. This is exactly how it was when she had her tonsils out."

Jonathan exhaled sharply, still gripping Rowan's hand. Alice knew he was struggling. He hadn't been at the tonsillectomy—he'd been scheduled to speak at a conference in Las Vegas, and Alice had assured him there was no need to miss it.

"The doctor said she'd be in and out of surgery in under thirty minutes and then home the same day. It's no big deal. It's not like the tonsillectomies we had back in the seventies when you were in the hospital for three days," she had told him.

So, Jonathan went to the conference. Then, to ease his guilt, he had overcompensated with a stop at Toys 'R' Us on the way home from the airport. Of course, he couldn't leave Ian out, so they had ended up with Christmas in July.

Now, he checked his watch every few minutes, his anxiety mounting. Before Alice could try calming him again, a woman peeked through the curtain and then gently stepped inside.

"Hello," she said, shaking both of their hands. "I'm Dr. Rose Effland, the surgeon who operated on your daughter. I do apologize that this is our first meeting. Normally, I speak with my patients and their families beforehand, but with this young lady, we didn't have that luxury. I imagine you both have a million questions, and I'll stay as long as it takes to answer each one. But first, would you like me to walk you through everything I did?"

Alice was grateful to let someone else take control, at least for the moment. Jonathan simply nodded. Dr. Effland rolled a stool over and sat down.

"First off, I want to say that I was fully briefed on how all of this came about. Dr. Mason told me how adamant you were, Mrs. Miller, about getting an ultrasound done today when it hadn't been scheduled for another month. IST is extremely difficult to detect, and even more so in children because it's so rare. However, I want you to know that, as both a doctor and a mother, I applaud you for advocating for your daughter. Your instinct told you something was wrong, and you didn't back down. If you hadn't been so vigilant, I'm not sure how long it would have taken us to find it—if we ever had. Usually, IST is detected during a hospital stay with continuous monitoring or through the use of a Holter monitor. The fact that we caught it during a twenty-minute ultrasound is, quite frankly, a miracle."

The word miracle struck Alice hard. She immediately thought of her conversation with Wendi. *Maybe He was listening. Maybe He did answer my prayer. And this time, the answer was yes.*

She snapped back to the present as Dr. Effland continued.

"It may not seem like it right now, but your daughter is incredibly lucky. I mean, as it pertains to the IST and the fact that we caught it in time. That being said, she will have to be even more closely monitored."

"What do you mean when you say she'll need even closer monitoring?" Alice asked, her voice wary. "Can IST come back?"

"No," Dr. Effland said, shaking her head. "The sinus node was ablated by sixty-eight percent. That should, for the most part, keep it from generating the dangerously high heart rates it was producing before. However, there's a possibility of a different issue—bradycardia."

Alice frowned. "Bradycardia?"

Dr. Effland nodded. "It's when the heart beats too slowly—under sixty beats per minute. Essentially, it means the heart's natural pacemaker isn't functioning properly, or its electrical pathways are disrupted. By altering Rowan's sinus node, we may have created a new challenge. That's why she'll need continued monitoring."

Alice felt as though the floor had dropped out from under her. She was trying to absorb everything, but it was too much. "So… in fixing one part of her heart, we may have damaged another?"

Dr. Effland sighed. "It's possible, but there was no other option. The IST had to be addressed immediately. If the bradycardia does develop, we can regulate her heartbeat with a pacemaker. It's not ideal, but it's manageable. The good news is that I don't see anything indicating her POTS has worsened. She still has a chance to grow out of it."

Alice nodded slowly. It was all too much to process, but she managed to ask, "What happens next?"

Dr. Effland stood and moved to Rowan's bedside. "First, let's see what's going on with our sleepyhead." She took a small flashlight from her coat pocket, lifted Rowan's eyelids, and shined the light into each eye.

Jonathan stiffened. "What's wrong? Why are you doing that?"

Before Dr. Effland could answer, Rowan stirred. "Mmm… what's happening?"

Dr. Effland smiled. "Ah, there she is. I thought I was going to have to break out the smelling salts."

Alice grinned. "You missed dinner, so we were about to order pizza without you."

Rowan's eyes fluttered open fully, and she looked at Dr. Effland. "Did you fix it? Is my heart fixed? When can I go back to cheerleading?"

Dr. Effland chuckled. "That's a lot of questions. The short answers are: chances are good, I truly hope so, and I don't know. But I promise, we're going to figure it out."

Chapter 15

Rowan ended up needing to stay in the hospital more than one night. At first, she wasn't amused by the extended confinement, but she quickly came around when she was showered with attention—not just from her family but also from her friends at school and their church congregation. Visitors arrived in a steady stream, bearing flowers, stuffed animals, candy, and handwritten notes. The constant love and support did wonders for her morale, and Alice was more than grateful. The steady flow of people in and out of the hospital room gave Alice a chance to sit quietly and reflect.

At present, it seemed like God's plan was to rally Rowan through this, and Alice was more than happy to let Him take the wheel. Even if, for her, that only meant having time to get her head on straight and process everything that had happened—and everything still to come. She and Jonathan had avoided discussing the potential complications that could arise following Rowan's surgery. Neither of them had been ready to face it.

But the previous night, before Jonathan headed home from the hospital, they finally had the conversation. There was no question that Alice would be the one staying with Rowan. However, they disagreed on how much to tell her about the potential risks.

"She's not a baby, Alice. She's sixteen. She can handle it," Jonathan had argued. "I just don't want her to be blindsided if the ablation damaged her heart further instead of fixing it."

Alice, however, was firmly on the other side of the debate. "Why worry her needlessly? We should stick to the facts of *what is* rather than burden her with *what-ifs*. That's for you and me to handle."

Alice could see the uncertainty and strain on his face. "Ok, how about a compromise..we will let Dr. Mason take the lead on that one. He is very good at getting down on her level. He works with sick kids everyday and she will probably have questions we cannot answer anyway."

Jonathan nodded in agreement and said, "Ok, sounds like a good plan. If Rowan does have questions, we can be there for her if she does not like the answers."

Alice smiled and nodded; glad they were both on the same side again.

***

When Dr. Mason came in on the second day he had assured them that nothing was wrong, but he wanted Rowan to remain on the heart monitor for another full day. Her heart had been beating within normal limits for the past two mornings, which was a good sign, but Alice remained only cautiously optimistic, waiting for the other shoe to drop. In front of Rowan, however, she masked her nerves, keeping a bright smile on her face and maintaining a light-hearted tone. It was working—Rowan was in good spirits. She had gotten her pizza and Starbucks as promised, but Alice could tell she was growing anxious. She had already asked several times when Dr. Mason would be in so she could ask about going home.

Alice wasn't sure how Dr. Mason would answer, so she stuck to reassuring her daughter. "He has other patients besides just *you*, punkins' but I'm positive he'll be in at some point. Daddy is coming after he drops Ian off at school. Want him to bring you something to eat?"

Rowan had already refused the hospital breakfast—something Alice couldn't blame her for, given its appearance. But at the mention of food from outside the hospital, Rowan's eyes lit up.

"Can I get a mocha Frappuccino and a piece of banana bread from Starbucks?"

Alice inwardly cringed. Although Rowan hadn't been placed on any dietary restrictions—at least not yet—she was nervous about all that sugar and caffeine. Still, Dr. Mason had allowed her to indulge her first night here, so Alice relented. Keeping Rowan in good spirits felt like the best plan for now.

"Absolutely," Alice said. "And I think we'll double that order because this hospital coffee is for the birds."

She picked up her phone to text Jonathan but then decided to call instead. With Rowan's earbuds in, she was already absorbed in her virtual world and wouldn't hear anything.

"Hey," she said when Jonathan answered. "Rowan wants her usual—mocha Frappuccino and banana bread, please."

Jonathan chuckled. "That's her signature order, so she must be feeling pretty good. Has Dr. Mason or Dr. Effland been in yet?"

"Not yet, but a nurse came in around five this morning to check her vitals. She said Dr. Mason would be here sometime this morning before heading to his office."

Jonathan was quiet for a moment. "We haven't really talked about this yet, but what are we going to do about Dr. Mason? On the one hand, we're being told he's the best for both her heart and POTS. But on the other, he *missed* a diagnosis that could have killed our daughter."

Alice had been expecting this. She had seen the way Jonathan distanced himself from Dr. Mason the night before. She had felt the same anger at first. But while Jonathan had gone home to bring back necessities for their extended hospital stay, Alice had spent the entire night researching IST. She pored over medical journals, case studies, and even online support groups, reading personal experiences from parents and patients alike.

By early morning, she had reached a conclusion. Dr. Effland had been right—IST was incredibly rare in children and even harder to diagnose. And as she read through Dr. Mason's professional profile and patient testimonials, one thing became clear: he *was* as good as they said. There were countless accounts of him diagnosing conditions other doctors had missed and managing POTS so well that his patients could lead normal lives. Alice realized something else—he had humbled himself. He had admitted he'd overlooked something and had taken immediate action to correct it. That mattered.

So, she told Jonathan about everything she had found. And she told him her decision.

"I think we should stick with Dr. Mason," she said.

Jonathan hesitated but finally sighed. "If that's what you think is best, then that's what we'll do. But God, Alice, I was *so* scared. I still am." "I am, too," she admitted. "But we'll get through this like we always do—together. And I promise you this: I will continue to advocate for Rowan. If that 'momma bear' instinct kicks in again, I won't back down. If I had backed down this time, we could have lost her. That *won't* happen again, and I'll make that clear." Jonathan was silent for only a beat before saying, "Sounds good, coach. Consider me on the team. And I have no doubt you'll let Dr. Mason know exactly where we stand. You can be *very* scary, you know. You've scared the crap out of me more than once." Alice chuckled. "Oh yeah? Well, don't you forget it. By the way, I love you." "I know. How could you not? I mean, have you *seen* me? There's a whole lot of hotness going on here. Even Ruth at the coffee shop in town will tell you—she's been after me for years."

Alice laughed. "Isn't Ruth like eighty?"

"Why yes, she is. But she's a *very* young eighty, and she's made no bones about it—she totally wants me."

"I see," Alice said, amused. "Well, I'll be sure to advise her to back off next time I see her. But in the meantime, *Sir Hotness*, your daughter has a Starbucks order, and I need the biggest coffee they have. This hospital coffee tastes like mud."

Jonathan laughed. "Okay, tell *Her Highness* I'm on it. I'll drop Ian off and then carry out my royal duties. See you soon."

Alice hung up the phone and glanced at her daughter, who was laughing sporadically at something on her screen—probably a viral video. She checked the monitor. Rowan's heart rate was steady at 68. *Perfect.*

Alice felt confident they had made the right choice to stay with Dr. Mason. But deep in her heart, the fear still lingered. She hoped that, in time, her heart would catch up with her mind because getting this wrong wasn't an option. Not when the stakes were this high.

Chapter 16

A bout forty minutes later, Jonathan arrived with all the requested provisions. As they all chowed down on the goodies, Dr. Mason came in, pulled up one of the chairs in the room, and sat down next to Rowan's bed. "So, how are you feeling this morning?"

Rowan sat up a bit straighter. Alice knew the first question before she even opened her mouth. "I feel pretty good. Have I been here long enough? Can I go home? And if so, when can I go back to cheerleading?"

Dr. Mason smiled. "I hope your coach knows the level of your dedication to the team. You are one tenacious young lady when it comes to cheer." Alice could see the pride in her daughter's face.

"I have been cheering since middle school. I can cheer any position on the squad."

Dr. Mason patted her leg. "Of that, I have no doubt. However, you're going to have to take it easy for a while, and unfortunately, that means no cheer just yet." Rowan's face fell.

"However, is that assistant coach gig still available? Because of that, I can approve."

"Yeah, I guess," Rowan said in a small voice. "Will I ever be able to cheer again?"

Dr. Mason looked a bit uneasy, and Alice knew the answer wasn't something he could promise. Her heart warmed toward him; it was evident it pained him to have to tell her so.

"That is part of my end goal for you, I promise. However, we must get through some steps successfully first before we revisit cheer or any other strenuous activity. So, here's how things are going to play out, and there are different options. We fixed your heart, but in doing so, we *may* have created a new problem with it. Now, that would have been the outcome for anyone who had undergone that... I mean, procedure."

Dr. Mason went on to explain how her heart might, at some point, start to beat too slowly and why. Jonathan and Alice exchanged a knowing glance, having heard all this information from Dr. Effland the night of the surgery. Rowan didn't ask for any further clarification, and Alice was relieved that Dr. Mason kept it light, avoiding unnecessary specifics. The here and now was enough for anyone to process, let alone a sixteen-year-old girl.

Dr. Mason continued, "There is only one way to determine that. I need to monitor your heart activity twenty-four hours a day, every day, for the next four weeks. If all goes well, we can reduce monitoring to every other week. If that goes smoothly, we can discuss weaning off the monitoring altogether. We can do this in the hospital, as you are now, but you've been stable over the last several days, so I feel comfortable having you wear a portable electrocardiogram machine—a Holter monitor, or ECG for short."

He explained that the portable machine would involve the same sticky pads with leads that connected to a small device worn on a belt. "If you choose the portable machine, you don't need to stay in the hospital. However, you cannot take it off, even when sleeping or bathing. The device has a retractable cord, so you can place it on a nightstand or bathroom counter when needed. The chip inside allows me to pull up data from my office. This way, you can return to school and help with the cheer squad—but no actual cheering, not yet."

Alice wasn't sure what to think. She was torn between wanting Rowan to be in the safety of the hospital and knowing that weeks spent in this room would crush her daughter. Other than the cheer restriction, Rowan seemed surprisingly okay with the conditions of her release. Rowan loved attention, but what sixteen-year-old girl didn't? The school was willing to accommodate her return instead of homeschooling during the monitoring period.

The day after the surgery, the high school principal, Ms. Harper, called Alice to check on Rowan and discuss a game plan.

"I have met with all her teachers and the guidance counselor, and we feel that getting back to a regular routine—as regular as we can make it—will help Rowan deal with this on an emotional and psychological level. Of course, you and Jonathan have the final say. If homeschooling is what you decide, we're prepared to help coordinate that. All her teachers—the whole staff, really—are willing to put in the extra work to support Rowan. I'm getting constant emails from teachers asking about her well-being, and some of them aren't even her teachers. I've had offers of in-home tutoring from staff and students. In short, we can provide Rowan with all the support she needs to keep her on track. The last thing anyone wants is for her to be held back due to absences. I have received authorization from the school board to implement any of this based on what you and your husband decide."

There were some drawbacks to small-town life—fewer resources, limited shopping options, and everyone knowing your business—but there were advantages, too. When someone was in need, the community showed up. The entire faculty and student body at the high school were eager to help.

At discharge, Alice, Jonathan, and Dr. Mason discussed the "here and now." Rowan decided she wanted to return to school. It wasn't often that a teenager chose school over an alternative, but Rowan had missed so much that she craved the interaction. Alice knew her main motivation was staying involved with cheer in any way she could. They agreed to tell Rowan information on an "as-needed basis" unless she asked questions. If she asked about "what ifs," they would be honest, but otherwise, they wouldn't overwhelm her with unnecessary details.

Alice turned to Rowan. "What do you think?"

Rowan was quiet for a moment, then smirked. "Do I still get to leave class early and have Blake push me in the wheelchair?"

Dr. Mason chuckled. "That's going to be a no. I need the data to show me how your heart responds to regular activity."

Rowan's eyes lit up, but before she could say anything, Dr. Mason added, "But no cheer, kiddo. For now."

Rowan sighed, resigned to the non-negotiable restriction. "Well, I guess I'd rather do this monitoring thing at home. The food here really sucks... stinks! I meant stinks! Sorry, Momma."

Alice laughed. "That's okay. The food here does suck especially the coffee."

Rowan's eyes went wide at Alice's choice of words. Then Dr. Mason chimed in and nodded in agreement.

"Okay," Dr. Mason said, "the nighttime monitoring looks promising. I'll have a nurse come in and get you set up with the portable ECG and explain how it works. I've called my office, and they'll be in touch to schedule your follow-up a week from today. We'll stick to that schedule for the next month. Once we review the data, we'll make decisions about whether you can go off the monitor and for how long. How does that sound?"

Rowan nodded. "Sounds good. Even if I can't cheer, being an assistant coach is better than nothing."

Dr. Mason smiled. "This is a big responsibility on your part, too. I need you to follow instructions and keep up with your journal. The more information I have, the sooner I can answer your cheerleading question. This is a team effort. What do you say?"

Rowan nodded. "Yes, I got it. I'll do whatever it takes if it gets me closer to cheering again."

Dr. Mason stood to leave. "Alice, Jonathan, if anything seems off—anything at all—call my service immediately. They'll contact me directly, no matter the hour."

He looked at Alice. "This is a team approach. I learned a few days ago that there is no 'I' in team. It's a mistake I won't make again."

Alice nodded and sat up straighter. "No, I don't believe you will. I'll make sure of that."

Chapter 17

After the nurse came in, hooked up the monitor, and explained how it worked, Rowan was finally released to go home. Leaving the hospital was bittersweet for Alice. As she got into the car, she felt like she was leaving a safe haven, stepping into a world filled with uncertainties she did not want to think about.

They stopped for provisions—well, "Rowan provisions" more like. They stood in line at the grocery store with a cart loaded down with Ramen noodles, brownie and cake mixes, and a twelve-pack of bottled Starbucks vanilla coffee. Alice gladly put the items in the cart but made sure to balance them with fresh fruit, sugar-free yogurts, and various flavors of one-hundred-percent fruit juice.

Upon arrival home, they were greeted by the sight of their front porch overflowing with covered Tupperware containers filled with what Alice could only imagine was every kind of casserole known to man. The sight warmed her heart. Family—that's what this was. This was what it looked like to have people in your corner through both the good and the bad. The last thing Alice wanted to do was cook, and it was clear she wouldn't have to for many days.

"That's only today's offering," Jonathan said. "You should see the fridge and freezer. We have enough pre-made meals to last us a month or more. I have no idea where we're going to put it all." Alice smiled. "It's nice though, isn't it? The people we have in our life, in our corner."

Jonathan put an arm around her as they walked up the path. "Indeed, it is. As scary as all of this is, it's comforting to know that so many people are making it a priority to take care of us. Besides, if we give Ian free rein, half of this stuff will be gone in two days flat. That'll solve the storage issue."

Rowan was out of the car in a flash. Both Alice and Jonathan simultaneously shouted, "Rowan, slow down!" She halted mid-step, then walked the rest of the way into the house, glancing back with a sheepish, "Yes! Right, sorry!"

Alice shook her head, knowing she was going to have to watch her daughter like a hawk. Rowan had already been brooding on the way home over Alice's purchase of a baby monitor.

"You're kidding, right? So, I lose my privacy on top of cheer? No way you're putting that thing in my room."

Maybe it was over the top, but Jonathan backed her up. "Look, Punkins, this monitor is set to go off if your heart beats too fast or too slow. We need to be able to hear that. I mean, unless you're not planning on sleeping with your earbuds in."

Alice knew this was a good argument. Rowan fell asleep every night listening to music.

"Fine, I won't sleep with them," Rowan grumbled.

Alice had anticipated that. "Whether you use your earbuds or not, the monitor is staying. If not, Daddy and I will never be able to sleep. Look, we won't turn it on until you're down for the night. I won't be listening to your phone calls if that's the issue."

Rowan sighed. "Fine, but only when I'm about to go to sleep, okay? You're big on compromise, Momma, and I think that's a fair one."

"Okay, agreed. I accept the terms of the compromise," Alice said.

Jonathan cuffed Rowan lightly on the shoulder. "Excellent negotiation skills, my girl—top-notch. Your mom's a tough cookie to crack."

Rowan seemed to take a little pride in "negotiating" her own terms, a small smile creeping onto her face as she walked toward the stairs. Halfway up, Ian emerged from the kitchen, chomping on a muffin nearly the size of his head.

He eyed Rowan. "What, no hello for your brother who's been fielding your social circus for the past three days while you napped twelve hours a day in 'La Hospital Royale'?" With a flourish of his arms, he added, "And could you pretty please send a message by text, snail mail, or carrier pigeon, for all I care, to your chicks in the henhouse? I can't keep answering questions about the merits of push-up bras versus underwire or regular lipstick over lip-plumping gloss."

Rowan gave him a look of pure sisterly disdain. "Oh yeah? Still, sneaking into my room to drool over my *Teen Glamour* magazines? You're such a little perv."

"Okay, okay, neutral corners," Jonathan interjected. Then, turning to Alice, he said, "Well, getting back to normal took all of three minutes."

To Alice, however, the banter was music to her ears.

***

By Sunday, Alice had felt so safe in her little cocoon that she was hesitant about church.

"Pastor Carl said he could come over after the service to visit," Alice protested.

Jonathan shook his head. "Rowan's going to school tomorrow, so you're just trying to put off the inevitable. She needs to get back to a routine, just as Dr. Mason ordered. We need to go to church, Alice. If we're going to lean on our faith, then we need to feed our faith. It'll be good for Rowan to go— for all of us. The congregation has put us front and center, and they need to see us as much as we need to see them."

Alice reluctantly agreed but was more than a little apprehensive about Rowan leaving the house. Jonathan didn't seem to understand her deep need to keep Rowan wrapped in a protective bubble. Her mind agreed with him, but her heart wanted to keep things exactly as they were—safe and contained.

At church, the reception was overwhelming. Rowan was elevated to near-superstar status, her monitor a source of fascination. The older members of the congregation were wary but impressed by modern medicine. When a few of Rowan and Ian's friends encouraged her to jump up and down to trigger the alarm, Alice moved to intervene but stopped when she saw Rowan shake her head and explain why she couldn't. *Okay*, Alice thought, hopefully she is *getting it* now.

Rowan and Ian usually sat with their friends. There was a section of seats that was unofficially for teenagers. As they took their seats, Alice tried to relax. The worship music began and even though Rowan did stand up, she did not jump around and dance to the music with the ferocity she usually did with her friends. Alice kept one eye on her, and when Rowan looked over at her, Alice smiled and gave her a thumbs up. Rowan smiled and mouthed, "Is this ok?" Alice nodded, and her daughter went back to watching the band and giggling over Corey, who was up on-stage playing bass guitar. She had gone bonkers when he sent Rowan a text while in the hospital saying how he hoped she was doing ok, and the team missed seeing her in the cheer squad during games.

She quickly turned a deep beet red when Jonathan and Ian heard about the text, thanks to Alice blabbing about it. "Really, mother?" she had said. Alice knew it was a serious infraction when she heard the word "mother" instead of momma.

"Awwwe...ain't that sweet." Said Ian, "Geez, what a total candy ass...I mean rea..."

"Zip it, Ian," said Rowan, "You're just jealous because the only girls that even remotely flirt with you are the ones selling Girl Scout cookies outside the Walmart." Rowan retorted back.

Jonathan began to laugh hysterically, and Ian shot him a look. Jonathan immediately cleared his throat and put on a serious look, "What? Those caramel coconut ones are the bomb; maybe you can, you know, hook me up with a box or two through your studly connections."

Rowan thought this comical, and Jonathan joined back in. Ian began to trudge up the stairs, shaking his head.

"We'll work on it, dad. The content, the delivery, all of it. It's weak; I'm not buying it, and you shouldn't be selling it." Alice could see the small smile on Ian's face and knew he was proud of yet another successful comedic exit.

After service, there was a fellowship gathering in the recreation hall, which was complete with cookies and punch. The church did it once a month and it was nice having time to spend with fellow parishioners. Pastor Carl approached Alice, placing a comforting hand on her shoulder. "I won't pretend I know what you and Jonathan are going through, but I want you to know you don't have to go through it alone. We weren't meant to do life alone. That's not how God made us."

Alice nodded but made no reply.

"I sense a test of faith," he added gently.

Alice looked up at him. "Yes, you could say that. I just had this conversation with Wendi. But try as I might, I can't stop myself from asking why. I think I could handle it better if I just knew why."

Pastor Carl sighed. "No, you wouldn't. Even if God gave you an answer right now, it wouldn't change how you feel. Knowing the *why* doesn't make it any easier. Sometimes, knowing makes it worse. But having faith that the answer will come—that's what gets us through."

Alice considered his words and, for the first time in days, felt a small measure of peace.

Pastor Carl smiled. "Besides, everything looks better when eating cookies and drinking punch. So, what do you say?"

119

Alice shook her head with a quiet chuckle. "Okay, okay. Let's go. But fair warning—Ian and his friends have already been in there for fifteen minutes. So don't get your heart set on too many cookies."

"Way ahead of you," he added with a wink. "I hid some in a container in the dishwasher."

Alice looked at him questioningly. "The dishwasher?"

"Yep. No teenager in my house ever goes near it."

She smiled, feeling lighter than she had in days. Pastor Carl slipped his arm through Alice's to formally escort her into the dining hall. "Two cups of punch and dishwasher cookies coming right up."

Chapter 18

T he fellowship gathering went well and passed without incident. It would seem that Jonathan was right on that score. As they gathered to leave, Pastor Carl met them at the door.

"Well, that went well. Rowan seems to be in good spirits, grinning ear to ear the whole time. So, are you all coming to the dance next Saturday?"

Alice hesitated. "I'm not sure if that is a good—"

"We will all be there, Pastor. Wouldn't miss it," Jonathan interrupted.

Alice shot Jonathan a look that could only be described as pure frustration.

Pastor Carl, sensing the tension, quickly said, "Great! I'll see you then," before making a hasty retreat.

Alice rounded on Jonathan. "Do you really think that Rowan coming to a dance, where she will no doubt be jumping up and down with her friends, is a good idea?"

Jonathan shook his head. "No, I don't think it's a good idea for her to be dancing like that. But I do think it's a great idea for her to be there, with her friends, having fun. She needs real face-to-face contact, not just sick visits in her room. She needs to leave the little nest you've built for her at home. She needs normal—even if it's a new normal."

Alice sighed. "Who even knows what the new normal is? We thought we had a handle on things before, and we didn't. Then something new came along, and we weren't prepared for that either. You keep pushing the envelope, and I'm just not ready to do that."

"Exactly," Jonathan said. "You're not ready, but this isn't just about you—it's about all of us, and most importantly, it's about Rowan. Isn't it better for her to learn and understand her limitations now, under our watchful eyes? Would you rather shelter her within the four walls of our house until she leaves for college, where she'll no doubt push herself too far? We need to let her figure out her boundaries—with us there to guide her."

Alice looked down and shook her head. "I just don't know what to do. I'm so scared. Sometimes, I go into her room at night just to make sure she's okay. Sometimes, I sit in her chair and just watch her sleep."

Jonathan gently tilted her chin up so she would look at him. "Yes, I know. I've woken up and found you there many times. I get it—I'm just as scared as you are. But how do you think she would feel if she woke up and saw you sitting there watching her? We can't afford to make her feel suffocated. The stakes are too high. This dance is a family event, so we'll be there too. If she starts doing too much, we'll be there to remind her to take it easy. She's still a teenage girl, Alice, and teenagers push boundaries. I sure did. We said we'd get through this as a family, so we need to go to this dance."

Alice gave a small nod. "Okay, we'll go. But I'll be keeping both eyes on her at all times. That's my compromise—take it or leave it."

Jonathan kissed her forehead. "Agreed. Compromise accepted."

For Rowan, the church dance was like attending a presidential gala. Alice smiled and went along with it, even as their shopping trip took them to three malls across two counties. In the end, Rowan found the perfect dress, complete with matching shoes, and Alice threw in a trip to Claire's for jewelry. To top it off, they treated themselves to manicures and pedicures on the morning of the dance. It was a full-fledged girls' day, and Alice found herself enjoying it.

To her credit, Rowan walked at a normal pace and took breaks without much prompting. While Alice recognized that as a good sign, they had only been shopping—nothing too strenuous. Still, no matter how good things seemed, Alice couldn't shake the fear lurking in the back of her mind.

On the way home, they made one last stop at Starbucks before bursting through the front door, their arms loaded with shopping bags and shoe boxes.

Ian took one look at the haul and said, "All this for one dance? Am I hitching a ride in the royal carriage, or am I one of the peasants pulling it?"

Rowan dropped her bags on the couch. "The carriage is Blake's Mustang, and no, you're lumping it into the dance with Mom and Dad. And unlike you, who will probably slither into the same jeans and T-shirt you wore yesterday, I need a new outfit."

Ian scoffed. "I'm not running for Congress, princess. It's a church dance. I expect to be out behind the building playing soccer with the guys within fifteen minutes of shoving half a platter of Miss Betty's fried chicken in my face. Besides, it's no secret who that outfit is for."

Rowan raised an eyebrow. "Meaning?"

"Meaning," Ian smirked, "that jockstrap Corey is going to be there, and you're hoping he checks off your royal dance card."

Rowan smirked back. "Jealous much?"

Ian laughed. "At what? That he throws a football and then stands around while everyone else does the work? Let's see him on a soccer field and find out what he can really do. Not too damn much, I'd wager."

"Language, Ian," Alice said with exasperation.

Ian looked momentarily apologetic—emphasis on momentarily—before heading upstairs.

Alice called after him. "And Ian, this is a church dance, so at least wear the cleanest jeans and shirt on your floor. And I'd watch the language. Pastor Carl has superhuman hearing and will have you serving punch all night."

Ian kept walking. "Yeah, yeah. Clean shirt, clean jeans, clean language. Got it."

Rowan grabbed her bags in one swoop and called out, "Momma, will you curl the back of my hair? I want to use that beach wave spray we bought. And can I wear some of your expensive perfume? Also, can I borrow that navy blue purse, or do you think the cream-colored one looks better? I had them both in mind when I picked out the dress."

Alice smiled, loving the fact that her teenage daughter still wanted her help. "Yes, yes, yes—and I think the navy blue will look best. Let me know when you're ready."

Jonathan had been listening from the living room and grinned. "Well, now I don't know what to do. Khakis and a tie, or jeans and a blazer? Should I gel my hair back and go for the man bun? Old Spice for sophistication, or Polo cologne to be bold and hip? There may be hot chicks at this shindig."

Alice laughed and pulled him into a hug. "You mean like Ruth from the coffee shop downtown?"

Jonathan sighed dramatically. "Well, yeah, but also the librarian."

"Ms. Mimms?! She's eighty!"

"Hey, a babe is a babe."

Alice rolled her eyes. "Come on, sir. I'll help you get ready for the ball, but I'm keeping my eye on you. Spry or not, I'll take both Ruth and that librarian down if I have to."

Chapter 19

When Alice, Jonathan, and Ian arrived at the dance, Rowan and her entourage were already on the dance floor. Alice was pleased to see that while Rowan was dancing with her friends, she was not as energetic as the other girls. Rowan gave a small wave, and Alice, not wanting to embarrass her daughter, smiled and gave her a little wink to convey that she was dancing at just the right pace. Rowan immediately turned back to her friends, and just like that, the moment was over. Alice thought back to her conversation with Jonathan—well, a slight tiff, if she was being honest with herself—and realized that maybe, once again, she was being a little too overprotective. She vowed to try to relax and enjoy the evening.

Alice was quickly on her own as Ian spotted Luke and several other boys from his soccer team while Jonathan made a beeline to Rick and Pastor Carl. They were all participating in a golf tournament the following weekend, and judging by Jonathan's excitement, you would think he was a five-year-old headed to Disney World.

She knew he wouldn't mention it now, preferring instead to wait and see the look on their faces when he pulled out his new driver. It had been quite pricey, but Jonathan was such a selfless person and rarely asked for things for himself. When Alice happened to see it on his Amazon wish list while ordering printer ink, she decided to add it to the cart. When it was delivered in a long rectangular box, he had torn into it like a kid on Christmas morning. He had then inhaled his dinner at record speed and bolted out the door to the driving range without a word as to when he'd be back.

True to his word, Ian and his friends had hunkered down at a corner table, each piling their plates high with fried chicken, potato and pasta salad, and an assortment of desserts. Alice knew that once the food disappeared, so would they— off to the back side of the church to play soccer, basketball, or both for the remainder of the evening. Pastor Carl always turned on the floodlights during dances, knowing most of the younger boys had little interest in the event itself. More often than not, he ended up outside with them, running around and joining in. Both pastors were phenomenal at engaging all age groups, which was a big reason why their congregation was the largest in the surrounding areas.

Alice made her way over to Pastor Wendi, who was currently manning the dessert table.

"Satisfying your sweet tooth?" Alice teased as she approached.

Wendi laughed. "More like guarding the desserts. It's a good thing I walked over when I did, or this table would have been wiped clean by the boys out back—your son being the biggest culprit."

Alice rolled her eyes. "Ian is on a seafood diet, in the sense that whenever he 'sees' food, he eats it. Tis the nature of a growing boy."

A small pang of worry surfaced as she thought about Rowan's appetite and how she often willed her daughter to eat more than the meager amounts that typically made up her meals.

As if sensing her thoughts, Wendi asked, "So, any updates? Any new strategies to get a handle on this thing?"

Alice gave a small shake of her head. "Rowan still has the Holter monitor on, and so far, the machine has only alerted us a few times. Each instance has been minor—her heart rate spiking or dropping briefly—but of course, I react as if the smoke detector has gone off and the house is on fire. Despite Jonathan's suggestion to give it a minute, I called Dr. Mason immediately. By the time his service reaches him and he calls back, the episode is over, and he's left to deal with a neurotic mother."

"Alice, you're not a neurotic mother, just a mother. A mother with a chronically ill child and a serious condition to manage. You may feel like you're losing it, but honestly, we all marvel at how well you and Jonathan handle this. We've all said that if we were in your shoes, we wouldn't be managing half as well."

"Well," Alice sighed, "they say God doesn't give you more than you can handle, but sometimes I wonder if He understands how heavy this burden is. Most days, it feels like more than I can take, and I could really use a lighter load."

Wendi nodded. "Sometimes, our perception of a heavy load doesn't match God's idea of one. Maybe He believes you can handle more because someone else close to the situation can only handle much less."

Just then, a group of younger kids ran up to the table, eager to grab more cookies. Wendi handed each a plate and told them to pick three.

"I'm sure there will be a few parents unhappy with my generosity when they try to get their kids—hyped up on sugar—into bed," Wendi joked.

Alice watched the kids run off, their hands full of cookies. How she wished her biggest worry for Rowan was something as simple as too much sugar before bedtime.

Lisa approached the table. "Wendi, I have it on good authority that the DJ has been requested to play the Cupid Shuffle, and you're expected on the dance floor ASAP."

Wendi grinned ear to ear, clapping her hands. "Oooh, that's my jam!" She grabbed Alice's arm. "Let's go, girl. You need to loosen up a bit."

Alice tried to resist, but Wendi mockingly cupped a hand to her ear and said, "What? This music is so loud... I can't hear you," as she dragged her toward the dance floor. As Alice attempted to follow along, she noticed Rowan and her friends joining the line dance, laughing and smiling. Alice smiled to herself—this was Rowan's version of 'three extra cookies.' For the first time in a long time, she let go of her worries and followed the moves. Before she knew it, she was doing the Cupid Shuffle like a pro. After making it through both the Cupid Shuffle and the Macarena, she retreated to a table with a cup of punch, content to watch the rest of the dance unfold.

Ian was nowhere to be seen, but she knew wherever he was, he was either throwing or kicking a ball. Jonathan was across the room with Pastor Carl and a few other men, deep in conversation and looking happy.

Rowan and her friends stood in a cluster, sipping punch and surveying the room. Alice followed her daughter's gaze and wasn't surprised to see her eyes locked on Corey, who was standing with a group of football players doing the same thing. The current song ended, and Christina Perri's "A Thousand Years" began to play. Alice knew this was one of Rowan's favorite songs.

She glanced at Corey. He was looking at Rowan.

"Come on, Corey, ask her," Alice whispered to herself.

As if on cue, Corey got up and walked straight to Rowan. Her eyes widened as she glanced at her friends, who were all smiling and giggling. He stopped in front of her, said something, and then, taking her hand, led her to the dance floor. Alice smiled and let out a small sigh of relief. Watching her daughter engage in the simple joys of teenage life was mesmerizing.

"Okay, I totally get it," Wendi's voice broke through her thoughts. "But seriously, if I turned around and saw my mom staring at me while I danced with a boy, I would beg for the floor to open and swallow me whole."

Alice looked up, startled. She hadn't even heard Wendi approach.

"Come on, Momma Bear. It's a slow dance, she's good. We're low on ice, punch, and chips. The younger boys are going to be back in here soon, and there will be chaos if there are no provisions."

Alice lingered a moment longer, enough to see Rowan and Corey talking while they danced. Then, Corey pulled Rowan close, her head resting on his shoulder.

"Earth to Alice... come in, Alice."

Alice finally broke her gaze and stood up. With one last glance at her daughter, she smiled. "Low on punch, cookies, and chips, you say? We'd better get a move on. You're right, that won't do. That won't do at all."

Chapter 20

"I was totally freaked out to come over there and ask you to dance," Corey said as he pulled back just enough to look down at Rowan.

"Why would you be freaked out? Did you think I would say no?" Rowan asked.

"Well, yeah, kind of. I mean, we've been texting for a while, like friendly chit-chat, but never really went out or anything—although I wanted to. Also, before the dance, I wasn't even sure you were allowed to dance, you know, because of the heart thing."

Rowan looked up at him and said, "Yeah, the heart thing. I'm not just Rowan anymore. I am 'Rowan, the girl with the heart thing.'"

Corey winced. "Sorry, didn't mean to bring it up."

"Don't worry about it," Rowan said. "It's not like the subject ever really goes away. I have a constant reminder every minute of my day and night." She motioned to the little wires and the box of her Holter monitor. "It's not the best fashion accessory, and I—wait, did you just say you wanted to go out with me?" Rowan was trying to hide her excitement but knew it probably showed on her face.

Corey smiled. "Yeah, I was wondering if you heard that part and were just ignoring it so as not to let me down."

Rowan felt herself turning beet red and lowered her face. Corey gave a small laugh, and Rowan looked up. "What?" she asked.

"You look even cuter when you blush."

"I didn't blush," she said, a hint of irritation in her voice.

"You totally blushed," he teased. "So, do I have to beg, or will you take pity on me and agree to be my girlfriend?"

Rowan gave a little smile and looked up at him. "You don't want to be my boyfriend, Corey, trust me. I have so much baggage. I'm damaged goods. You deserve a girl who can go up a flight of stairs without getting out of breath or do all the normal things I can't seem to do or things I can do but have to do in a weird way."

"I totally understand, and I know all about what's going on with you, and I don't care. It doesn't matter. It doesn't change the fact that I want you to be my girlfriend, Rowan. However, if you'd rather just be friends, I under—"

"No!" Rowan said in an alarmed voice. Then, softer, "No, I'd love to be your girlfriend."

Corey smiled. "So do I actually need to ask you to prom, or, due to our official dating status, is that implied?"

"Not implied," Rowan said seriously. "You'll have to officially ask me. It's on my bucket list, you see."

Corey looked at her and whispered in her ear, "I don't want to hear any more of this bucket list nonsense. Everything is going to work out. However, I am quite pleased that being my girlfriend made the cut on said list. So, will you go to prom with me?"

Rowan squinted her eyes. "Hmmm... Am I getting a corsage?"

Corey smiled. "Of course. Can't go to prom without one."

Rowan smiled. "Yes, I will go with you, but I can't dance too much, though. Are you sure you want to waste a perfectly good dance with someone who will have to sit down a lot of the time? I mean, a lot of the cheer—"

Corey shook his head. "Not them. You. I want to go with you. If we have to sit a good deal of the time, then we do. We'll just make fun of all the bad dancers. Or we can just sit together and talk until a slow song comes on. Those are the only dances I am looking forward to anyway," he said with a wink.

Corey pulled her back into him, and Rowan felt like she was melting into him, feeling very conflicted. Part of her couldn't wait for the dance to be over so she could tell her momma everything. But part of her—the part that involved being in Corey's arms—wished the night would never end.

After a little peck on the cheek and saying goodnight to Corey, Rowan made a beeline for her mom, who was helping with the cleanup of the dance.

"Do we have to stay for cleanup, Momma? I want to go home."

Alice, on immediate high alert, came around the table. "Are you feeling funny? Was your monitor beeping?"

"No, nothing like that. I just need to talk to you! I don't want to do it here, though," she said, giving Ian a sideways glance as he unceremoniously dumped leftover cookies into a gallon-sized Ziploc bag.

"Trust me, Princess, I have no desire to hear about your court at the royal ball," Ian said.

Rowan rolled her eyes. "Can we go?"

Wendi glanced at Alice. "We got this, Alice. Plenty of help. Also, I am the eyes and ears of this whole institution, and trust me, you're going to want to hear the scoop."

Rowan looked down, a bit embarrassed. Wendi made eye contact with her and said, "You go, girl!" which made Rowan giggle.

Alice now had the feeling that this was not heart-related but boy-related. And at that point, she couldn't get to the car fast enough.

"Ian, let's go. They have plenty of people to help clean up."

Ian protested, "Hold up, there may be more cookies on the other table."

"You have a bag of cookies the size of your head. Let's go," Alice said.

She practically had to drag Jonathan away from his gaggle of friends.

"What's the big hubbub, bub?" he asked when he looked over at Rowan, who seemed to be fine.

"Nothing is wrong. I just want to get home."

Jonathan gave her a questioning look.

"All I know is that there may be information to be had by Rowan about a certain boy, and she does not want to talk about it here... so let's get a move on,"

"Okay, okay, calm yourself, jeez. You act like there's been a major intelligence leak from the Pentagon or something."

Alice smirked. "It may be far bigger than that—at least in the mind of a teenager. Look, this is *normal*. Rowan wants to talk to her momma about something *normal*. Everything else has been so abnormal, so I *want* this normal. I've been praying for some *normal*."

Jonathan pressed a quick kiss to her forehead. "Well then, let's get you home ASAP so you don't miss the normal. Will I be included in the normal?"

"Possibly, but not right away. I think it's a momma-and-daughter kind of normal," Alice said with a big smile.

As they walked out, they said their goodbyes, and Rowan all but jumped into the car.

On the way home, there was some idle chit-chat—but not from Rowan. Her phone was *blowing up* with text messages. She typed furiously, her fingers flying over the screen, a constant grin plastered on her face.

Alice felt giddy with anticipation.

Her teenage daughter was having a full-blown *teenager* moment—and she wanted to talk to *her* about it.

Most of their conversations lately had been about Rowan's heart. Conversations that *had* to happen. Conversations that Rowan resented. Because of that, their talks slowly faded away.

Alice missed her daughter.

She missed the healthy Rowan—the one who would come home from school and cheer practice and give a play-by-play rundown of her day, spilling all the drama that came with being a teenager. Those talks had dwindled, replaced by discussions about what she could and couldn't do.

Alice knew that was *her* doing.

Rowan would be in the middle of venting about some cheer drama, and Alice would interject—

"But you weren't cheering, were you?"

"You're drinking enough at school, right?"

Rowan would get so upset, but Alice *couldn't* help it.

The drama and the lives of all these high schoolers were *paramount* to Rowan. But Alice only cared about one of them—*Rowan.*

The monitor, the blood pressure, the salt pills, the hydration—it had become *her* focus.

So, this time, Alice vowed this conversation would *not* include her health...and she could hardly wait to hear every detail.

They arrived home, and Rowan was the first out of the car. She didn't even wait for Jonathan to unlock the door;

instead, she used the spare key they had outfitted with a small magnet and kept it on the back of the porch light.

As she pushed the door open, she looked back and called, "Momma, come upstairs!"

Alice glanced at Jonathan, then picked up her pace.

Ian quipped, "What's up with *Her Highness*? Is she expecting the prince's guard to come to outfit her for a glass slipper?"

Jonathan, watching Alice disappear into the house and immediately turn left up the stairs, chuckled. "Possibly, but whatever it is, it doesn't look like *us dudes* are invited."

Ian shrugged, grabbing his bag of cookies. "Whatever. As long as *whatever it is* doesn't finish off the milk," he said, waving the oversized bag in the air.

Jonathan's eyes widened. "Whoa—how did you get extra macaroons? They ran out of those in the first hour."

Ian smirked. "I got connections."

"Hmmm… so in other words, neither Pastor Carl nor Pastor Wendi knows you have them. Or that you squirreled some away," Jonathan said with a conspiratorial smile.

Ian rolled his eyes. "Alright, name your price, man."

Jonathan grinned. "Okay, I'll take the macaroons off your hands."

"What?! Like *all* of them? No way!" Ian protested.

Jonathan smiled slyly. "They're stolen cookies, so what you have to ask yourself, son, is—*what would Jesus do?*"

"Oh, that's good, Dad. It's low and underhanded, but it's good," Ian admitted. Then, with a defiant look, he countered, "How about half the macaroons, and I won't tell Mom you '*couldn't get the lawnmower started*' and then went to play golf?"

Jonathan let out a slow, impressive nod. "Well played, my son. *Well played.* Okay, you've got yourself a deal. Now, let's go check out the milk situation."

Chapter 21

S hopping for prom took all day, mostly because Rowan needed frequent breaks. Fortunately, there was a Starbucks in the mall, so she didn't complain too much. Her biggest frustration was trying on dresses while wearing the Holter monitor. Several times, she asked if she could take it off, just for a few minutes, but Alice refused. She gave the excuse that Rowan needed to see which dress worked best with the monitor since she would be wearing it at the dance anyway. But that wasn't the real reason. Alice wasn't willing to go even a second without that monitor recording. Missing one event—just one—could mean masking a potential problem, and Alice couldn't take that risk.

As a peace offering, Alice threw in a few new pairs of jeans, along with the promised manicure and pedicure. Once the shopping was done, Rowan was eager to get home and start getting ready for the big night. The moment they walked through the door, she tore through the bags, laying out her dress, shoes, and jewelry, leaving the rest in a heap. Within five minutes, the music was blasting from her room, and Alice smiled to herself. Right now, her daughter was happy and focusing on something other than her heart. That was worth everything.

Still, there was one last battle to come—Alice had to give Corey the rundown about the monitor and Rowan's limitations.

"You're kidding, right?" Jonathan asked when Alice had told him about her plan. "I really think that's overkill. Rowan fully understands how that monitor works and what she can and can't do. This will do nothing but upset and embarrass her. I mean, you're not with her all day at school. She knows the drill, Alice."

"Yes, but we won't be there with her tonight," Alice countered, irritation creeping into her voice. "She'll only be surrounded by a few adults who know what's going on. We can't just let her run amok. What if something happens? I need to know that he would know what to do. I still keep waiting for the other shoe to drop"

Jonathan sighed. "And what if something does happen? What if the monitor goes off? What if she starts feeling bad? It's not rocket science, Alice. Corey has enough sense to call 911 and then us. What else do you expect him to do? What would any of us do in that situation? Don't do this, Alice. Please. Just let her be a teenage girl going to prom with her boyfriend. You always say we need to make things as normal as possible for her. What's more normal than this? She lives with this every second of every day. She deserves to put it on the back burner for a few hours. If another shoe drops we will deal with it."

Right then, Rowan called from upstairs. "Momma, can you curl a few pieces of my hair in the back? It looks stupid."

"Coming!" Alice called back.

Jonathan started to stand. "Oh, I got this one."

Alice pushed him back down playfully. "Don't get too cocky, or I'll throw one of those metaphorical shoes at you."

Jonathan laughed. "Of that, I have no doubt."

***

When Rowan finished dressing, she came downstairs to wait for Corey to pick her up. Alice could tell she was both nervous and excited. She moved from the couch to the window and back again, unable to sit still.

"Rowan, relax. It's not like he's going to stand you up. It's obvious he really likes you," Alice said.

Rowan didn't seem to hear her. She was back at the window again.

Jonathan walked into the room and smirked. "Prince Charming hasn't pulled up on a white horse yet, huh?"

Alice shot him a look. He put up his hands in mock surrender. Just then, headlights shone through the front window, and Rowan jumped up.

"Should I answer the door, or should I go upstairs?"

"Why would you go upstairs? You've been pacing for the last half hour," Jonathan said.

Rowan looked at her father as if he had three heads. Jonathan turned to Alice with an expression that clearly said, "What? What did I say?"

"Go on upstairs, and I'll answer the door," Alice said. "I know what you're thinking, and you don't want it to look like you were waiting for him."

Rowan gave Jonathan an exasperated look before rushing up the stairs.

"I don't understand why you women have to overcomplicate things," Jonathan said, shaking his head with a smile. "I don't remember you doing any of this when we were dating."

"Oh, I did," Alice said, grinning. "You were clueless then, and you're clueless now. So why don't you go open the door, and I'll see if Rowan needs any last-minute costume and makeup adjustments."

Jonathan laughed. "Okay, but I'm glad I'm not a woman. This is way more complicated than I can understand."

Alice smiled knowingly. "God knew that when he made Adam. That's why he created Eve—because Adam was clueless too. Now, go open the door and bring Corey in."

As Alice climbed the stairs, she heard Jonathan greeting Corey. She gently pushed open Rowan's bedroom door. Rowan stood in front of her full-length mirror, turning from side to side, scrutinizing her appearance.

"You can keep spinning in circles, but from every angle, you look beautiful," Alice said.

She knew Rowan's nervousness wasn't about her outfit. The wardrobe scrutiny was just a stall tactic.

Rowan let out a frustrated sigh and flopped onto her bed. "I feel like I'm going to embarrass him tonight. I have all these stupid wires all over me. What if I get dizzy, or worse, pass out? I'm not sure this was a good idea. He's gorgeous, sweet, and kind—why would he want to saddle himself with me? I really like him, but I'm terrified I'll get attached and then he'll dump me because of all my issues. Wouldn't it be easier to just tell him I'm sick and can't go?"

Alice took her daughter's hand. "Easier for who? Corey knows all about your condition, yet he's still waiting downstairs for you. I think you mean easier for you, and honestly, that's selfish."

Rowan shot her mother a sharp look, but Alice pressed on. "Yes, I said it. Is this a 'break up with him before he breaks up with you' situation? You haven't even given him a chance, and you're already ready to cut and run. That's not like you at all, Rowan. So tell me—what's this really about?"

Rowan covered her face with her hands and started to cry. "What if he falls in love with me? What if I fall in love with him and then..."

"Then what?" Alice prompted her gently.

"What if something happens to me? Something really bad, so bad that a normal life isn't possible? What if it's even worse than that? What if I...?"

Alice lifted Rowan's chin. "What if what?"

Rowan's voice broke. "What if I die? What if he loves me, and I love him, and then I die? How can I start something like that when I don't know the answers to those questions? I've already lost so much, Momma. I don't know if I can handle investing in something else only to have it taken away from me."

Alice's heart clenched. She hadn't realized Rowan carried such a heavy burden. Had she seen glimpses of it before and ignored them, unwilling to acknowledge the depth of her daughter's fear?

"I wish I could tell you I understand what you're going through, but I can't," Alice admitted. "It wouldn't be fair to pretend I do. I only know how this affects me. You're more than justified in feeling this way. But here's what I do know— yesterday is gone, and tomorrow isn't promised for anyone. If you bury your head in the sand and avoid risks, you'll end up with a life that's safe but empty. I would rather have five years of happiness and adventure than thirty years of playing it safe and missing out."

Rowan seemed to be processing Alice's words. It hurt Alice deeply to see her daughter wrestling with such heavy emotions at sixteen.

"So you really think this is okay? That I'm not making a mistake?" Rowan asked, hope flickering in her eyes.

"I do. Corey knows the situation, and he's here, right now, waiting for you. And I didn't realize you were carrying all this worry. You shouldn't because you are going to be okay. I promise you, Rowan, you're going to come through this."

"How can you know that, Momma?"

Alice squeezed her hand. "Because I'm your momma, and mommas just know things. Okay?"

Rowan hesitated, then took a deep breath. "Okay, I'm doing this. Can you tell him to give me a few minutes? I'm pretty sure my makeup is wrecked."

"Sure," Alice said, grinning. "But don't take too long. He's been alone with your father for fifteen minutes now. If he's run out of corny jokes, he's probably showing him your baby pictures."

Rowan laughed. "Daddy run out of corny jokes? Not possible."

Alice smiled. "You're probably right. And I'm not sure I'd like it if he did."

As Alice backed out of the room, she saw Rowan grinning at her reflection. At that moment, Alice felt something close to peace.

Chapter 22

Rowan and Corey arrived at the dance just as things were getting into full swing. They had started the evening at a local pizza place for dinner. Corey had offered to take her to a nicer restaurant, but Rowan had wanted the night to feel as normal as possible—and normal for teenagers didn't involve fine dining.

On the dance floor, Rowan kept up with the fast songs, albeit carefully, and Corey matched her pace without hesitation. He was sweet, attentive, and completely unfazed by the box and wires of her Holter monitor. He made sure she stayed hydrated, retrieving bottles of water from the small cooler they had brought, and always found an empty seat for her when she needed to rest.

But perhaps most thrilling of all, Rowan could feel the eyes of other girls on Corey—and she couldn't help but enjoy their envious stares. Halfway through the dance, Rowan began to feel overheated. She sat down, fanning herself as she tried to cool off.

"Do you want to go outside for some air?" Corey asked, crouching beside her.

Rowan looked up at him gratefully. As much as she didn't want to miss a second of the dance, she knew overheating was a serious concern for people with POTS. "Thank you," she said, sighing. "Yeah, that sounds like a good idea."

They stepped outside into the crisp night air, heading toward the benches near the front of the school—the same ones where students waited for their rides after the buses had already left on school days.

"Stay put; I'll grab you another water," Corey said, disappearing back inside.

Rowan sat down and took a deep breath, letting the cool air fill her lungs. Within a minute, she could already feel her body cooling down. Her monitor beeped a few times, but she brushed it off. No alarms, she reminded herself. Just minor fluctuations, the kind Dr. Mason had assured them were expected. Corey returned moments later, handing her a bottle of her favorite flavored water before sitting beside her.

"Are you having fun?" Corey asked, reaching for her hand.

Rowan smiled. "Yes, I'm having a great time."

Corey laced his fingers through hers and smirked. "Is that because you're here with me or because of the music and snacks?"

"Yes, yes, and yes—in that order," she teased.

Corey chuckled. "I'm glad you were on the sidelines with the cheerleaders at the game last night. I know it's not the same as actually cheering, but calling out the cheers has to be better than nothing, right?"

Rowan hesitated. She didn't want to talk about her illness—not tonight. Just for one night, she wanted to be a regular teenager.

"Well, I go back to my doctor next week, and I'm hoping he'll clear me to actually cheer again," she said, keeping her response short, hoping he'd take the hint.

But he didn't.

"Is it scary?" he asked after a beat. "Having these issues with your heart?"

Rowan furrowed her brow, considering the question. "At first, yeah. Sometimes it still is. But at this point, I'm pretty resigned to it. I have to be. I hate that it defines me, controls me. It feels like it's the most important thing about me now." She exhaled heavily. "I know I should be grateful—I see kids at Dr. Mason's office who have it way worse. Some are in wheelchairs, others need oxygen. And I tell myself, they probably look at me and think, I wish I could walk on my own, or I wish I didn't need a breathing tank. But knowing that doesn't change how I feel."

Corey squeezed her hand. "That doesn't make you a bad person, Rowan. I get it. You probably look around school, see everyone living their normal lives, and it stings a little. Their biggest worries are homework and what they're wearing."

Rowan nodded, unable to speak past the lump in her throat.

"Hey," Corey said softly. "I didn't mean to upset you, I just—"

She forced a smile and stood up. "It's fine. I'm cooled down now, so let's head back inside, okay?"

This time, Corey got the message. He stood and took both of her hands, pulling her up with ease.

"You got it," he said.

As Rowan followed him back inside, she felt a familiar flutter in her chest—but for once, she knew it had nothing to do with her heart condition.

It was all Corey.

Chapter 23

After the dance, Rowan sailed through the rest of the week on a high, so she was not amused when she found out she would have to miss school that Friday for a doctor's appointment.

"Can't you just reschedule? We have a home game on Friday, and even though I can't cheer, I'm still on the squad. I'll be in uniform calling cheers."

"No, Rowan, I'm sorry, but you know you can't miss this appointment. We have to schedule your next visit at the end of each appointment because Dr. Mason is booked solid. If I cancel this one, you may not get back in for months," Alice told her.

Rowan wasn't ready to give in. "My monitor has only beeped a few times in the first two months, and it hasn't gone off once in the last month. Can't you call him and ask him to review the Holter monitor results? If he says everything looks fine, I'll go next time. I don't want to spend all day at his office for nothing."

"Rowan, it's not just the monitor, and you know that. You have to do your stress test, ultrasound, tilt table, and blood work, too. Varsity plays every Friday night, so you can go next week. I'll be mindful of that in the future and try my best to avoid Friday appointments. Now, I'll buy nachos and popcorn for your whole gang at the next game. How about that?"

"Well, that sounds like a pretty good plan," Jonathan said. "And I'm getting in on that popcorn and nachos deal for sure."

Rowan's face went beet red as she looked at both of them. "Oh, great! Nachos and popcorn... well, that makes everything okay then. This is such bullshit! I am so sick and tired of being sick and tired... I am so over this crap!"

"Whoa," Jonathan said. "I get that you're upset, but you need to drop that attitude down a few notches. I'm not fond of the language being used in anger or you talking to your mom like that, but I know you're upset, so I'll let it slide—this time."

Rowan turned on him. "I am not going to that stupid appointment. I am going to the game if I have to walk there."

She turned on her heels, her head held high in defiance and stomped up the stairs. Alice stood frozen. She had never seen an outburst like that from Rowan—sure, little teenage spats here and there, but never this. The screaming, the language—at least, not from her.

Ian emerged from his room and stood at the landing. "Jumpin' Jesus on a pogo stick, what in the actual hell is going on? Can't a man relax with some gaming and a full bag of chips without the whole house—"

"Ian, not now, and I am definitely not in the mood for your comedic wit," Jonathan said, watching Alice, who had yet to move or say a word.

Ian looked from his mom to his dad, then glanced at Rowan's closed bedroom door. He descended the stairs, concern replacing his usual sarcasm.

"Has something happened? Like with Rowan— is she okay?"

"She is," Jonathan said. "Physically, at least. She's having 'a moment,' as you kids say."

"That much is obvious. I heard her cussing like a sailor all the way upstairs. Very 'un-your-royal-highness' for her." Ian said. "So, what's the deal?"

It was clear Ian wasn't going to let this go. Alice finally found her voice. "She has to miss the football game on Friday because I scheduled a doctor's appointment without realizing it was on a Friday. She's furious."

Ian nodded but said nothing. Alice made a move toward the stairs, but Ian stopped her. "Can I talk to her?"

Alice looked at her son. He wasn't joking around. "What are you going to say?"

"Look, it's a teenager thing, okay? There are some things you guys just don't get. And I know you were both teenagers, like, way back before electricity, but you don't get it."

Ian headed upstairs. "I got this."

Alice and Jonathan exchanged a look but said nothing as Ian knocked on Rowan's door.

"I do not want to talk to either of you right now! Just go away and leave me the hell alone!" Rowan shouted.

Ian slowly cracked the door open and shoved a large bag of potato chips through. "I come in peace and bearing gifts." He opened the door slightly more. "It's just me. I told the parental units to chill out—and to butt out."

Ian hesitated. He rarely entered his sister's room. Holding up the chips, he said, "These are basically potatoes with a lot of salt on them, so, for you, they're healthy. Let's chow down before Mom comes in and overrules us."

"What do you want?" Rowan asked warily.

"To chill. And to find out what the hell is going on. Pretty strong words flying around down there. For me, that's par for the course, but one does not normally hear such talk from a high-standing member of royalty."

Rowan gave a small smile and shifted to make space on the bed. Ian took this as approval to sit.

"So, out with it," Ian said.

"I'm just really tired," Rowan muttered.

Ian made a move to stand. "Oh, well, okay, no problem."

"No, not that kind of tired," Rowan said quickly. "I mean 'life' tired. 'Being sick' tired. I just want to be normal. Is that too much to ask?"

Ian shook his head. "No, it's not too much to ask. But Mom didn't make you sick, Rowan. Yelling at her won't fix this. In case you didn't notice, this is hard on us too. Not as hard as it is for you, but we all have to deal with it."

He leaned back. "Neither Mom nor Dad has been to one of my soccer games since you got sick. It sucks looking over at the sidelines and seeing no one there rooting for me.

Mom runs around documenting every move you make in her journal, obsessing over every ingredient in our food, going to four different stores to find the brand of water you like, and a small part of her wilts every time she sees you unhappy. I come downstairs for a midnight snack and find Dad on the computer, researching your illness and clinics across the country."

Rowan looked down, guilt flickering across her face.

"I know that," she said softly. "That's part of it. It affects my family, my friends, my boyfriend—everyone. People make sacrifices for me. I have to make sacrifices for me." She let out a breath. "I just wanted to go to the game, and now, because Mom made that appointment, I won't be able to."

Ian shrugged. "Mom didn't schedule it just to ruin your game. She probably didn't even realize it was a Friday." He leaned in. "Look, this heart thing is Mom's full-time job. She's trying to make everything better for you every day, and sometimes you don't seem too grateful for that."

Rowan glared at him, but her eyes were glassy with tears.

"All I'm saying is, she's not the enemy. She worries enough about you physically—don't make her carry the emotional bullshit too."

Rowan chuckled. "Can you ever have a conversation without swearing?"

Ian grinned. "Nope. So, you good?"

Rowan nodded her head and went in to give her brother a hug.

"Whoa, just whoa, don't be getting all mushy on me. The boundaries of our relationship have been clearly established."

So, Rowan reached over and flicked his ear.

"Mildly painful, but definitely more acceptable," Ian said as he stood up. "Ok, I got to get out of this room now. All this girlie bright pink in here is going to make me go blind; it's like someone puked up a bottle of Pepto Bismal in here."

After Ian left Rowan pulled at the leads attached to her machine, rearranging them for comfort. She laid back and thought about this whole heart thing. About her momma and how she kept fighting this illness head-on, relentlessly punching back at it. How recently Rowan felt like her momma was holding something back. Holding back what Rowan did not know and, if she was honest with herself, she did not want to know. What Rowan did know was that from now on she would let her mom take the wheel and silently ride shotgun as if her life depended on it, which, she realized, it probably did.

Chapter 24

O n Friday, both Jonathan and Alice took Rowan to her appointment with Dr. Mason. The usual procedure took place. First, labs were drawn so that by the time Rowan finished all her testing, the results would be back for Dr. Mason to review. After completing her ultrasound, EKG, EEG, tilt table test, and finally, the stress test, they were put in a room to wait for Dr. Mason. Rowan did her usual thing—sitting on the table with her earbuds in. She had gained almost a full minute during the stress test, and Alice was grateful for even the smallest of victories. The monitor, which she had come to think of as Rowan's lifeline, had been blissfully quiet over the last month. Alice didn't want to jinx it by thinking too much about it, and although Rowan was getting excited about the progress, Alice kept her optimism in check.

After about half an hour, Dr. Mason entered the room. Rowan immediately took out her earbuds, sitting up straighter in anticipation of the question Alice knew would be first out of her mouth.

"What did all the tests say? My monitor hasn't gone off even once in the last month. So, is it fixed? Can I go back to cheerleading? I've been feeling really good, like excellent good."

Dr. Mason smiled as he sat down on the stool and pulled up Rowan's chart.

"I was wondering how far into the room I would actually get before you asked the coveted cheerleading question."

Rowan said absolutely nothing, and Alice could tell her daughter was literally holding her breath.

"So, the answer is yes. However..." Rowan grinned from ear to ear, nearly vibrating off the table with excitement.

"Whoa, hold on a second. There's a 'but' coming."

A small bit of wind left Rowan's sails, but she sat patiently, waiting for the explanation.

"Your test results are very encouraging. Your heart enzymes are irregular but not terribly so, which isn't unusual for someone whose heart is healing from an ablation. I'm impressed with the stress test—you lasted fifty-two seconds longer than the last time. The ultrasound showed that the valve has not worsened, which is great, but we will continue to monitor it. My only concern is your tilt table test, which helps gauge how your POTS is doing. Your blood pressure still isn't regulating as it should with movement, so I don't see any signs that the POTS is improving. However, on a positive note, it's not getting any worse. Lastly, the data I reviewed from the Holter monitor indicates that your heart continues to beat faster than it should at times, but not often, and it regulates itself within a few seconds."

"So, on that front, I'm cautiously optimistic that the ablation was a success. But understand that when it comes to the heart, things can change. My only real concern is that some of the data shows that, at times, your heart beats too slowly. We discussed this after your ablation—how the cure might come at a price. While these occurrences are few and far between, they're still happening."

"But I can still cheer, right?" Rowan asked.

Dr. Mason nodded. "Yes, I will release you to cheer, but we need to have some guidelines in place. I want to increase the dosage of Propranolol, which helps regulate blood pressure, and I want you to take three salt pills a day instead of just two. Hydration is still a key component, and it's imperative that you continue on that regimen—especially now that you're going back to cheerleading. Additionally, I'm going to put you on a medication for the bradycardia called Atropine. This will help maintain a normal heart rate by preventing your heart from beating too slowly. So, the hope is that the ablation worked for the tachycardia and the Atropine will help with the bradycardia."

Rowan perked up and said, "Anything you say, I'll do—as long as I can cheer."

"Very good. So, between cheers, you'll need to put on your cuff and take both a blood pressure and heart rate reading. Your heart rate should be between sixty and one hundred beats per minute. Your blood pressure should be at or very close to 110/70. If either of those numbers is too high or too low, you need to sit and hydrate. Wait at least ten minutes before taking the readings again. If they're back to normal, you can cheer. If not, you'll repeat the process every ten minutes until they stabilize."

Rowan was grinning ear to ear. "So, does this mean I don't have to wear that stupid machine anymore?"

Alice began to interject, "Rowan! You're being rude and—"

"It's okay," Dr. Mason said, waving her off. "I wouldn't want to wear that stupid machine either." He looked at Rowan and winked. "The answer to that is no—at least not right now. But understand while things seem to be getting better, they could just as easily get worse again. It's too early to make a definitive call on that. So, for now, you don't have to wear it. But if you don't outgrow the POTS, we may need to monitor for a few weeks here or there just to keep an eye on things."

Alice spoke up. "So, you're saying that with parameters in place, Rowan can cheer. Are those parameters permanent? If things start fluctuating again, does that mean a total relapse or just a bump in the road?"

Dr. Mason nodded as if he expected these questions. "I really wish I could give you a definitive, black-and-white answer, but I can't. I appreciate how frustrating that is. The reality is that nothing about Rowan's case is cut and dry. All her medical issues feed into each other—they're all connected. If one thing goes wrong, it could affect everything else. I know that's not what you want to hear, but it's the best I can give you. The bottom line is that all we can do is pick a course of action and see if it works. If it doesn't, we adjust accordingly."

Alice looked over at Rowan. Despite Dr. Mason's lukewarm reassurances and lack of definitive answers, she decided to focus on the here and now. Rowan was glowing with happiness, and that was enough—for now. But in the back of her mind, Alice knew she would be watching. She would be ready if this thing reared its ugly head again.

Chapter 25

As the weeks and then months went by without incident, Alice gradually became more relaxed about Rowan's activities. However, she wasn't quite ready to completely let go of the reins just yet. To her credit, Rowan tolerated it. Life was returning to normal—not just at home or church, but in their family traditions as well. Before Rowan's illness, they had taken frequent camping trips, usually five or six times a year. That had all stopped when Rowan got sick. Now, Alice decided to take a leap of faith.

"Wait, for real? We're really going hiking and camping this weekend?" Ian asked, eyes widening in excitement.

"Yes, well, yes, in the sense that we are going camping, but we're not going to hike up the trail. Instead, we'll drive in at the bottom," Alice told him.

Ian's enthusiasm dimmed just a bit. "Oh, okay."

Alice ruffled his hair, knowing he hated it. "It's just a precautionary measure. I know it's not Mount Kilimanjaro, but Travers Trail might still be too much for Rowan. There's no point in pushing her only to make her feel awful by the time we get there. But here's something you might like—Corey is coming with us."

Ian's head snapped up. "Really!?"

He quickly reeled in his excitement, trying to appear indifferent, but Alice knew he really liked Corey. Since

Rowan and Corey had become "official," Corey often came over just to watch sporting events on TV with Ian and Jonathan while Rowan was off doing, as Corey and Jonathan would say, "dumb girl stuff."

"Yes, really. And if you don't mind, I wanted to ask if Corey could share one of the large tents with you. Your dad and I will take the other large one, and we'll get Rowan a smaller tent for herself."

Alice half-expected Ian to complain about Rowan getting her own tent, but instead, she saw the gears turning in his head. Corey also loved camping and hiking, and Ian was clearly already imagining all the fun they would have together. Corey never treated Ian differently because he was younger— one more thing Alice and Jonathan liked about him.

While the kids were at school and Jonathan was at work, Alice focused on preparing for the camping trip. Being ahead on her book schedule meant she had some time to focus solely on her family, and she was excited. She pulled out all the necessary equipment, inspecting each item to make sure it was in good condition.

In the days leading up to the trip, she made a checklist of everything they needed and had it all assembled by the front door when Jonathan came home.

"Wow, you've been busy. And it looks like I got here just in time to avoid doing anything," Jonathan said with a smirk.

"Nice try, but wrong. I packed for the trip; you are packing the car and unpacking when we get to the lake."

"Isn't that why we have two healthy, strong young men on this trip?"

"Oh sure, by all means, put Ian in charge of packing. Just don't be surprised when he throws out your sleeping bag to make more room for cookies and chips. And Corey won't be much help—he has makeup practice, and his dad will be dropping him off directly at the campsite. So, my dear, the packing is all you. Get on it." Alice nudged him playfully.

Jonathan sighed dramatically. "Alright, alright, as you wish," he said with a grin, heading out of the kitchen to bellow for Ian to get his butt in gear.

Once they arrived at the river, everyone—except Rowan—began setting up. Spirits were high, and the weekend away felt like a much-needed break.

As the second day dawned, the trip was going perfectly, and Rowan had had no issues so far. She and Ian played tug-of-war, with Corey being the rope. Alice pulled Ian aside at one point and reminded him that, no matter how close he and Corey were, his girlfriend always trumped. To his credit, Corey split his time evenly between them.

Alice kept one eye on Rowan as she sat at the picnic table drinking water. Sidling up next to her, she asked, "How are you feeling? Anything going on?"

"I'm good," Rowan assured her. "Other than getting a little overheated, I'm okay. I've been sitting here for a while and feel fine. Should we get ready for dinner?"

Alice followed Rowan's gaze as she nodded toward the side of the campsite.

"Are you sure you feel up to it? It's pretty hot out," Alice asked.

"Yep, it's tradition!"

"Alright," Alice agreed, "but if you start feeling bad, come back, okay?"

"Got it."

Alice watched as Rowan walked toward a meadow brimming with wildflowers. Since she was little, Rowan had always wandered over to the field, often hand-in-hand with Jonathan, to pick a bouquet for Alice. Alice would make a big show by arranging them in an empty soda can and proudly displaying them at the center of the picnic table. Ian had never seemed particularly interested, but Rowan had always beamed with pride over her floral arrangements.

Alice watched her and reflected on how, not so long ago, they wouldn't have been here... couldn't be here. She lulled herself into what she hoped was not a false sense of security and thought to herself, "*we shall see.*"

Chapter 26

After dinner, Alice suggested taking the boat out to the floating dock to cool off with a swim. The kids splashed and dove into the lake while she and Jonathan lay back on the dock, reminiscing about past trips.

On the way back, Ian cut the small outboard engine, grinning mischievously. "Guys against girls," he declared.

Rowan scoffed. "That's not fair! With Corey here, there are three boys and only two girls."

"Well, life's not fair sometimes, Princess. Get up and man your post," Ian teased.

Rowan stood. "Fine, but Corey is in the neutral zone—he works for neither side."

Ian pretended to ponder it. "Okay, I agree to those terms."

Alice knew what was coming—her family's version of chicken. Instead of sitting on shoulders in a pool, they stood straddling the sides of the boat, rocking it to see who would fall off first.

"It's pretty hot out. Maybe we should just head in," Alice suggested.

The collective "Really?" look from everyone, including Jonathan, answered that question.

"Nothing cools a person off like cold lake water," Jonathan said. "But hey, if you're scared, just say you're scared."

Alice knew why they were pushing, but when Rowan met her gaze with determination, she couldn't say no.

"We got this, Rowan. Your dad is so uncoordinated he falls up a set of stairs," Alice teased.

Corey hesitated. "Uh...what exactly am I supposed to do?"

"It's our version of chicken. Just stand in the center and try to keep the boat steady. You're playing for both teams," Ian explained.

Soon, everyone was in place. "Go!" Ian shouted.

The boat rocked violently, Corey struggling to keep balance but soon getting the hang of it. Laughter and shrieks filled the air until, finally, the boys went flying into the water.

"What the actual hell, Corey?" Ian sputtered, splashing water at them. "You weren't supposed to keep the boat that steady! Three boys lost to two tiny girly girls."

More good-natured ribbing followed as they headed back to shore. That night, as the kids took the boat back out for evening fishing, Alice and Jonathan were curled up by the fire.

"Well, I think we can call this trip a success. What about you?" Jonathan asked.

Alice smiled. "Definitely. I was nervous, being so far from the hospital, but Rowan had a great time. So did Ian, even if he had to share Corey."

"What about you?" Jonathan took her hand. "Did you enjoy yourself? You deserve a break."

Alice leaned against him. "I really did. It felt so right, so normal. I had forgotten what that felt like."

Jonathan chuckled. "Ian ate his weight in hot dogs, Rowan still screams when she has to take a fish off the hook, and you stole all the covers. Yep, I'd say it was perfectly, wonderfully normal."

Alice laughed, resting her head on his shoulder. Yes, it was perfectly, wonderfully normal indeed.

Chapter 27

With their first successful family camping trip behind them, life gradually settled back into its usual rhythm. Daily routines resumed, and Alice found herself more productive than she had been in years. She was writing at an incredible pace, staying at least a month ahead of schedule for her current book while already toying with ideas for the next one.

But with success came new challenges. If the book did well, there would be demands—book signings, readings, promotional events. She couldn't afford to decline, not after the way her career had taken a backseat during the height of Rowan's illness.

"We'll be fine, Alice. This isn't new. This happens every time you finish a book," Jonathan reassured her one evening.

"Yes," Alice admitted, "but it's never happened while we had a chronically sick child."

"So, you being here will make her less sick?" He met her gaze, his tone calm but firm. "She's been doing great. It's been almost two years since your last book tour, and your editor would have a baby cow if you refused. They support you by publishing your books—you support them by promoting them."

Alice sighed. "My head knows you're right, but my heart isn't convinced. Sometimes, I wonder if we've just been lulled into a false sense of security. I can't help it, I continue to keep waiting for the other shoe to drop."

Jonathan smiled. "Then my advice is to keep all your shoes on the floor so none of them can drop. And in the meantime, go where you need to go. I've got this."

He always made things sound so simple.

She didn't have to wait long. Within weeks, her editor had her on the move, juggling home life and jet-setting across the country. The first trip was the hardest. She texted Jonathan and Rowan obsessively, asking about Rowan's wellbeing. She knew she was probably driving Jonathan crazy—and absolutely driving Rowan nuts—but she couldn't shake the nagging feeling that something wasn't right.

That feeling never quite went away.

At the moment, Alice was home on a temporary reprieve—two weeks before she had to finish up the last leg of her tour. But writing was the last thing she wanted to do. She was burned out on words, exhausted from flights and hotels and bookshop meet-and-greets. What she needed was something physical to shake the restless energy from her system.

So, she turned to cleaning.

A full-scale purge, from attic to basement. She boxed up years' worth of accumulated clutter, sorting through forgotten memories and useless junk alike. When she finally finished, she figured she had just enough time to sit outside in the fresh air with a cold glass of lemonade and a quick scroll through Facebook before starting dinner.

As she stepped onto the porch, her phone rang.

She glanced down at the screen.

Coach Lauren.

Alice froze.

A strange sense of foreboding wrapped around her as she answered.

"Lauren? What's—"

Lauren cut her off. "Alice, it's Rowan. She went down."

The words hit her like a physical blow.

"Okay," Alice forced out, trying to keep her voice steady. "Heart too fast? Too slow? Is she—"

Lauren interrupted again, her voice high with panic. "Alice, listen to me. Rowan clutched her chest and screamed in pain. She went down. She had a pulse—it was weak, erratic—but then she went limp. And I checked again and—" Alice heard a strangled sob come out of Lauren. "Her heart wasn't beating too fast *or* too slow. It wasn't beating at *all.*"

The glass of lemonade Alice was holding slipped from her hand to the porch, and she watched it, and her whole world, shatter into a million pieces.

Chapter 28

A lice arrived at the hospital with no memory of driving there. She knew she had called Jonathan, but she couldn't recall a single word of what she had said to him. As she ran through the doors of the ER, she heard Jonathan scream her name from behind. He was sprinting toward her, seemingly appearing at her side in an instant. Without breaking stride, they nearly crashed into the reception desk.

Jonathan gasped, his voice frantic. "Our daughter, Rowan Lee Miller, was brought here by ambulance. Her... her..." But he couldn't get the words out.

Alice took over. She wasn't about to waste time explaining all of Rowan's medical issues to the receptionist— she just needed to see her daughter.

"Our daughter was brought in from Lakeside High School. What room is she in?"

Alice recognized the receptionist from previous visits. She had been working during some of Rowan's earlier ER admissions, and Alice vividly remembered her lack of urgency and how she had taken her sweet time looking up Rowan's information. Alice had no patience for that now.

But this time, the receptionist seemed to remember them, too. Without hesitation, she began typing rapidly on her keyboard.

"She's in Room 12. Go through the double doors and take a left. Even-numbered rooms are on the right side of the hallway."

Alice noticed the slight look of urgency on the woman's face. What did she know that they didn't?

Jonathan and Alice raced through the doors. As soon as they opened wide enough to squeeze through, they rushed down the hall. Room 12 wasn't far. Alice shoved the door open as if escaping a burning building.

Inside, the room was a flurry of movement. Medical staff surrounded Rowan, setting up oxygen and inserting two IVs—one in her hand, another in her arm. A nurse was attaching leads for an EEG and EKG while a doctor in a white coat was prying open Rowan's eyelids, shining a light into her unresponsive eyes. Alice watched as syringe after syringe of medication was pushed through the IV ports, sending who knew what into her daughter's body.

A warming blanket was draped over Rowan. An automatic blood pressure cuff was activated, and a pulse oximeter was clipped onto her finger. Alice's eyes flicked to the monitor.

Her oxygen saturation was only 91%.

Her heart rate was 41 beats per minute.

Jonathan looked at the numbers, his face drained of color. Without speaking, they instinctively reached for each other, gripping tightly as they moved toward the corner of the room—out of the way but still able to see Rowan.

The numbers on the monitor ticked upward. Slowly. Alice willed them to keep going, to climb to safer levels. As Rowan's vitals improved, the room gradually emptied. Within minutes, only one person remained.

Dr. Gregory.

Alice's breath caught. She remembered him. He was the first doctor who had treated Rowan nearly two years ago. But this time, his demeanor wasn't warm or reassuring. There were no smiles, no light-hearted greetings. He got straight to business.

He shook both of their hands briefly before motioning for them to sit in the two chairs beside the bed. Neither of them moved. Instead, they rushed to Rowan's side. Alice covered Rowan's icy hand with her own.

She looked up sharply at Dr. Gregory, her panic growing.

"She'll warm up quickly," he assured them. "Her blood pressure bottomed out, and she was going into shock. That's why we have the warming blanket on her—to prevent it from getting worse."

Alice felt paralyzed. She turned to Jonathan and saw the same dazed, frozen expression on his face.

She swallowed hard, trying to fight off the sharp, throbbing pain that was already brewing at the base of her skull—a migraine building from stress.

"What happened to her?" Alice's voice cracked. "Her cheerleading coach said her heart stopped. But surely, she was mistaken, right?"

Dr. Gregory leaned forward, gripping the bed rail. "I'm afraid the coach was right. According to EMS, Rowan likely suffered a heart attack, which led to cardiac arrest. That means her heart stopped beating altogether."

Alice staggered.

Jonathan sucked in a sharp breath. "She—her heart *stopped*?"

Dr. Gregory nodded grimly. "When EMS arrived, her coach and another person were performing CPR. Rowan had no pulse. They used a defibrillator to shock her heart, and thankfully, it worked. By the time she arrived here, her heart was beating, but it was dangerously slow. Her blood pressure was critically low as well. We administered epinephrine to raise her heart rate and midodrine to stabilize her blood pressure."

He glanced at the monitor. "Her vitals still aren't great, but they're significantly better than when she first arrived. Her oxygen saturation is still low, but when EMS brought her in, it was 86%. I was on the verge of intubating her, but her airway relaxed just enough that a simple oxygen mask sufficed. Progress is slow but steady."

Tears blurred Alice's vision. She bent down and kissed Rowan's forehead.

"What *caused* this?" she whispered. "She was doing so much better for months. And why isn't she waking up?"

Dr. Gregory exhaled, his expression guarded. "The short answer is—we don't know. As for why she's still unconscious... Rowan was without an adequate oxygen supply for approximately ten minutes."

Alice flinched.

Dr. Gregory continued. "The people performing CPR knew what they were doing, which is crucial. However, even with effective CPR, the recipient only receives about 10-14% of the oxygen they need—along with carbon dioxide. The chest compressions only provide 40% of normal circulation. CPR is a temporary measure, meant to keep a person alive until advanced life support can take over."

Alice's hands clenched into fists.

"Basically," he said, "CPR kept her *alive* long enough for EMS to intervene. It worked. Whoever performed it saved your daughter's life."

Alice barely registered his words. Her mind was fixated on one thing.

"But she's still unconscious," she whispered.

Dr. Gregory hesitated. "Yes. The lack of oxygen to her brain, even for a short time, is likely the cause. As her oxygen levels stabilize, we expect her brain to—reboot."

Alice's head snapped up. *"Expect?"*

Dr. Gregory's silence was deafening.

Alice felt her knees buckle. Jonathan grabbed her, holding her steady.

Finally, Dr. Gregory spoke. "It's unlikely that she won't wake up, but… it is a possibility."

A sob caught in Alice's throat.

Jonathan found his voice. "So, what happens now? Do you have any idea what caused this?"

Dr. Gregory shook his head. "No. As I told you before, this is beyond my specialty. However, as soon as Rowan arrived, I had my nurse pull her file and contact both Dr. Mason and Dr. Effland. They've been informed of her condition and will collaborate on the next steps."

Alice barely heard him. Her mind was racing, spiraling with worst-case scenarios.

Dr. Gregory's voice softened. "For now, Rowan isn't going anywhere. Once her vitals stabilize, we'll move her to the ICU. Both Dr. Mason and Dr. Effland have privileges at this hospital, so they'll be handling her care from here."

Alice swallowed hard. "What do we do in the meantime?"

Dr. Gregory looked down at Rowan, then back at them.

"There's only one thing you can do."

He met Alice's eyes.

"Sit with her. Hold her hand. Talk to her."

His voice was gentle.

"And hope she hears you enough to *fight* her way back."

Chapter 29

Rowan was moved to the intensive care unit about an hour later. Dr. Gregory had come in and informed both Jonathan and Alice that he had spoken with both Dr. Mason and Dr. Effland, who would be in to see Rowan soon. Dr. Mason planned to come after his last patient at his practice, and Dr. Effland would arrive following her last surgical procedure of the day.

Alice couldn't understand why they weren't already there. *Why aren't they at her bedside?* Her frustration bubbled up, but before she could voice it, a nurse entered the room, her presence calm and reassuring.

"Hello, my name is Genny, and I'll be Rowan's nurse for the night. Right now, your daughter's vitals are stable," she said. "Though I say that with a grain of salt—her stability could be the result of the intravenous medications we're giving her. Dr. Mason has already ordered a series of tests. He won't be able to provide many answers until we get those results."

Alice nodded, trying to absorb the information.

"A technician will be in soon with a portable ultrasound machine. In the meantime, I'm going to draw some blood so we can keep things moving," Genny continued as she prepped Rowan's arm. "We have her leads attached, and we're running an EKG every fifteen minutes. The results go directly to the nurses' station, along with continuous monitoring of her vitals. There's even a dedicated technician whose sole job is to review patient monitors in real-time. If anything changes, we'll know immediately."

Alice exhaled slightly. Despite everything, the nurse's calm demeanor was somewhat reassuring.

"If you have any questions before the doctors arrive, just push the call button. I'll do my best to answer them."

Genny glanced down at Rowan with a warm smile. "Your daughter is beautiful."

Alice managed a small smile in return. She liked this nurse. Genny's soothing presence made her feel slightly more at ease.

Dr. Mason is already working on Rowan's case, and he isn't even here yet, Alice reminded herself. She felt a twinge of guilt for her earlier annoyance. She knew he had other patients. But Rowan was her *only* daughter. Wanting him here immediately was natural, even if it wasn't realistic.

Alice swallowed her frustration and instead asked, "Do you know why Dr. Effland is coming? She's a surgeon… Does that mean Rowan needs surgery?"

Genny filled the last vial of blood and placed it in a test tube holder. "I can't say for certain, but surgical consultations are standard in cases like these. It doesn't necessarily mean surgery is required, but they need to rule it out."

Alice nodded, rubbing her temples.

"Are you okay?" Genny asked.

"Just a migraine. I'm prone to them," Alice admitted.

Genny nodded. "I can't give you anything since you're not a patient, but the gift shop downstairs sells those little packets of pain relievers."

Alice pulled a small pillbox from her purse and shook it lightly. "I've got it covered, but thanks."

As Genny removed the needle, Rowan began to stir.

Alice and Jonathan bolted to her bedside.

Rowan's eyes fluttered open, then closed again. She repeated this several times before managing to keep them open.

"Where... am I?" she asked groggily.

Alice summoned every ounce of strength, pasting on a smile. "Well, young lady, you gave us quite the scare. There was an... issue with your heart, and now you're in the hospital. Dr. Mason will be in soon to explain everything. But right now, your vitals are stable, so you're doing great."

Jonathan shot Alice a sharp look, but Alice returned one of her own, silently conveying that she wasn't going to tell Rowan everything just yet.

Before Jonathan could say anything, the door opened, and a technician wheeled in a portable ultrasound machine.

Jonathan leaned down toward Rowan. "Hey, kiddo, Mom and I are going to step out for a bit. There's a lounge just down the hall for families. We'll be back after your test."

Rowan gave a sluggish nod, then closed her eyes again.

Once outside, Jonathan turned to Alice, frustration evident in his expression.

"Why did you tell her she was fine? Why didn't you tell her the truth? Do you think watering this down is doing her any favors?" His voice was tight and controlled but clearly upset.

Alice held her ground. "Tell her *what*, exactly? We don't even know the full story. Throwing words like 'heart attack' and 'cardiac arrest' at her right now would only terrify her. The last thing we need is for her to panic and send her heart into another tailspin."

Jonathan clenched his jaw but said nothing.

Alice softened her voice. "We don't know how long it will be before Dr. Mason arrives, and we have no idea what the test results will show. Worrying her right now won't help anything."

Jonathan exhaled sharply, then walked over to the window, looking down at the city below. Alice let him have his space.

After a long moment, he finally spoke. "You're right. I know you're right. But if I feel this overwhelmed just *knowing* what happened, I can't imagine how she'll process it all at once. I just… I don't want her to feel like we kept this from her."

Alice walked over, wrapping her arms around his waist. She rested her head against his back. "I know, and I get it. But telling her now would only lead to a barrage of questions we *can't* answer yet. Wouldn't that be worse? She may be mad at us later, but right now, keeping her calm is what's best."

Jonathan placed his hands over hers, squeezing gently. "I'm scared, Alice. More scared than I've ever been about anything. My daughter is broken, and I can't fix her."

Alice felt his body tremble. She tightened her hold. "I know. I'm scared, too. Terrified. But for now, we need to show her that everything is under control. If she sees how afraid we are, she'll feed off that energy. We walk back in there as a united front. We'll deal with each thing *together*—one step at a time."

Jonathan turned to her, giving a small, weary smile. "Is it hard being right all the time?"

Alice smirked. "It's exhausting, but someone's gotta do it."

Jonathan chuckled, shaking his head. "Alright, Coach. Send me in."

Chapter 30

A couple of hours later, Dr. Mason entered the room, accompanied by Dr. Effland. Rowan had been drifting in and out of sleep, surprisingly not asking many questions. But the moment she heard Dr. Mason's voice greeting Alice and Jonathan, she perked up.

He smiled down at her. "Hello, my dear. You've had quite the day. How are you feeling?"

"I feel groggy. Out of it. I'm so tired I can barely keep my eyes open." She paused, then frowned. "Why am I here? What happened? I was cheering at the game, and now I'm… here."

Dr. Mason glanced at Jonathan and Alice, silently asking for permission to proceed. They both nodded.

"The short answer? You had a cardiac event. Well, two."

Rowan blinked. "What does that mean?"

Dr. Mason softened his voice. "Given that you were cheerleading at the time, your heart most likely went tachycardic. Then, in an effort to correct itself, it overcompensated and slowed down too much. The result was too much pressure on your heart. It couldn't regulate itself and began to spasm."

He paused, then continued, his voice gentle but firm.

"That spasm led to a heart attack. The stress of that caused your heart to go into cardiac arrest—or more simply put, your heart stopped beating altogether."

Dr. Mason let the words sink in.

Rowan's eyes widened. "My heart stopped? Like, completely stopped?"

"Yes, that is what I'm saying."

Silence filled the room.

Alice could see the fear creeping up Rowan's body. She gave her daughter's hand a reassuring squeeze, sensing the whirlwind of unspoken thoughts racing through her mind.

Alice stepped in, her voice steady. "What happens now? What's the next step?"

Dr. Effland took over. "Well, as we had discussed before, the downside to the ablation I performed would be that by altering the heart, it may not be able to beat properly on its own. It may have fixed one issue but caused another. Given the amount of time since the ablation, we had high hopes that it was a success all around, but it appears that is not the case. Therefore, given the circumstances, we believe the best course of action is implanting a pacemaker. It will regulate your heart's rhythm—preventing it from going too fast or too slow."

Rowan's expression faltered. "For how long?"

Dr. Mason sighed. "It's permanent."

Tears welled in Rowan's eyes. "But… why can't I cheer if it's supposed to fix everything?"

"We need to give your heart time to heal," Dr. Mason said gently. "We'll take it one step at a time."

Rowan asked, "So, when is this happening? When am I getting this pacemaker thing in?"

Dr. Effland fielded this question after glancing at Dr. Mason, which was not lost on Alice. "The sooner, the better, so we would like to take the rest of the day and night to stabilize you and do it first thing in the morning. Given the severity of your condition, you'll need to stay in the hospital for constant monitoring for an indeterminable amount of time. A sweet kid like you, I bet you'll have lots of visitors with many gifts. So, if you still wanted that pony you didn't get, now is a good time to ask for it."

If that was Dr. Effland's way of lightening the mood it failed miserably. Rowan looked utterly defeated. She lowered the head of her bed slightly, rolled over away from both doctors, and softly began to cry. All Alice could do was stand by helplessly and watch her daughter's world caving in around her.

Chapter 31

Rowan's nurse, Genny, entered the room with Dr. Mason and another doctor Alice did not recognize. "Genny is going to take some additional blood for a few more tests I want to run," he explained. "I know it must seem like we've taken a gallon already, but I want the clearest picture possible. She's also going to switch out one of Rowan's IV bags for a solution called IV infusion vitamin therapy. This will help boost her immune system. Infection is dangerous for anyone, but for Rowan, it's a full-on enemy. It's imperative we keep her infection-free." That being said, I'd like to introduce a colleague of mine, Dr. Kent, an immunologist. I want to bring him in on Rowan's team. Dr. Kent said nothing but smiled at Rowan and then Alice and Jonathan. Dr. Mason then glanced at both Alice and Jonathan and subtly gestured toward the door. For now, let's give Genny some space to work." Turning to the nurse, he continued, "Genny, let's get Rowan into one of the thicker, more comfortable gowns we use for long-term patients. She's had those leads on for hours—they're probably going to start itching soon." Genny nodded, already moving toward Rowan with quiet efficiency. Alice could tell something unspoken had passed between the doctor and nurse, a silent understanding. The hair on the back of her neck stood on end.

Alice leaned down and whispered to Rowan, "We'll be right back, punkins. Let Genny get you all fixed up."

Rowan barely acknowledged her.

As they followed both doctors into the lounge, Alice had a sinking feeling they'd be spending a lot of time in that room over the next few weeks. Once the door closed, Dr. Mason gestured toward the table and chairs.

Once they were all seated, he looked pointedly at them, his expression grave. Instinctively, Alice and Jonathan clasped hands.

Alice's stomach was clenched. "What is it you haven't told us yet?" she asked. "What's so bad that you couldn't say it in front of Rowan?"

Dr. Mason nodded. "Everything I said in there was accurate. However, there's another serious one—that I felt was best discussed with you first. You can decide if Rowan should know this information now or later."

Alice and Jonathan exchanged a glance. Without speaking, they turned back to Dr. Mason, silently agreeing for him to continue.

"A human heart is essentially a large muscle," he began. "Rowan's heart has sustained considerable damage, both in muscle tissue and scar tissue from the ablation. The IST, the ablation, the POTS, the bradycardia, the MVP, and now—most critically—her two cardiac events have taken a significant toll. Her heart has drastically weakened.

"In addition, her MVP has worsened. The spasming of her heart caused further damage to the mitral valve, and the buckling of that valve has become more pronounced. When we implant the pacemaker, we won't have a choice—we have to repair that valve as well. It's now buckling to the point where blood is regurgitating backward through the valve.

"Fixing the valve will cause more scar tissue. Now, while the heart has some ability to regenerate muscle tissue, it's a slow process. More often than not, scar tissue develops instead of working muscle. The two are not interchangeable. Scar tissue cannot function like muscle tissue."

Alice's throat tightened. "Reconstruct her valve? What does that mean?"

Dr. Mason explained, "We will remove the part of the mitral valve that no longer closes properly. Then, stitches will be used to connect the valve edges together. Finally, we'll place an annuloplasty ring to tighten the width of the valve."

Jonathan shook his head, staring at the floor. "You said her heart is weakened. How do we fix that?"

Dr. Mason sighed. "There is no medical treatment for a heart with diminished performance."

Alice and Jonathan locked eyes, then turned back to the doctor.

"Okay," Alice said, struggling to keep her voice steady. "What does this mean for the pacemaker? Are you saying it might not work?"

Dr. Mason exchanged a glance with Dr. Kent before turning back to them. "Your daughter's heart is now so weak that the pacemaker is a band-aid at best. But it will buy us time.

Jonathan's voice was barely a whisper. "Time? Time for what?"

Dr. Mason's face was unreadable as he said, "Time to find your daughter a new heart."

187

***

After Dr. Mason and Dr. Kent left, Alice and Jonathan remained frozen, hands still clasped. Neither spoke. Neither moved. It was as if staying perfectly still could somehow undo what they had just heard.

Finally, Jonathan rose, lacing his fingers behind his head as he began pacing the room. He came to a sudden stop in front of a chair, gripping the armrests so tightly his knuckles turned white.

Then, with a gut-wrenching scream, he hurled the chair across the room.

The impact against the wall was deafening. Half of the chair lodged into the drywall before crashing to the floor. Jonathan collapsed to his knees, sobbing uncontrollably.

Alice rushed to him just as the door burst open.

Dr. Mason and Genny entered first, followed by an orderly.

The orderly hesitated. "Should I call security?"

Dr. Mason never took his eyes off Jonathan. "No. Just tell maintenance we had an incident in the lounge and leave it at that." He then looked pointedly at the orderly.

The orderly nodded, indicating that he understood, and slipped out.

Jonathan, still kneeling, muttered weakly, "I'm sorry about the chair." His voice cracked. "Thank you for not having me escorted out of the building."

Dr. Mason placed a firm hand on Jonathan's shoulder. "You owe no one an apology. And no thanks are needed. Trust me, if I didn't think I'd lose my privileges at this hospital, there'd be another chair sticking out of that wall."

He gave Jonathan's shoulder another squeeze before quietly leaving.

Alice sat on the floor beside him, cradling his head in her lap, running her fingers gently through his hair. She hummed softly, soothing him as one would a frightened child.

A few minutes later, Genny returned. "Rowan's asking for you."

Alice hesitated. "Can you tell her I'm talking to her brother on the phone? I'll be there in five minutes."

Genny nodded. She lingered for a moment, glancing around the room, then smiled. "Does Rowan like makeup?"

Alice gave a small nod. "As much as any teenage girl."

"Good," Genny said. "I'm about to go on break, but I thought we could have some girl time while you're "on the phone with Ian."

Alice's chest swelled with gratitude. "You're in the middle of a twelve-hour shift, and you want to spend your dinner break giving my daughter a makeover?"

Genny grinned. "Some of my best care comes after hours, and I need to go over the meal options with her. She can have anything she wants until midnight before the procedure."

"Thank you, Genny," Alice said earnestly. "You're truly a wonderful nurse. If she's not impressed by the hospital menu, tell her we'll bring her something."

Genny flashed a thumbs-up before slipping out.

Alice turned her attention back to Jonathan, who was beginning to sit up.

"Welcome back," she said softly.

He surveyed the wreckage. "Dear God… Alice, I'm so sorry. I totally lost it. I hardly even remember doing it."

"No harm done. Well, no harm to any person, at least. The wall… not so much." She gave him a weak smile.

Jonathan let out a shaky laugh before standing. He goes back to the window. "I've never felt so helpless in all my life. Our daughter may die, Alice and all I can do to help her is to stand around and watch. As hard as this is for me and for us, how much harder is it going to be when we tell her?

Alice begins to pace. "We are not going to keep that from her, however bad I want to. But we tell her nothing until after this surgery. I don't want her going into that, knowing that all they are doing is "buying time." *We* are barely holding it together with the knowledge of it, let alone her. The right time will present itself."

"Ok," Jonathan said, "But at some point, we have to tell her that she needs a new heart. We cannot keep that from her."

Alice inhaled and exhaled deeply. "Agreed. However, if we look terrified, she will be terrified. So, for now pull it together and get your game face on.

Chapter 32

T he next few days passed quickly. For the most part, Alice never left Rowan's side. She did have a doctor's appointment, and Jonathan was insistent on accompanying her, but despite his concern, she made him stay at the hospital. "Dr. Wyngarden's office is right across the street from the hospital. We won't be gone long, and we can pull Ian out of school to be here with Rowan. He's pretty much been given a pass on missing school," Jonathan said. Alice said, "You're making more of this than it needs to be," "Exactly, my point. They have been getting worse for some time now", Jonathan spoke. "You kept refusing to go, insisting it was just the added stress, and now suddenly you wanted to be seen as soon as possible. Is there something you are not telling me?" Alice shook her head and said, "Look, it's not something I am worried about, so neither should you. With everything that's been going on, it's no wonder they have been getting worse. A change in medication or something else to go with the Imitrex will be all that is needed. Quite possibly she may order some tests for good measure. I won't be able to relax if you are not here with Rowan."

Tests were, in fact, ordered for Alice, and after explaining all that was happening with Rowan, the doctor personally called the hospital and scheduled all necessary testing to be done there over the next few days. Alice was grateful that she wouldn't have to spend much time away from Rowan.

Still, time seemed to be slipping away too fast. Every time Alice looked at the clock, whole hours had flown by. Every minute that passed brought them closer to the surgery, tightening the knot of anxiety in her chest.

Later that night, prior to the surgery, Dr. Mason came in and, once again, led them back to the lounge.

"I've put Rowan on the donor list," he said, "and she's pretty high up."

Jonathan leaned forward. "Does that mean finding a heart will be easy—and, more importantly, fast? I mean, thousands of people die every day."

"Yes, that's true," Dr. Mason acknowledged, "but it's not that simple. Rowan's blood type—AB-negative—must match the donor's blood type, or the donor must have type O-negative, which is the universal donor blood type. Both are rare, and the percentage of people who have them is low."

He continued, "The size of the heart is also a critical factor. The donor heart must fit inside Rowan's rib cage.

"Then there's distance. Since we need a heart, that means it must come from a deceased donor—either from a traumatic death or if life support is discontinued. The maximum time to harvest a heart, crossmatch it, transport it, and implant it in the recipient is four to six hours. You may think that's a lot of time, but given everything that must be done—from A to Z—to get that heart into Rowan, a donor that's too far away won't work.

"The longer the heart has ceased beating before implantation, the lower the chances of a successful transplant. Given the severity of Rowan's condition, the ideal scenario would be for a donor heart to be harvested and implanted within sixty minutes—what we call the golden hour."

Alice frowned. "The golden hour? What does that mean?"

"It's a medical term often used in trauma or emergency care to emphasize that an injured or critically ill person must receive definitive treatment within the first sixty minutes from the time of injury or the appearance of severe symptoms. For our purposes, it means that the shorter the time between harvest and implantation, the better.

"Although Rowan hasn't suffered physical trauma like a car accident, her heart attack and cardiac arrest qualify as trauma, given that the heart is now failing due to both of those things. Her heart is weakening by the day because of that. I'm not saying that a heart transplant requiring more time—due to distance or other factors—won't work, but the time factor is crucial.

"For example, if a heart becomes available in California and both Rowan and another patient in California are suitable matches, the patient in California would receive it. That's because the odds of a successful transplant are higher for that patient than for Rowan due to the sheer distance involved."

Dr. Mason sighed. "I know this is a lot to take in. Do you have any questions?"

Alice swallowed hard. "How long does she have before her heart gives out?"

Dr. Mason hesitated. "As I've said, Rowan's heart is very damaged, and it's hard to—"

"Dr. Mason," Alice interrupted sharply, "just tell us. No sugarcoating. How long?"

He exhaled heavily. "It's not an exact science. Based on all the testing, her monitored activity, and imaging, my baseline estimate is four weeks. But it could fail sooner... or it could last longer." He continued, "I'm hoping that the pacemaker will buy us more time, but there are other risks—organ failure or infections. The heart and brain are the epicenters of the body's functions. When one starts to fail, it can trigger other organ systems to fail as well. There are simply too many variables for me to give you anything beyond an educated guess."

Jonathan cleared his throat, his voice tight. "What are her chances of getting a heart in time?"

Dr. Mason rubbed his jaw. "I don't like to deal with statistics and averages, at least not something like this. There are definite cons—the challenges we discussed were the extent of Rowan's heart damage.

"But there's also a significant pro: Rowan is young, and aside from her heart, she's healthy. She has no infections and, so far, no other organ damage. That gives her a stronger chance than most." He paused. "For now, I'd say we should be cautiously optimistic."

Alice let out a frustrated sigh. "Cautious optimism isn't really telling us anything."

Dr. Mason nodded. "Unfortunately, that's the best I can do."

Chapter 33

At seven o'clock the next morning, Rowan went into surgery to have the pacemaker placed in her heart and her mitral valve repaired. She was in surgery for four and a half hours. By the time the clock reached three hours—the original estimated time frame—Alice was practically hyperventilating.

The waiting room for the OR had games and books, and Jonathan and Ian played endless rounds of checkers. Alice knew they needed something to occupy their minds, to avoid talking about what was happening.

Finally, Dr. Effland entered the surgical waiting room. Alice and Jonathan jumped up, nearly speaking at the same time.

"What happened? Why was she in there so long?"

Dr. Effland gestured for them to sit. "Rowan is stable now, but we ran into a few complications. During surgery, we had to stop several times because her blood pressure kept fluctuating—either too high or too low. However, the pacemaker is in, and the valve is repaired. We'll monitor that valve daily using an ultrasound. Once we got in there, we saw that the valve was in worse condition than we originally thought, which added extra time to the surgery."

Alice let out a shaky breath. "She's okay, though?"

"She's in recovery now, still under anesthesia. I can take you both to her on my way back. You'll be there when she wakes up."

Jonathan glanced at Ian. "What about our son? Can he come, too?"

Dr. Effland gave him an apologetic look. "I'm sorry, but no. Only two visitors at a time."

"It's okay, guys," Ian said. "You go. I'll just hang out here. I'll text Pastor Carl and let him know Rowan is out of surgery. I'll text Corey, too."

Alice hugged her son. "That would be great, honey. Thank you. Tell Pastor we'll check in again later."

As Dr. Effland led them through the hallways, she added, "Dr. Mason will check on her during his evening rounds."

When they arrived outside the recovery room, Dr. Effland stopped. "This is your stop. Once Rowan wakes up, the anesthesiologist will check her vitals. If everything is stable, she'll be moved back to her room."

Alice nodded. "Thank you for everything you're doing for her."

Dr. Effland's expression softened. "I hope to do a lot more. Surgeons usually rotate being on call, but for Rowan, I've put myself on a twenty-four-hour call. If we get that heart, I want to be the one to transplant it. I've operated on your daughter twice now, and I want to see this through." She smiled. "That being said, I have another surgery to get to. I'm praying I'll see you again soon—under better circumstances."

"There's no such thing as too much prayer," Jonathan said.

Dr. Effland started to walk away, then hesitated. She turned back and hugged Alice. "It's risky business getting emotionally involved with a patient, but that little gal has stolen my heart—no pun intended."

Alice watched her disappear down the hall before following Jonathan into the recovery room. They didn't talk; they just sat on either side of Rowan, each holding one of her hands.

Thirty minutes later, Jonathan broke the silence. "I'll head back to the waiting room, get Ian, and then go back to Rowan's room."

Alice nodded. "She'll be hungry when she wakes up— she hasn't eaten since last night. She mentioned wanting Chinese food. Maybe you and Ian can pick some up? And..." She hesitated. "Maybe we should tell him. Everything."

Jonathan looked taken aback. "Tell him before we tell Rowan? Are you sure that's a good idea?"

Alice sighed. "I honestly don't know what's best. On one hand, Ian will be there for Rowan—help her through it, lighten the mood like he always does. But on the other hand,... this is her battle, her reality to process. She might not want anyone else to know right away. I'm at a loss."

Jonathan considered her words before responding. "Let's tell Ian, but we'll make it clear that Rowan doesn't know yet. We need to include him in this. If he processes it now, he can be there for her tomorrow when we tell her. We get through this as a family, remember?"

"Tomorrow?" Alice frowned. "I think we should wait a few days. What if her heart starts regenerating muscle? What if we jump the gun—"

"Tomorrow," Jonathan said firmly. "She needs time to process it. Right now, Dr. Mason says she has about four weeks. I pray it's longer—much longer—but we can't pretend this isn't happening. We held off telling her before surgery, but we need to face this head-on."

Rowan stirred, and Alice shot Jonathan a look. *Happy face on.*

Jonathan squeezed her hand. "Hey, princess."

Rowan blinked groggily. "Is it in? The pacemaker?"

Alice smiled. "It is, and it's working well. You'll be back in your room soon. Are you hungry?"

Rowan sat up slightly. "Yeah... and thirsty." She turned to Jonathan, her voice teasing. "Daddy, how much do you love me?"

Jonathan laughed. "I feel a food and drink order coming my way. How many stops am I making?"

Rowan grinned. "Three... maybe four, depending on if Ian is here."

"Four, then," Jonathan said. "He's here, and he's probably cleaned out my wallet in the vending machine."

Rowan chuckled. "Okay—Angelo's pizza, with the works. Pink drink from Starbucks, large. And... twenty-five, no, wait—fifty munchkins from Dunkin' Donuts."

"Fifty?" Alice raised an eyebrow. "Don't you think that's a bit much?"

Rowan and Jonathan exchanged glances and said at the same time, "Ian's here."

Alice shook her head with a small laugh. "Fair enough."

***

The evening passed without incident. They ate pizza and munchkins while watching *Ghostbusters,* a family favorite. Ian was unusually quiet, which was understandable after hearing the news. He had taken it hard, breaking down in tears.

He played it off to Rowan, claiming he was just tired from his game. But Alice saw the way Rowan watched him, concern flickering across her face. Ian noticed, and to his credit, he snapped into character—cracking jokes, keeping the mood light.

After the movie ended, Alice walked Ian and Jonathan to the elevators.

"Can I be here when you tell her?" Ian asked.

Alice studied him. "It's going to be an emotional conversation and not one you can joke your way through. Do you think you can handle that?"

Ian nodded. "If we're doing this as a family, then I need to *be* family. I want to be here, Mom."

So, it was decided. Jonathan would bring Ian to the hospital in the morning, and together, they would tell Rowan.

By the time Alice returned to Rowan's room, she was fast asleep. Alice wasn't surprised—she had held on longer than expected after surgery.

Alice grabbed her tote bag, tore a blank page from her journal, and scribbled a note: *Went to the lounge for coffee. Be back soon.*

She had no intention of sleeping. She would spend the night watching Rowan breathe, watching the rise and fall of her chest.

The lounge was quiet. The last time she had been in there was a blur, so she hadn't noticed there was a Keurig, a dorm-sized fridge, and a variety of coffee and tea pods. A man stood next to the machine, stirring cream into his coffee.

He smiled at Alice. "Much better than the vending machine sludge, right?"

Alice chuckled. "Anything is better than *that.*"

The man stuck out his hand. "Stephen. Room 210."

Alice shook his hand. "Alice. My daughter's in 208."

Stephen said, "The man in 206—John is his name—bought it and donated it to this ward. Apparently, he's an all-day coffee drinker and couldn't take one more cup of "mud". I picked up a variety of coffee pods to do my part, and that nurse, Genny, is keeping us in half-and-half. She's an amazing nurse." Alice smiled. "She *is* an amazing nurse. I love it when she's on shift, and Rowan absolutely adores her. I think I've seen John and his wife. He's an older gentleman, yes?" "Yes, and his wife's name is Emily. I've talked to them a few times—they're nice people. Their son was involved in a motorcycle accident. Unlike my daughter, their son has a chance of coming out of the coma. "Last time I talked to John, he said his son was showing signs of brain activity. Certain things they do register on the monitor, proving his brain is still functioning at some level. They are prepared, however, for the possibility that he may have sustained enough trauma to be paralyzed. How paralyzed, they don't know yet. He may also have irreversible brain damage and require total care if he does wake up. "But John says it doesn't matter *when* he wakes up or the condition that he is in. They're prepared to care for him as long as they can.

"I envy them—that there is *hope.*"

Stephen sat down at the table with his coffee as Alice began making her own. When she was done, Stephen gestured toward the seat across from him.

"Feel free to sit down. I don't bite."

Alice took a seat. "Just for a few minutes. I don't like to be gone from Rowan's room for too long."

"Rowan—that's a beautiful name," he said.

Alice smiled. "My husband was reading *Interview with the Vampire* by Anne Rice. Rowan was the name of one of the main characters in the book. At first, when he mentioned it, I remember making a face. I thought it was a weird name. But then it kind of grew on me, and when we found out she was a girl, we just started calling her Rowan."

"Did you have any boy names picked out, just in case? I've heard of that happening."

Alice smiled. "It's funny you say that. Actually, if she had been a boy, we still would have used the name Rowan because it's gender-neutral. Ever heard of the comedian Rowan Atkinson?"

"Ah, yes, I have. You're right—gender-neutral." He took a sip of his coffee. "So, Rowan has an issue with her heart, yes?"

Alice gave him a surprised look.

"It's a small ward," Stephen said. "Everyone knows everything once you've been here long enough."

Alice nodded. "Yes. My daughter has a heart condition. Well… *had* a heart condition. Now, she's actively in heart failure, and she's on the transplant list. She doesn't know yet. We're telling her in the morning.

"She had to have a pacemaker implanted and her mitral valve repaired early this morning. My husband and I didn't want to tell her everything going into that surgery."

Stephen nodded solemnly. "Totally understandable. You and your husband must be terrified."

"That's the understatement of the year. We're officially playing beat the clock. The pacemaker was implanted to *buy time,* but how much time is anyone's guess."

She hesitated, then added, "Though we haven't talked before, I've seen you around the ward. Who are you here for?"

Stephen looked down but said nothing.

Alice's stomach tightened. "Sorry. That's really none of my business."

Stephen lifted his gaze, his expression unreadable. "No, it's fine.

"My daughter was involved in a car accident."

Stephen exhaled, his fingers tightening around his coffee cup.

"She and her friend, Bailee, were on their way back to school to watch the varsity football game. Some jackass, who knocked off work early that Friday, decided to have an extended liquid lunch before heading home. He veered over the center line and hit my daughter head-on.

"The drunk, of course, walked away with little more than superficial wounds.

"Bailee was killed instantly.

"Kelsey—my daughter—was barely clinging to life when EMS arrived. She suffered substantial trauma throughout her body, including a TBI... that stands for traumatic brain injury.

"She's been here for two months on life support. Three separate doctors have informed both me and my wife that she is brain dead... that she will never regain consciousness."

He paused, swallowing hard.

"I've accepted that. Made my peace with it.

"But Karen—my wife—she refuses to give up.

"It's amazing what you can find on the internet if you look hard enough. I've researched Kelsey's condition extensively, and everything I've read supports what the doctors are telling us. But Karen... she's done her own research, and she is *not* convinced.

"Like I said, you can find *anything* on the internet if you look long enough. You'll find exactly what you *want* to hear, no matter how obscure or uncreditable the source is.

"She latches onto these tiny nuggets of information, zones in on them, and clings to them like gospel. She presents them to the doctors and then gets furious when they try to explain that none of it applies to Kelsey—that it's unreliable, that it's unfounded. "I wanted to turn those machines off a month ago.

"I *know* Kelsey would want that. But Karen won't even discuss it.

"Eventually, insurance will stop paying, and we'll have no choice but to leave."

Alice hesitated before asking, "How much more time are they giving you? What happens when that time runs out?"

Stephen sighed. "We have about two more weeks. That's the maximum they'll cover with her being declared brain-dead. After that, Karen says we'll take her home and hire nurses and aides to come in daily to care for her.

"But, again... with the brain-dead diagnosis, insurance won't pay for that. And we *certainly* can't afford it."

He let out a hollow laugh. "I've looked into all of it. That kind of care is at *least* a thousand dollars a day—probably more.

"Believe me, Alice... if I thought for *one second* that Kelsey would wake up—"I would sell *everything* we own. to pay for that, but she is not going to wake up. Kelsey died two months ago, and everyone agrees except for Karen. She sits there day and night and talks to her, reads to her, and she exercises her arms and legs every day. I keep trying to tell her she is not sleeping; she is not in a trauma-induced coma state; Kelsey is brain dead. She just blows up and tells me to get the hell out of the room since I have "given up on our daughter." Which is why I am here now. I'm in the doghouse again. So, I must wait at least an hour before I go back in, and then I must apologize for not believing that my deceased daughter is going to wake up."

"I cannot even imagine being in that situation, what you must go through and relive repeatedly every day. Do you have other children?" asked Alice.

"No, we have no other children. Maybe if we had another child to focus on as well, Karen she may be more apt to see reason. My hands are tied. I could go to court to try to get an emergency injunction. I've even spoken to an attorney, and he said it would not be hard with three doctors saying she won't wake up. However, I would lose my wife. I cannot lose her on top of losing Kelsey. I think, on some level, she realizes the truth, but she is just not ready to give up on her. Maybe that makes me a bad father." Stephen said.

"I don't think that makes you a bad father at all. You are both just trying to do what's best for Kelsey, you are both just doing it differently." Alice said.

"Yeah, I guess. Well don't let me keep you. It should be safe to go back in soon, especially if I bring her a decent cup of coffee. I'll see you around, I'm sure. I truly hope everything works out for Rowan."

"Thank you, and I will say a prayer for your family." Alice said as she got up. As she walked back to Rowan's room, the wheels were turning in Alice's head. *So, Kelsey was brain damaged, never to wake up. A healthy human heart not fifty feet from Rowan's room.* Alice found herself walking right past Rowan's room and came to the door of Kelsey's room.

And then she saw it—Kelsey's medical chart hanging by the door. Her heart pounded as she glanced at the stickers on the front, and one stood out to her more than the others.

Blood type...

O-negative...

Alice closed her eyes. She knew the thoughts in her head were wrong, very wrong. *And yet... she didn't even care.*

Chapter 34

When Alice walked back into the room, she needn't have worried about being gone— Rowan was still asleep. Alice and Jonathan had decided they wanted Dr. Mason and Dr. Kent to tell Rowan about the need for a new heart. Alice was afraid they wouldn't be able to get through it without breaking down, and they didn't want Rowan to see her support system crumbling.

The doctors would be arriving in about an hour, so Alice called Jonathan.

"She's still asleep, but Dr. Mason and Dr. Kent will be here soon. Why don't you pick up a Starbucks drink for her and that breakfast sandwich she likes?"

"Way ahead of you. We already did that and are on our way to the hospital," Jonathan replied. "I talked to Ian again this morning to see if he changed his mind, but he still wants to come. He says we're lame and can't be counted on to make her smile."

Alice felt the tears coming already. *It's going to be a long day.*

"There's more. Ian already told Corey everything— swore him to secrecy. Apparently, Corey's going to text later and see if Rowan's up for a visit."

"Actually, that's a great idea. If anyone can make her smile, it's him," Alice said.

Jonathan continued, "I also called Carl and Wendi. I should have asked you first, I know, but I really needed some guidance last night, Alice. They're not going to reach out to us today—just waiting for us to call when we're ready. And again, people are lining up to bring meals and baked goods. I know it's a lot of food, but it'll be nice to have something ready when we take turns at the hospital or when Ian comes home from school. We need to keep things as simple as possible right now.

"Lastly, I talked to David today. He's going to take over all my projects for now and pass the smaller jobs to the junior architects. I don't want to worry about anything except focusing on Rowan—on *us*."

Alice choked up. *This man, the love of my life, always putting himself and everyone else on the back burner for his family.* She thanked God every day for blessing her with Jonathan.

"Of course, I got you the largest cup of coffee and some banana bread."

Alice smiled through her tears. "You two have been busy. All I've done is sit in the lounge this morning talking to Stephen. He's the father of the girl in room 210."

"Oh? What's their story?" Jonathan asked.

"It's not important right now. We can talk later. I'll see you soon."

As Alice ended the call, Rowan stirred. When her eyes focused on Alice, she blinked sleepily.

"Daddy's bringing you breakfast. They should be here soon."

"They?" Rowan asked.

"Yes, Daddy and Ian. Also, Dr. Mason and Dr. Kent will be here around ten to talk to us about the surgery and everything else."

Rowan frowned. "Why is Ian coming? What's wrong?"

"Oh, you know Ian—he'll take any excuse to get out of school." Alice tried to sound casual, but Rowan wasn't buying it.

Alice decided to distract her. "I do have a surprise for you, though."

Rowan raised her eyebrows.

"Corey is coming to see you after school. If you want him to, of course."

Rowan's eyes widened in horror. "*What?!* He's coming *here*? He can't see me like this! I have no makeup on, and my hair is a greasy mess!"

Alice laughed. "Don't worry. I'll run home, grab everything you need, and have it back here in plenty of time for you to shower and fix yourself up. Not that you need it— you wake up beautiful."

Rowan gave her a look. "You *have* to say that. You're my mom."

"That's true," Alice admitted. "But it doesn't mean I'm wrong."

Fifteen minutes later, Jonathan and Ian walked into the room bearing gifts—including another box of munchkins.

"You look like hammered shit," Ian said.

Rowan laughed, and so did Ian. Alice said nothing about the language. *He hadn't been in the room for fifteen seconds, and he already had her laughing.*

They had just finished eating when Dr. Mason and Dr. Kent walked in.

Alice felt her insides liquefy. Ian shrank back. Jonathan went white and seemed paralyzed.

None of this was lost on Rowan.

"Ian is here. My boyfriend is missing football practice to see me later. So, what's going on? I'm sixteen, not two."

Dr. Mason moved closer to the bed. "Rowan, we need to talk about what's happening. Your parents felt it was best coming from us in case you had questions they couldn't answer."

Alice knew this wasn't entirely true. She just didn't trust herself to stay composed. And she knew Jonathan would crumble.

Dr. Mason took a breath. "Your heart suffered a great deal of damage from the heart attack and cardiac arrest. This damage is *on top* of the scar tissue from the ablation, and the additional scar tissue that will develop from the pacemaker and valve repair. Are you with me so far?"

Rowan squeezed Alice's hand and nodded.

"That's how we got to where we are now," Dr. Mason continued.

Rowan's voice was firm. "So, what now? What's next? Did the pacemaker fix my heart?"

Dr. Mason hesitated. "Rowan, your heart is in very poor condition. It won't heal or improve on its own. To be plain... your heart is failing. You need a new heart."

Rowan just *stared*.

Jonathan moved behind Dr. Mason and took her other hand. Ian stared at the floor.

Rowan finally spoke, her voice sharp. "Why put in a pacemaker if I needed a new heart anyway? Will it keep my heart going until I get one?"

She wasn't crying. She wasn't scared. She was *furious*.

Dr. Mason had clearly expected this reaction. "The pacemaker is intended to keep your heart beating properly *until* we get you a new one. You're already high on the transplant list."

"Intended? How long will this pacemaker idea work?" Rowan asked, voice rising.

Dr. Mason hesitated again.

Rowan's anger boiled over. "*Stop dancing around me like I'm a moron!* How long? How long before my heart *stops working*?" Dr. Mason sighed. "Four weeks. Maybe more. Maybe less." Dr. Kent opened his mouth to explain the immunology, but Rowan turned away from them. "Get out," she said, voice flat. "Both of you. Get the hell out of my room."

Neither doctor said another word. They left.

For most of the morning, Rowan lay in bed, staring at her phone, crying softly, or both. Alice and Jonathan tried to talk to her, but she rolled away.

Corey had been texting nonstop. Rowan wasn't answering.

Alice took Ian's phone and texted Corey herself.

Alice: *Hi Corey, it's Mrs. Miller. Can I call you?*

His response was immediate.

Corey: *Yes! How is Rowan? She hasn't answered my texts. Is she mad at me?*

Alice excused herself and went to the lounge and called Corey.

"No, Corey. She's just had some really bad news." Alice hesitated, then told him.

Silence.

Corey then said, "So… if she doesn't get a new heart in time, she'll die.

Alice swallowed. She had never heard those words spoken aloud before. But that *was* what it meant.

"Yes," she said. "That's what it means."

Corey's voice was steady. "Mrs. Miller, I don't care if she has *four weeks or four hours*. I want to be there."

Alice smiled. "She's going to love that."

Corey didn't hesitate. "I'll be there *right* after school."

Alice sighed. "She'll kill you if you skip practice."

"I don't care."

Alice chuckled. "Well, you *might* get away with tomorrow. We'll see you then."

At least Rowan still had something to look forward to.

***

Alice walked back into the room to find that Jonathan and Ian had already left, their mission clear. She settled into the chair next to Rowan's bed and hesitated for a moment before speaking.

"This is a dumb question, but how are you feeling... you know, about all of this?"

Rowan shrugged. "Honestly, right now, I'm just angry. I mean, yeah, I'm scared to death, but I played by the rules. I did everything Dr. Mason told me to do, and now I'm basically dying." Her voice broke, and she started to sob.

Alice reached for her hand, squeezing it gently. "Rowan, I want you to listen to me. You are not going to die. It's not going to happen. People die every day—thousands of them, and most of them with healthy hearts. Other than your heart, you're young and strong. That's why you're at the top of the transplant list."

Rowan wiped at her eyes. "But I was reading about all the things that have to line up for a heart transplant. Blood type, heart size—there are so many things that have to match

213

perfectly. What are the odds that a heart will become available *and* be the right fit for me?"

Alice held her gaze. "You're right, all of those things matter. But I'm still telling you, you are not going to die. God would never let that happen."

Rowan looked at her mother like she had grown three heads. "I really wish everyone would stop talking to me like I'm a toddler. I *know* God lets bad things happen to good people all the time. Pastor Carl always says our lives are already mapped out, that the ending is written and only He knows when that is. What if this is the end of my story?"

Alice's grip tightened around Rowan's hand. "This is not the end of your story. *Okay?* That's what I'm telling you."

"How can you possibly know that?"

Alice gave her a small smile. "I've told you this before, because I'm your momma... and mommas *know* things. You've got to trust me on this one. Now, let's figure out what we're going to watch on Netflix before Ian gets back and commandeers the remote."

Chapter 35

T he next two weeks passed without any major incidents. For the most part, the pacemaker continued to keep Rowan's heart on an even keel. There were occasional blips on the monitor, but nothing alarming. The only noticeable changes were that Rowan was sleeping more and losing her appetite. Dr. Mason had anticipated this and increased her intravenous immune therapy from one to three bags per week.

Corey visited regularly, and though Rowan voiced concerns about his commitment to the football team, Corey couldn't have cared less. Alice knew he hadn't missed any games, so apparently, his coach had no issue with him skipping practice. According to Jonathan, as a star quarterback, Corey would play no matter what.

Alice glanced over at Rowan, who was taking her second nap of the day, despite it being barely noon. Jonathan arrived with sandwiches and chips, bringing Rowan her favorite—a turkey club with extra cheese. Alice saw the brief flicker of disappointment on his face when he realized she was asleep.

Handing Alice a sandwich, he sighed. "I really wish you'd let me go to this follow-up appointment with you. Corey said he'd be here by one since they have a half-day at school today."

"Yes, I know, but we agreed one of us would always be with Rowan," Alice reminded him. "We are just going to be reviewing the tests she ordered. If it were serious, she would have called me in for a sooner appointment. In the end, she'll either increase my dosage or switch my medication—it's as simple as that. After the appointment, I'll go home, grab a shower, and pick up some clean clothes before coming back."

Jonathan frowned but nodded.

Alice smiled. "Oh, and when Corey gets here, make yourself scarce, okay?"

"Make myself scarce? What does that mean?"

She smirked. "When you brought a girl home, did your dad sit in the living room with you?"

"Oh… right," Jonathan said, chuckling. "I wouldn't know. You were my first girlfriend."

Alice rolled her eyes. "Then just visualize it."

Jonathan squeezed his eyes shut dramatically. "Yikes. That is horrifying. Okay, I'll find something to watch in the lounge, but I'm checking in every fifteen minutes."

"I'd advise against that unless you want a very annoyed sixteen-year-old girl to deal with."

"Fine," Jonathan conceded. "Every twenty minutes."

Alice chuckled, grabbing her bag. "Good luck with that. Be back soon."

She hurried off, eager to get her appointment over with. As she pulled out of the parking lot, she murmured a quick prayer. *Everything is going to be fine. It has to be fine.* But no matter how hard she tried to push the doubt away, it lingered.

After her appointment, Alice went home to grab a shower. She was allowed to use the one in Rowan's hospital room, but nothing compared to being in her own space. She took care of a few housekeeping tasks—sorting the mail, bringing in more food that had been left on the porch. Nothing urgent in the mail, just bills, which she tucked into her bag to pay later that night after Rowan fell asleep.

Someone had dropped off a lasagna—one of Rowan's favorites—so Alice quickly made a salad and packed everything into a tote. The hospital lounge had a microwave, making dinner a simple fix. A huge container of brownies had also been left, and as Alice transferred them into a Tupperware container, a thought struck her. She divided them into two containers and grabbed paper plates and silverware.

Armed with food and fresh clothes, she headed back to the hospital—her *new* home. Jonathan and she had originally planned to take turns on "night shifts," but Alice couldn't bring herself to leave. Either she stayed, or they both stayed. The one time she had tried to go home, she lasted less than two hours before she was back at Rowan's bedside.

When Alice arrived, she was pleasantly surprised to find Rowan awake, playing *Monopoly* with Corey, Ian, and Jonathan. Seeing them all engaged in something familiar, something *normal*, filled her heart with relief.

She set the food down, and Ian's eyes lit up. "Is that Mrs. Butler's homemade lasagna?"

"It is," Alice confirmed. "And it's for all of us."

Rowan barely glanced at it. "He can have mine. I'm not hungry."

Everyone fell silent.

Rowan sighed. "Look, I'm just not hungry. I'm not going to force-feed myself. Maybe you can save some for later."

Jonathan started to protest, but Alice shot him a look that said, *let it be.*

Everyone else ate, enjoying the food—especially the brownies. Alice felt another pang of concern when Rowan didn't even want one. *Another red flag.*

Midway through *Back to the Future*, one of Rowan's favorite movies, she fell asleep. Corey didn't want to wake her but had to leave. He kissed her forehead and left a handwritten note on her bedside table.

Shortly after, Jonathan and Ian got ready to head out. They wanted to say goodbye, but she was still asleep.

Ian, however, was in full protest mode. "Why do I have to go to school tomorrow?"

Alice sighed. "The school and the board are being flexible with your absences, *but* only if you keep up with your assignments. You need to go in, turn in last week's work, and collect what you've missed this week. That way, you can stay on the soccer team. You have a game Thursday, and your coach is going to lose it if you can't play."

Ian rolled his eyes. "Do you really think I give a rat's furry ass about a game?"

Alice shot him a warning look. "First, watch the language. Second, Rowan *loves* watching the videos Nate's dad records of you playing. When you don't play, it's just another reminder of how much this is affecting everyone. You can come back after practice tomorrow, okay?"

Ian exhaled, glancing at Rowan. "Fine... but Mom, why is she sleeping so much? And she barely eats."

Alice hesitated. *Because her heart is failing. Because she's running out of time.* But she couldn't burden him with that.

"I don't know for sure. They think it's the medication. Maybe her body just needs to adjust."

Ian didn't look convinced but nodded anyway, grabbing his backpack.

Jonathan turned to Alice. "I'll check my emails in the morning and swing by the office to drop off a zip drive. I'll check in on a few things, then come right here."

Alice kissed him. "Take your time. David's got things covered, but I know you need to check in at least once a week."

"She *is* sleeping more. And eating less," Jonathan murmured, glancing at Rowan.

"I know," Alice admitted. "But her vitals fluctuate all the time. Let's see what Dr. Mason says before we panic."

Jonathan sighed. "It's just... it's been two weeks. He said four or less. And we've heard *nothing*."

Alice held up a hand. "He also said her heart *could* last longer than four weeks. The sleeping and not eating just started. Let's wait for morning rounds."

Jonathan hugged her. "I have no idea how we'd get through this without you. We *wouldn't* get through this without you. Even if your cool, calm demeanor is a little *annoying* sometimes." He smirked.

Alice smiled. "You never know what you're capable of until you have no choice. You'd do it if you had to."

Jonathan kissed her forehead. "God willing, I'll never have to find out."

She walked them to the elevator. "Go home, get some sleep. I'll see you in the morning. I've got everything under control."

Jonathan nodded and left.

As soon as the doors closed, Alice walked back to the room and stood looking out the window, her body trembling.

I do not have everything under control.

She wiped her tears quickly.

The clock was ticking… It's time to do something about it.

Chapter 36

R owan woke up about an hour later, hungry. Alice all but ran into the lounge to warm up some lasagna for her. Rowan did her best, but she only managed to eat half of it and none of the brownies before indicating she was full. She asked if Corey was coming back the next day.

"As far as I know, he is," Alice said.

This response garnered a smile. Corey never came empty-handed. Flowers, stuffed animals, candy—he always brought something. As it was, she already had three stuffed animals from him arranged around her bed.

Rowan set one of the stuffed animals she had been sleeping with down and said, "It's been two weeks now, Momma. I'm getting scared. What if they don't find a heart before..."

"They will," Alice interrupted.

"But maybe they won't. I have to think about that," Rowan said.

"No, you don't. They will find one," Alice insisted, with more confidence than she felt. Rowan nodded and picked up another stuffed animal.

"Momma, can I have one of your journals? Do you have an extra one in your bag?"

Alice reached for her bag. "Girl, one thing your momma always has is at least two journals."

She pulled out a spiral-bound one and ripped out the few pages that were written on, folding them up and stuffing them inside the other journal she was carrying. Then she handed the blank one to Rowan. Alice watched as Rowan picked up the pen from her tray, the same one she used to fill out her daily meal menu and opened the journal. Alice sat down next to her and pulled out her laptop. Rowan shifted slightly, twisting herself away from Alice.

Rowan saw Alice notice and said, "I want to write some stuff down. It's kind of private."

Alice noticed the tears in her daughter's eyes and stood up. Picking up the second container of brownies, she said, "Why don't I give you some space? I'll be back in a little bit, and if you feel up to it, we can rent a movie."

Rowan nodded. She was already writing when Alice left the room.

Kelsey Wentworth's room was only two doors down.

Alice had been discreetly monitoring the room and had noticed that, just like with her and Jonathan, Karen Wentworth seemed to be on the *night shift,* so to speak. That didn't mean she was absent during the day. As far as Alice knew, she never left the hospital.

Just like in Rowan's room, there was a recliner in Kelsey's—one of those hospital loungers that folded out into a makeshift bed. Surprisingly comfortable, but still no substitute for home. Alice assumed that Karen slept during the day while Stephen was there, then stayed up all night after he left, sitting at her daughter's side, waiting. Hoping.

Or maybe *denying.*

Alice inhaled deeply, steadying herself before walking to Kelsey's room.

Within seconds, she was face-to-face with Karen.

"Hello, I'm Alice, from room 208," she said softly. "I spoke with your husband in the lounge the other day." She held up a plastic container wrapped in foil. "I thought I'd come over, introduce myself, and bring you these. You've never had a brownie like these before. They're homemade—from scratch—by a lady in our church. They're legendary."

Alice offered a warm smile, hoping to bridge the space between them.

Karen didn't smile back.

Instead, she gave Alice a wary, guarded look, hesitating before finally opening the door wider, wordlessly letting her in.

Alice stepped inside and was immediately struck by the difference. Though it was the same type of room Rowan had, Kelsey's felt *different.* Heavier. *Darker.*

And it wasn't just the dim glow from the monitors or the faint antiseptic scent lingering in the air. It was the stillness. The suffocating, unnatural *stillness.*

Machines beeped rhythmically, their quiet hum the only indication of life. Wires and tubes snaked in and out of Kelsey's fragile body, tethering her to existence.

She was so *still.*

If not for the shallow rise and fall of her chest, Alice would have thought she was staring at a corpse.

And from what Stephen had told her—*she was.*

Karen took the brownies but made no move to open them.

"I'm very sorry about your daughter," Alice said gently. "Stephen told me what happened to her. You must be devastated."

Karen's grip tightened around the container. She stared at the floor for a long moment, then finally spoke.

"The drunk bastard who hit them walked away with barely a scratch," she said, her voice thick with restrained fury. "I wanted to kill him—*would have* killed him if I had been allowed anywhere near him in the ER."

Alice nodded in understanding. "That's completely understandable. I think any mother would feel that way. Instinct tells us to protect our cubs at all costs." She hesitated, then added softly, "Stephen mentioned she's your only child."

Karen let out a shuddered breath. "Yes. Just her. We thought about having another, but Kelsey was—" She stopped, corrected herself. "*Is. She is* everything I ever wanted."

Alice could hear the desperation in her voice, the unrelenting need to keep her daughter in the *present* tense.

Karen shifted uncomfortably, then changed the subject. "I've seen a man and another child in and out of your room. I assume that's your husband and son?"

Alice nodded. "Yes, Jonathan is my husband, and I have a son, Ian."

Karen was quiet for a moment, then said, "Stephen says your daughter needs a new heart."

Alice swallowed, nodding. "Yes, she does. She's high on the transplant list, but as of yet, they haven't found one. They estimated her heart would last four weeks. Maybe a bit less. Maybe a bit more."

Karen's lips parted slightly, her expression unreadable. "How old is she?"

"She's sixteen," Alice said.

Karen exhaled shakily. "My Kelsey is eighteen," she said in a quiet, defeated voice.

For a brief second, Alice saw a crack in the armor. A moment of truth. A tiny sliver of doubt.

She pressed forward.

"Rowan is otherwise healthy," Alice said, her voice gentle but firm. "A new heart would mean she could live a full, normal life."

Karen's entire body stiffened. Her gaze sharpened, and she turned to Alice with a small, sideways glare.

"That's what *Kelsey* will have when she wakes up," she snapped. "She is otherwise healthy."

225

Alice met her gaze and decided to be blunt.

This would only go one of two ways.

"That's not what Stephen told me," she said carefully. "He said that three separate doctors have confirmed Kelsey is brain dead and will never wake up. That Kelsey has been *gone* for two months. It's only these machines that keep her heart beating."

Karen went white.

For a split second, her expression was one of pure shock—raw, unfiltered truth hitting her in the chest like a bullet.

Then, the shock turned to fury.

"How *dare* you come in here and presume to tell me *our* business!" she spat. "Stephen may have *given up* on our daughter, but I have *not*. As for those so-called *specialists*, they're a bunch of quacks, and I for one—"

Alice cut in. "Kelsey's blood type is O-negative."

Karen blinked. Confused. "Yes… same as mine. What about it?"

Alice's voice trembled. "My daughter needs your daughter's heart."

Karen sucked in a sharp breath.

Alice stepped closer, eyes pleading. "I am asking you as one mother to another. I can't imagine what you're going through, and I *would not* be asking this if there were any chance—*any* hope—of Kelsey waking up. But she *won't*. And deep down, on *some* level, you *know* that."

Tears streamed down Alice's face. "My daughter has a chance at life, Karen. Yours does *not*. Please… try to put yourself in my position."

For a moment, Karen didn't move.

Then she rose from her chair, grabbed Alice's arm, and *shoved* her toward the door.

"How *dare* you," she seethed. "How *dare* you come in here and ask me to *end my child's life* to save yours! You are *crazy*—certifiably *crazy!*

"My daughter is *alive* in there, and she is going to wake up! I swear to God, if you ever come near this room again, I will *kill you* with my bare hands!"

Alice rounded on her, fury overtaking her grief. "Your daughter *died* two months ago, Karen. And without Kelsey's heart, *my* child will die too."

Karen shoved her into the hallway, followed by the container of brownies.

"Don't talk to my husband again. Don't talk to *me*. If you ever come within ten feet of this room, I will *tear you limb from limb.*"

The door slammed shut.

Alice stood there, breathless, then crumpled to the floor, silent sobs racking her body.

Genny rounded the corner and knelt beside her, wrapping an arm around her shoulders, rocking her gently.

A passing nurse hesitated. "Should we call security?"

Genny shook her head. "No, I got this. Show's over. Everyone get back to work."

After a few moments, Alice calmed.

Genny didn't ask why she had gone into Kelsey's room. She already *knew*.

"I get it, Alice. I really do. But I *caution* you against trying that again. If they take out a restraining order on you, you could be banned from the hospital."

Alice wiped her eyes and looked at Genny. Her voice was hollow, but her resolve was firm.

"My daughter is dying." She exhaled.

"I promise you *nothing*. Not a damn thing."

Chapter 37

J onathan came into the room the next morning, and Alice knew immediately that he had already heard about the events of the previous evening.

"I saw Genny downstairs on the way back up to the room with Rowan."

"Yes, she thought Rowan might want to get out of bed and stretch a bit, so she took her down to the cafeteria to pick out whatever she wanted for breakfast and to grab some snacks for the rest of the day. Rowan wasn't very hungry, but she was happy to get out of bed for a while. I'm assuming that look you're giving me is because Genny told you what happened last night."

"Yes," Jonathan said. "While Rowan was picking out food, Genny mentioned it. Not to get you in hot water with me, but just so I knew what I was walking into today."

Alice didn't even have it in her to look guilty.

"I regret nothing. That woman is holding onto a pipe dream while our daughter lies here dying."

Jonathan shook his head. "Her own husband has tried to convince her of that, and she loses it. What on earth made you think she would listen to you?"

"Because we are both mothers. It's not the same with fathers, and I don't mean to say I love our kids more than you do. Mothers have a connection to our kids that goes beyond love. It's like a primal instinct to protect our young. That umbilical cord may be physically cut, but it never truly goes away. This is not over."

"Actually, it is. Whereas I totally understand why you did it, that doesn't make it right, and if I have to stay here at night and babysit you, I will. You need to stay away from Karen Wentworth. That cannot happen again."

Just as Jonathan finished speaking, Rowan came slowly walking back into the room, followed closely by Genny. She helped get Rowan into bed and then pulled out five or six packets of graham crackers from the nurse's station—Rowan's favorite.

"Well now, let's get the princess back on her throne. Then I am going home to catch a few winks, and I'll be back tonight at seven." Genny then looked at Rowan and said, "I'll bring my monthly bag of Ipsy makeup for you tonight. All the colors are all wrong for me, but I think they'd be right up your alley."

Genny gave her a wink and a pat on the leg as she walked out the door.

"Wow!" Jonathan said. "That's a breakfast and a half. Makes me hungry just looking at it."

Rowan gave the tray a little shove and said, "Go on and eat it. I'm not hungry."

Alice remembered how Rowan had barely touched her dinner the night before.

"How about just the fruit cup?" Alice prodded.

"Not right now, maybe later. I just want to sleep. That walk to the cafeteria was fun until I had to walk back."

On instinct, Alice looked at the monitor and saw that Rowan was in bradycardia. This wasn't new, but she kept an eye on it because it usually rectified itself within fifteen to twenty seconds. When that time frame passed, Alice looked at Jonathan and then at her watch. One minute went by, then two. At three minutes, Alice hit the button for the nurse. She didn't recognize the nurse who walked in. She may have been a floater from another floor. How Alice wished Genny was still on shift.

"She's been bradycardic for over three minutes. Please page Dr. Mason," Alice said.

"That's not necessary. Your daughter has a standing order for Atropine when she goes bradycardic. I'll get it and be back shortly."

When the nurse left the room, Alice looked at Jonathan and saw that he was staring intently at the heart monitor. She wasn't even sure if he was breathing. When the nurse returned, she administered the medication.

"Can you please page Dr. Mason and tell him we'd like to speak to him?" Alice asked.

"Of course. I'll do it as soon as I chart this dose," the nurse said.

Alice and Jonathan kept their eyes on the monitor. Slowly, Rowan's heart rate began to climb back up. Alice let out a breath she didn't realize she'd been holding. It seemed the fight was over. Jonathan pulled a chair over next to Alice and took her hand.

"This is going to keep happening more and more, isn't it?"

"Yes," Alice said softly, the only answer she could muster.

Later that day, Dr. Mason came in. Rowan was asleep. It seemed she was sleeping more than she was awake.

"So, you had a bad bradycardic scare today. She did respond well to the Atropine, so that's a positive sign. Unfortunately, her heart is going to continue to break down and rely more and more on the pacemaker. I do have some good news—one of the patients ahead of Rowan on the transplant list received a heart, which moves Rowan up on the list. That greatly increases our chances of finding her a heart."

Alice paced the floor and said, "She sleeps more than she's awake. I can barely get any food into her. She seems weaker by the day. It sure doesn't seem like we're even going to get the four weeks you said we had."

Dr. Mason sighed. "To be fair, I used four weeks as a guideline. I said she could have more or less. This isn't an exact science. I wish I could give you guarantees, but I can't. For now, the pacemaker is doing its job, and she's still responding to the medications. The body naturally takes care of itself. That's how it's wired, so to speak. When the heart is tired, the brain shuts things down to conserve energy. Sleeping rejuvenates the body, so when things get... complicated, for lack of a better word, the body will sleep. I assure you, this is normal for her situation. I'm increasing the immunotherapy to one bag per day. I'm more concerned about infections at this point. With her heart in this weakened state, infections could become a serious problem."

Alice stopped pacing and looked pointedly at Dr. Mason. "You said a donor heart can either come from someone who has died or from someone who is clinically brain dead and whose machines are turned off, yes?"

Dr. Mason's expression tightened. "I know where this is going. Doctors talk to each other too."

"Then you know," Alice continued, "that Kelsey Wentworth's blood type is O- negative, the kind, as you said, was the *universal* blood type.

Dr. Mason shook his head. "I cannot confirm Kelsey's blood type with you. That information is protected under HIPAA."

Alice's face was set in stone. "It's not hard to figure out. There's a sticker on the front of her chart outside the door."

"Yes, I'm aware of the stickers. It's a safety measure to ensure information can be obtained quickly. But as far as Kelsey Wentworth is concerned, I've spoken with her physician. I did so for the same reason you spoke to Karen Wentworth. I didn't tell you because the answer wasn't favorable, and I didn't want to upset you further. The bottom line is that Mr. and Mrs. Wentworth are not prepared to take their daughter off life support."

Alice's anger flared. "That's inaccurate. *Karen Wentworth* isn't willing to take her daughter off life support. Her husband, Stephen, very much wants her off. He told me himself that three doctors have declared Kelsey brain dead, that she'll never wake up. Can't you do something?"

"Mrs. Miller, I know that won't work. We tried that."

233

Alice's head snapped up. "You mean you have already asked her for Kelsey's heart?"

Dr. Mason shook his head, "We had a fourteen-year-old child who had a missed diagnosis of Lyme Disease, and his liver went into rapid failure. She declined the request."

"And the boy?" Alice asked.

Dr. Mason didn't answer, just shook his head, Alice not needing any clarification of what became of the boy.

"Mrs. Miller, I implore you to let us do our job and do everything we can to find your daughter a heart."

Alice wiped her tears, and her resolve hardened, and said, "I'll tell you what Doc, *you* do everything you can to find my daughter a heart and I will do everything *I* can to find my daughter a heart, and we'll see who finds one first."

Dr. Mason didn't respond. He just gave Alice a look of utter pity and walked out of the room.

Chapter 38

T
he next morning was Saturday, and Dr. Mason and Dr. Kent, Rowan's immunologist, came to discuss the most recent results of her echocardiogram, ultrasound, and blood work. Rowan was sleeping, and Dr. Mason whispered to Alice and Jonathan, "Let's go to the lounge and talk."

Alice quickly grabbed the menu sheet the cafeteria brought around every morning so Rowan could pick her meals for the next day—though cafeteria food was always a last resort—and turned it over to write on the back: "Ran to the lounge for a coffee, be right back." Rowan mostly slept now and would likely still be asleep when they returned, but Alice never wanted her to wake up and feel alone.

The walk to the lounge was short, but Alice felt the weight of whatever was coming pressing down on her chest, making it difficult to breathe.

Her legs moved as if she were knee-deep in mud, her body sluggish and uncooperative, her mind screaming at her to move faster while simultaneously telling her to turn back, to run in the opposite direction. She wasn't ready for this.

She would *never* be ready for this. As they entered the small room, the scent of stale coffee and hospital-grade disinfectant filled Alice's nostrils. A man sat at the table, his hands wrapped around a steaming cup, staring into it as if the secrets of the universe were hidden at the bottom.

John.

Alice recognized him immediately. He was the man who had donated the Keurig to the ward, the one whose son was in a coma. She had seen him several times in passing, always polite, exchanging quiet pleasantries in the hallway or near the vending machines. But beyond that, they had never really spoken.

Dr. Mason gave John a small nod. "Would you mind giving us some privacy?"

The man looked up, his tired eyes flickering between Alice and the two doctors. He gave a brief, knowing smile and stood without protest. He didn't ask questions. He didn't linger. He simply walked out, leaving his still-steaming coffee on the table.

That confirmed it.

Alice's stomach twisted, bile rising in her throat.

This news was *not* good.

The doctors didn't even want to discuss it in front of Rowan—*asleep or not.*

Alice's heart pounded, her ears ringing with the rhythm of her own blood. Dr. Kent was the first to speak. His voice was clinical, measured, as if he had practiced these words so many times that they had lost all meaning to him. "Rowan's white blood cell count has spiked again, which means we'll need to put her back on intravenous antibiotics, as well as continuous immunotherapy. Her body is struggling to fight off infections, despite the treatments." Alice's fingers curled into fists at her sides. She barely registered Jonathan standing stiffly next to her, his silence like a lead weight pressing against her ribs. Dr. Mason cleared his throat, shifting slightly, his hesitation setting off every alarm in Alice's brain. "We also reviewed her heart scans." He paused. "The sinus node in her heart is continuing to deteriorate. It's now skipping beats more frequently, and we're seeing longer periods where her whole heart is beating far too slowly."

Alice exhaled sharply, the weight in her chest growing heavier.

Dr. Kent continued, "The pacemaker is no longer able to compensate. The damage to the muscle tissue is too severe."

Alice felt the room start to tilt.

Her fingernails dug into the skin of her palm, grounding herself.

"What does this mean?" she asked, her voice barely above a whisper.

The two doctors exchanged a brief glance before Dr. Mason spoke again, choosing his words carefully. "It means that Rowan's heart is going in and out of—"

"Yes," Alice cut in sharply. "I *know* she's going in and out of bradycardia at regular and irregular intervals, along with some lingering bouts of tachycardia. I *get* that." She exhaled, eyes burning. "At this stage, I probably know as much as you do about the heart. *When I ask what this means, I'm asking you what this means for her.*"

Dr. Mason hesitated, his features taut, his hands pressing against the table as if bracing himself for impact.

237

"We are on the database *day and night* looking for a heart," he said. "We have a whole team dedicated to this, and we are staying on top of it."

Alice felt something snap inside her.

Her composure. Her restraint.

Her sanity.

"For the love of *God*," she yelled, her voice cracking. "*WHAT DOES THIS MEAN?!*"

Dr. Mason looked down, then back up again. If he was offended by her outburst, he didn't show it. His eyes were filled with something far worse than anger.

Pity.

Regret.

"It means that unless we find a heart for your daughter within the next several days—a week at the most—there will be nothing further we can do for her."

Alice gasped, her hands flying up to cover her face, shaking her head in rapid succession as if the sheer force of denial could undo what had just been said.

No.

No, no, no.

This was *not* happening.

She looked up desperately. "What about life support? Can't we keep her heart beating until a donor is found?"

Now it was Dr. Kent who spoke. "The infections she has now, despite the immunotherapy, are a result of her other organs suffering from a lack of oxygenated blood. Her heart can no longer pump enough to sustain them. Her liver will begin to fail, unable to filter out toxins the way it should." He paused. "We can try to slow this down with constant antibiotics, but that is only a temporary measure. A band-aid. It buys a *little* more time to find a donor. But that's all."

He inhaled deeply before adding, "It may be time for you to start making some decisions about what you will or will not tell her."

Alice blinked, her throat raw, her body trembling.

"She's young," Dr. Kent continued. "But she's not a child. This is a difficult decision, and it is entirely yours to make, given that Rowan is a minor. But I strongly advise you to tell her the situation. There may be things she wants to say… or do… in the time she has left."

A cold, nauseating realization swept over Alice.

Jonathan had said *nothing*.

Not a single word.

He hadn't even lifted his head.

She turned to look at him, her breath catching at what she saw.

Silent tears trailed down his face, his expression utterly vacant.

In that moment, Alice understood.

A small part of her husband had just *died* right before her eyes.

This decision would be hers.

Hers alone.

Jonathan would play no part in it. He always took her lead when it came to Rowan, and she knew, with absolute certainty, what she had to do.

They would tell Rowan *nothing.*

There was no reason for her daughter to lie there, *waiting* for her heart to stop beating. Knowing—*with near certainty*—that sixteen-years was all she was going to get.

And if Alice was honest, there was *selfishness* in her choice too.

She *couldn't* watch Rowan go through that.

Rowan would see right through her.

Dr. Mason and Dr. Kent nodded, understanding without Alice needing to say a word, and silently walked out of the room.

Alice stood there, frozen, her mind spinning so fast she could barely form a single coherent thought.

Then, she heard herself whisper, "This is *her* fault."

Jonathan finally looked up, his voice hoarse. "Who? Whose fault?"

Alice turned to him, exasperated. "The *tooth fairy*, Jonathan. *Who the hell do you think I mean?* That *bitch*—that *selfish* bitch, two rooms down. This is *all* her fault."

Jonathan's eyebrows lifted, first in surprise at the sheer venom in her voice, then in quiet exasperation.

"No, it's not," he said softly. "And deep down, you *know* that."

Alice didn't raise her voice. Didn't speak. Didn't blink. She turned and stormed out of the room. With every step, her resolve grew stronger.

When she reached Kelsey Wentworth's room, she slid the door open and strode in, her purpose clear. Karen Wentworth looked up from her constant perch at her daughter's bedside. Her husband, Stephen, stood by the window, looking barely able to hold himself upright.

"What the hell are *you* doing in here?" Karen spat. "Get out. Get out *now!*"

Her husband turned, but he didn't move toward Alice. Instead, he simply watched, curious. Alice wasted no time.

"My daughter has *days* to live," she said, her voice devoid of emotion. "If she doesn't get a heart, she will die. Meanwhile, your daughter lies here, hooked up to machines that you *think* are keeping her alive. But they're not. *Not really.* My God, can't you see? She's *gone!* They've told you over and over. *Your own husband* told me. She is *never* going to wake up. And while she lies here, her *healthy* heart beats—*for nothing.* Meanwhile, my daughter, who is actually alive, is going to *die.* I am begging you—please, listen to these doctors and let her go. *My daughter needs her heart.*"

Alice's voice cracked into gut-wrenching sobs. Karen stood up, striding toward her until they were nose to nose.

"My daughter is *going* to wake up," she screamed. "She will! I don't care what those so-called 'specialists' say. I *know* my daughter. She is *going* to wake up!"

Alice didn't back down. She met Karen's eyes with steely resolve. "Your daughter died two months ago, and *you know it.*"

Karen let out an animalistic scream and grabbed Alice by the arms. "*Get the hell out!*

Genny rushed into the room. "Call security," Karen shouted. "I want this woman *arrested!*"

Jonathan arrived as Alice felt herself being led out—not by him, but by Stephen. As security entered, Karen continued screaming for Alice's removal.

"This isn't over," Alice seethed.

Jonathan turned her around, gripping her firmly. "Stop it!"

He then looked at Karen. "I plead with you not to call the police, our daughter has only a few days, and my wife needs to be here. She knows this, and I promise, she won't come in here again."

Karen does not back off, however. "I want her arrested or removed from the hospital, your choice."

Karen's husband looked back at his wife, his eyes dark as coal. "We are *NOT* going to have this woman *arrested* or *removed.* We will not be the reason she misses even one minute of sitting by her daughter's side. How would you feel about that if the roles were reversed? *Sit down* Karen and leave this to me."

Karen hesitated for only a moment before silently returning to the bed, gently taking her daughter's hand as if nothing had transpired. With Jonathan on one side and Genny on the other, Alice was guided away, back to her own daughter's room. As she stepped inside, the crushing reality settled over her—like Karen, she, too, would sit at her child's bedside, holding her hand, and watching her die.

Chapter 39

After Alice had calmed down, Jonathan nodded his head towards the door, and Alice followed him out. He led her past the familiar hallway, past the blinking machines and quiet murmurs of nurses, past the smell of antiseptic and stale coffee, until they reached the lounge.

Alice barely had time to process before Jonathan pushed the door closed behind them with a quiet but forceful *click.*

When she turned to face him, his expression nearly stopped her cold.

It was a storm of emotions—disbelief, frustration, sadness, and something deeper, something more fragile.

His voice, when he spoke, was tight, laced with controlled anger.

"What is *wrong* with you?" he demanded, his tone somewhere between heartbreak and outrage. "I want our daughter to live just as much as you do, but I'm *not* going to ask someone to end the life of their *child* for it to happen!"

Alice felt the burn of fury rising in her chest, bubbling up with every painful beat of her heart.

She spun toward him, her voice sharp, rising with emotion.

"*Living?* Is that what you think Kelsey is doing, Jonathan?" Her breath was ragged, her body trembling. "*Our* daughter is living—she's talking, eating, drinking, *thinking. That* is living.

"But Kelsey? Kelsey is not *living.* She is *existing.* There is a big difference.

"The only thing keeping her body functioning are those machines—machines that are doing all the work for her whole body. For all intents and purposes, she is *dead,* Jonathan. She holds the key to *our* daughter's chance at life. Stephen told me that they only have *two weeks* left and they cannot afford private care. Rowan has *days.* We cannot afford to wait! Kelsey will be taken off those machines and she will die, officially, and she will take her healthy heart with her."

Jonathan's jaw clenched. But he remained silent.

Alice pressed forward, her voice shaking with conviction.

"Stephen sees it. *I* see it. *Her doctors* see it.

"Why can't *you*—and her mother—see that?

"If they turned off those machines, she would pass in *minutes*, if that, and our daughter would have a heart. A healthy, *beating* heart."

Jonathan's expression darkened, his nostrils flaring as he took a sharp breath.

"So, you're saying," he shot back, "that if the roles were reversed, if it were *our* daughter lying in that bed, you would just... *end her life* and give her heart to another?"

Alice met his gaze, steady and unflinching.

"Yes."

Jonathan flinched, but otherwise remained still.

"Yes," Alice repeated, her voice unwavering. "If three doctors told me that Rowan was brain dead, I would end her existence to save another. You want to know why?"

She swallowed hard, blinking against the sting of tears.

"Because I know, in my *heart*, that if she could choose, Rowan would *want* that."

Jonathan looked down, shaking his head. He ran his fingers through his hair—a telltale sign of his frustration, something Alice had seen a thousand times over the years.

"Well," he muttered, his voice thick with emotion, "that's easy to say when it's *not* our daughter."

Alice turned away, her gaze locking onto the window.

She pressed a hand to the cool surface, watching commuters go home to their families, watching as people passed by on the sidewalks, their laughter ringing through the night air. College kids wandered in and out of bars, wrapped up in carefree conversations, oblivious to the fact that—just a few floors above them—her daughter was *dying*.

How?

Alice's world had stopped.

Why hadn't theirs?

"You should go home," she finally said, her voice barely above a whisper. "Check on Ian. Get some rest."

Jonathan sighed, running both hands over his face before dropping them heavily to his sides.

"I thought we agreed," he said, his tone quieter now, tinged with exhaustion, "that from now on, we would *both* stay here."

Alice didn't answer.

She couldn't.

She kept her eyes on the window, on the blur of headlights and distant voices.

Jonathan let out a bitter chuckle. "Ah, yes. The 'I want you to rest' statement—which really means, *I need to think and I want to be anywhere you are not.*"

His voice softened, but the weight of his next words nearly undid her.

"When did we stop being a team, Alice?"

She turned then, slowly, and looked at him, really looked at him.

The dark circles beneath his eyes. The way his clothes hung slightly looser than they had a few weeks ago. The slight hollow in his cheeks. The lines etched deeper across his forehead.

For the briefest moment, guilt crept in, weaving itself between the cracks in her anger.

But then—Rowan.

It always went back to *Rowan*.

The guilt vanished, replaced by a dull ache in her chest, one that would never fully fade.

She inhaled shakily. "Actually, no," she murmured. "I don't need to be alone to think." She paused, turning back to the window. "But I think *you* do."

Silence stretched between them, thick and heavy.

She heard him sigh, then felt the warmth of his hands on her shoulders. His grip was gentle. He pressed a soft, lingering kiss to the top of her head.

Then, the soft swish of the door opening and closing.

He was gone.

Alice remained still, her hands pressed against the glass, her breath clouding the window.

Outside, the world carried on.

And inside, hers continued to fall apart.

Chapter 40

Alice returned to Rowan's room and stood over her bed. The medications sometimes made Rowan's limbs jerk in her sleep, and her golden honey-colored hair had fallen across her face. Alice gently swept it back. When Rowan was born, she had a full head of deep brown, silky-soft hair. Alice had held her, and she and Jonathan had marveled at their perfect baby. But it was her eyes Alice had fixated on—their rich, deep blue, just like her own. Even as a newborn, Rowan had opened them wide, seeming to study Alice intently.

Now, Alice willed her to wake up, to open those beautiful eyes, to immediately search the room for her mother's face. After every procedure, every test, Rowan always looked for Alice first. No matter how scared she was, Alice would force a smile and a thumbs-up, and she would see the relief wash over her daughter. Rowan took her cues from Alice. If Alice wasn't worried, Rowan wouldn't be either. It was an exhausting act to maintain, like trying to plug holes in a dam while more kept appearing.

Alice moved to the window, wedging herself into the large windowsill, watching another day fade into night. No new heart. Another day lost. She spent the night writing furiously in her journal, watching the moon blur in and out of focus, then later, the first light of dawn creeping across the city skyline.

Will today be the day? she wondered.

249

But something had changed in her overnight. As she had gone over the situation and scenarios in her mind, again and again, and one thing remained clear. Her daughter would not die. She was fully committed to that affirmation. She would not sit idly by and watch her waste away. Especially while the heart that could save her beat uselessly two doors down.

Kelsey Wentworth will save my daughter's life—whether Karen Wentworth wants her to or not.

Jonathan arrived just after 9:00 AM and brought coffee and buttery croissants from the bakery in town. They had yet to tell Ian about Rowan's latest decline—today was his last rec game of the season, and they didn't want to burden him before it.

Thoughts of Ian playing yet another soccer match with no one there to cheer him on stabbed at Alice's heart. She sometimes forgot how much this was affecting him, too. Not only might he lose his sister, but his parents were essentially absent, giving him only the bare minimum of attention. At fourteen, Ian was self-sufficient, but no child should have to be. Thankfully, friends' parents had stepped in, hosting sleepovers and pizza nights, letting him escape into video games and laughter. Ian understood the gravity of the situation, but it was clear that visiting Rowan had become too much for him. His visits dwindled, and his calls and texts increased instead. It was his way of keeping his sister close without witnessing her decline firsthand.

Rowan, ever the big sister, reassured him constantly. "It's okay," she told him. "You don't have to be here all the time. I know you care."

Jonathan handed Alice the coffee, and she tore into the croissants, realizing just how hungry she was. It was a peace offering, and her return gesture was a hug and a kiss on the cheek, signaling that all was well between them. Or at least, that they were pretending it was.

"You sleep okay?" Jonathan asked.

Alice nodded. "Yeah, I slept fine."

In truth, she hadn't slept at all. She had spent the entire night in the window seat, writing, thinking, and planning. But sometimes, it was easier to lie.

On weekends, Jonathan stayed with Rowan during the day while Alice caught up on errands—laundry, groceries, bills. But she always came back at night. She had tried to sleep at home before, but she never lasted more than a few hours before returning. The silence was unbearable, and the thought of Rowan's condition changing while she was gone kept her from resting.

Now, though, Alice had things to do. She kissed her daughter, taking note of her Starbucks order for when she returned. She kissed Jonathan with the promise of sandwiches from Lou's Hoagie Shack for their Sunday tradition of a Netflix movie night—a rare moment of normalcy in their shattered lives.

Ian would be joining them later. Sundays were his only semblance of family time. But even as Alice went through the motions, one thought haunted her.

How many more Sundays do we have left?

Chapter 41

T he heat and humidity hit Alice like a battering ram the moment the hospital's sliding doors whooshed open. Mid-July in Georgia was relentless, but the oppressive warmth was a welcome contrast to the sterile chill of the hospital. She closed her eyes briefly, inhaling the fresh scent of cut grass and lilac bushes lining the entrance. It was a fleeting comfort, grounding her for just a moment before reality came crashing back.

She reached her car, which felt like an oven, but to her, it was a cocoon—a place where she could momentarily escape. She took a deep breath, letting the heat soak into her skin, willing herself to stay composed.

Her usual routine was to spend these first few moments alone outside the hospital having a good, private cry before pulling herself together. But not today. Today, there was no time.

She had checked off all but one of her errands—the last of the groceries were put away, the dryer was humming with the final load of laundry, and the house was as tidy as it was going to get. Now, only one task remained. The one she had been avoiding.

Alice had driven past *Harland's Gun & Tackle* a hundred times, if not more, but never paid it any attention. Today, she pulled into the parking lot and spotted a space right by the door. Instead, she drove past it, choosing one toward the back. She didn't want to be seen.

She walked briskly to the shop, keeping her head down. The pharmacy and dry cleaners they used were in the same shopping center, and the last thing she needed was to run into someone she knew. She pushed through the heavy glass door and was immediately met with an icy blast from an ancient window air conditioner, rattling like it might give out at any second.

The shop had a distinct, musky scent—damp earth mixed with aged wood. To her right, a line of glass-fronted refrigerators displayed live bait. Further down, shelves were stocked with fishing rods and reels of every kind. But Alice's focus was on the long glass case to her left, packed with guns of all sizes, each accompanied by neat stacks of ammunition. Behind the counter, even larger rifles were locked in glass cabinets—guns meant for hunting, she assumed, though some seemed excessively large for anything short of taking down a grizzly bear. But she wasn't here to debate hunting ethics. She had other matters to attend to.

The man behind the counter looked to be in his early to mid-sixties, his face permanently flushed. What remained of his hair was a mix of salt and pepper. He perched on a stool, absorbed in the local paper—an image that momentarily transported Alice back to weekends on the porch with Jonathan, sipping coffee and reading the news. Those mornings felt like a lifetime ago, so distantly she questioned whether they had ever been real.

The man groaned slightly as he stood, bracing his back with one hand, his belly straining over his belt. He favored one leg, shifting his weight as he spoke.

"Morning," he greeted. "Hot enough for ya?"

There it was again. Just an ordinary comment from an ordinary person, blissfully unaware of how cruel life could be. God help her, but Alice wanted to *punch* people who had the luxury of mundane conversations—people untouched by the unbearable weight of waiting for a child's heart to fail.

"What can I do for you today?" he asked.

Alice's stomach churned. *What could he do for her today?* In her mind, she answered: *Well, you see, my daughter is dying. She needs a heart, and we can't find one. So I'm going to... I'm going to...* What, exactly?

Alice had never been one to lie outright, but this situation seemed to warrant it.

"Uh... well, we've had a rash of burglaries in our neighborhood," she said haltingly. "And, um, my husband... he works nights. So, I'm looking for a gun—for protection, I guess."

If the man noticed her awkward delivery, the hesitation in her voice, he didn't show it.

He nodded. "Yeah, seems to be the way of it these days. Used to be you could let your kids run till the streetlights came on, sleep with the doors unlocked. But those days are long gone. I won't even let my granddaughter play in the front yard without sitting on the porch, watching her like a hawk. Sad how things have gotten, huh?"

"Yes, it is most disturbing," Alice agreed, keeping her tone neutral.

Better to let *him* take the lead. She would simply follow along.

He smiled. "So, do you know what you're looking for? I've got everything from a handgun small enough to fit in the pocket of your jeans to something that could blow a hole the size of a horse through a barn door."

Alice forced a sheepish smile. "I, um… I'm not sure. I guess something small, something I can keep beside the bed."

She felt exposed, out of her depth. It was as if her true purpose was stamped across her forehead for all to see.

The man's eyes narrowed slightly. "Ever shot a gun before? I offer classes out at my gun range. Reasonable price."

"No, but my husband—um, my husband was in the military. He's going to teach me," Alice replied quickly.

"Well, you can't beat being taught by an ex-military man." The clerk gave her a knowing nod. "I'm surprised he isn't with you."

Alice tensed. *Why?* The word fired through her mind like a bullet.

She caught herself before speaking and softened her tone. "I mean… why? How hard is it to pick out a gun?"

The man raised his hands in a surrendering motion. "No offense meant. Just that usually, the teacher helps the student pick one out.

But no worries—I can help. It's all about size and weight. If you can't hold it right, you won't be able to shoot it right."

"Well, that's why he told me to just come see for myself," she said, forcing calm into her voice. "To find one that fits."

The clerk nodded and gestured toward a case. "Let's start small. If all you need is home protection, you don't need anything too fancy."

Alice nodded, but in truth, she wasn't thinking about home defense. She needed something small enough to fit in her purse.

The man retrieved a tiny handgun, barely larger than her palm.

"This here's real popular with women. Lightweight, easy to use. A .22LR mini revolver."

Alice took it from him. It felt light—too light. "This would actually stop someone?" she asked doubtfully.

"Oh yeah. If it's close-range, it'll do the job. And if you know how to aim right, it can do a whole lot more than that."

Alice had been in the shop too long. Longer than she had planned. Longer than she was comfortable with.

"I'll take it," she said abruptly.

The clerk smiled. "Alright. Just need to run a background check."

She froze. "What? Why? And how long does that take?"

"For handguns, it's quick. Give me your license, fill out a form, and I can run it in about ten minutes."

Alice hesitated, then steeled herself. She had made her decision last night. There was no turning back now.

"Alright," she said. "Let's do it."

The man handed her a clipboard. As she scanned the questions, her heart pounded.

Do you have a history of violence or mental illness?

Did *deciding* to take a life last night count? She exhaled, forced her hand steady, and checked *No.* Then completed the rest of the checklist.

Ten minutes later, the clerk returned. "You're all set. How much ammo you need?"

Alice barely whispered her answer.

"One."

The clerk chuckled. "Alright. One box it is."

In her mind, Alice corrected him. Not one box. *one* bullet. She only needed *one* bullet.

Chapter 42

M ovie night went well, which was a relief. Everyone needed a couple of hours to momentarily forget—if only a little—why they were having movie night in a hospital, yet again. Sometimes, they would play a game afterward, like *Catch Phrase* or *Uno*, but Alice could tell Rowan was tired.

Ian lingered for a while, sitting on his sister's bed, chatting about school and his latest gaming stats. He pulled out his phone to show her short soccer clips, videos his friend's dad had recorded just for him—just so he could share them with her. The guilt stabbed at Alice's heart. Her son was showing Rowan pieces of his life, knowing this was the only way she could experience them.

Still, it was sweet watching them interact, Ian trying to pretend this was normal, and Rowan pretending she wasn't exhausted, *oohing* and *ahhing* at all the right times. They slipped into their usual teasing, playful jabs turning into real laughter. But just as always, the laughter would fade, and the facade of normalcy would crumble.

It was well played, though.

They high-fived and fist-bumped—a substitute for a hug, the closest Ian could bring himself to. He didn't like to break down in front of Rowan. Even as her little brother, he was fiercely protective of her, of her fragility. He would walk out of the room with a smile but step into the elevator and sob uncontrollably all the way to the car.

Alice admired his ability to turn his emotions on and off at will. And then, she felt guilty that her fourteen-year-old son had to develop that trait in the first place.

Once Rowan had fallen asleep, Ian and Jonathan moved to leave. They exchanged hugs and kisses, made promises to see each other the next day, and said what had become a routine parting phrase: *Call me if something changes.* It should go without saying, but it was now a necessary ritual—a symptom of their new reality.

They both knew, at this point, that things could only change in one of two ways.

You say what you need to say to get to the next moment in time.

That's how Alice counted time now. *Moment by moment.*

For the longest time, they had lived by the mantra *one day at a time*. That was a distant memory now. Alice had once despised that phrase, but now, she would give anything to have the luxury of it back.

Not long after Jonathan and Ian left, Alice decided there was no point in trying to sleep. She already knew it would evade her again. With Rowan deep in slumber, she slipped off to the lounge for a coffee and a muffin for later.

When she entered the lounge, she noticed Stephen— Kelsey's father—sitting at the table, nursing a cup of coffee. He looked up briefly and offered the smallest, briefest grin before lowering his gaze back to the cup. It was cold—no steam rising from it.

Alice headed straight for the vending machine and shoved her card into the slot, jabbing the button for a banana muffin with more force than necessary.

Stephen sat up straighter and cleared his throat. "Alice, I just want you to know—"

She cut him off, raising a hand. "Yes, Stephen, I know. You agree with the doctors. You know that without those machines keeping her alive, Kelsey would pass within minutes—her heart could save my daughter's life. But *agreeing* with something and *doing* something about it are two very different things. Your words mean nothing to me, and they certainly mean nothing to my daughter."

His shoulders sagged, his fingers tightening around the cup. "It's easier said than done," he murmured. "Karen won't budge, no matter what I say. And believe me, the guilt is all-consuming."

Alice looked at him and *almost* felt sorry for him. *Almost.*

"If it's forgiveness you're after," she said coolly, "there's a chapel on the first floor. Maybe *He* can give you absolution. Or maybe not. But you certainly won't get it from me."

He looked up at her then, tears welling in his eyes. In the smallest of whispers, he said, "I know that. I don't expect it."

Alice said nothing.

She spent every waking hour *hoping, praying* that the girl across the hall would die—that they would either turn off the machines or her body would give up despite them—so her daughter could live.

Maybe *she* needed a visit to the chapel, too.

She picked up her coffee from the Keurig machine and walked out of the lounge without a word or a backward glance.

She had tried to put herself in his position. But when she walked back into Rowan's room and saw her daughter asleep—her waking hours growing fewer and fewer—she felt nothing for Stephen Wentworth.

Or his *conscience*.

She fully realized what kind of person that made her.

And she simply did not care.

The Wentworth's' loss would be Rowan's gain. And Alice didn't care about the consequences. Not for Stephen. Not for Karen. Not for herself.

She looked at her daughter.

Tomorrow, she thought, *my daughter is getting a heart.*

Rowan stirred, caught somewhere between sleep and wakefulness. Alice hurried to her bedside, gently running her fingers through her daughter's hair—just as she had when Rowan was little and had trouble sleeping alone.

Rowan settled for a moment, but then her eyes fluttered open.

"I had fun tonight," she murmured.

Alice smiled. "Me too. But it's nowhere near morning, so get some more rest." She kissed Rowan's forehead.

She moved to get up, but Rowan grabbed her hand.

"What's going on, Momma?" Her voice was quiet but steady. "I know there's something you're not telling me."

Alice froze. *What was she supposed to say? Don't worry, Punkins. Momma will have a new heart for you tomorrow, so get some shut-eye. It's going to be a big day?*

She forced a smile. "Oh, honey… there is. I just don't know how to tell you."

Rowan's expression grew serious. "I'm not a little kid, Momma. Tell me."

Alice let out an exaggerated sigh. "Well, there's no easy way to say this, but… Santa Claus isn't real. Daddy and I put your gifts under the tree. And while we're at it, there's no tooth fairy either." She giggled, trying to lighten the moment.

Rowan didn't smile.

"Look at me, Momma." She tightened her grip on Alice's hand. "I'm not doing so great, am I? You don't have to protect me. I'm dying. I've *been* dying. And I know I probably *will* die."

Alice's breath caught in her throat.

"I can *feel* it," Rowan continued. "I *know* when my heart isn't beating right. Sometimes, I feel like I need to *crawl* into the oxygen machine just to catch a breath. And I'm so tired all the time. My body doesn't have the energy to stay awake for more than an hour or two."

Alice opened her mouth, but Rowan cut her off.

"I need you to know that I'm okay. That I've come to terms with this. We've always been strong in our faith, and even after all this, I *still* am. I'm so tired of being sick, Momma. I almost *welcome* it. Pastor Carl always says we're just visiting here—that life here is temporary. If I go, I'll be free. No more pain. No more struggling to breathe. And no more watching my family lose a piece of themselves every day… because of me."

Alice shook her head. "Rowan, no—"

Rowan squeezed her hand. "I don't want to talk about it anymore. I just need you to know. *If this doesn't work out, I will be okay.* But I need *you* to tell me that *you* will be okay too. I *have* to hear that."

Alice's throat burned. She looked at her daughter—so young, so brave, so heartbreakingly *wise*—and felt an overwhelming swell of pride.

She couldn't imagine a world without her.

But if Alice had *any* doubts about her plan, they were gone at that moment.

Alice gently stroked Rowan's hair, just as she had when she was little. She willed her daughter's breath to keep coming, her heart to keep beating, even though she knew it was a losing battle. Then, all at once, it hit her—*My God, is what this feels like?*

Her mind drifted down the hall to the room where Karen Wentworth sat beside her own child, willing her to breathe on her own, for her heart to beat on its own. The realization struck Alice with force. Kelsey's parents were fighting a losing battle, refusing to let go—wasn't that exactly what she was doing with this plan? Refusing to give up?

Alice took a slow step back from the bed, thinking Rowan had fallen asleep, but just as she turned, Rowan's fingers tightened around her hand.

In a sleepy voice, she murmured, "Promise me, Momma."

She forced herself to speak. "I will be okay," she whispered. "I promise."

Rowan had no idea what that meant.

Neither did Alice.

Not yet.

Chapter 43

T he first thing Alice noticed when she woke up the next morning was that, despite only getting two hours of sleep, she had slept deeply—better than she had in weeks. She had spent most of the night either on her laptop or writing in her journal. Alice didn't understand people who could work through a problem with just thought. For Alice, the written word had always been how she coped. How she dealt with things. She never quite knew how she thought about something until she wrote her feelings out. However, what she had learned changed nothing. She was moving forward.

Alice shifted over to Rowan and gently stroked her head. As her daughter stirred, her eyes fluttered open. As always, there was that fleeting moment of disorientation before the harsh reality settled in. Alice watched the realization dawn on her face, the resignation setting in. But then, like always, Rowan turned to her and smiled.

She was so pale now, her features drawn and shadowed with deep purple smudges beneath her eyes. Alice watched as Rowan instinctively reached for the oxygen meter, turning it up slightly. Every time she did that, Alice felt another crack in her heart.

"Momma, do you remember when I was little, how we used to talk about what I wanted to be when I grew up?" Rowan asked softly.

Alice smiled. "I do remember. Every single morning, the same routine. It broke my heart when you got too old to want to do it anymore."

Rowan grinned. "Well, I've finally decided. I know what I want to be when I grow up."

Alice played along. "Oh yeah? I thought you wanted to be an archaeologist?"

"No, that was yesterday," Rowan teased. "I want to be an astronaut. That's the one. That's what I'm going to be."

"Are you sure this time?" Alice asked with mock skepticism.

Rowan nodded confidently. "Yep. This is it."

"Alright then," Alice said with a chuckle. "Astronaut it is."

Alice's mind drifted back to those mornings when she would brush Rowan's hair, pulling it into a ponytail, a braid, or pigtails while they played this game. Over the years, Rowan had been royalty, a famous actress, a concert pianist, a country singer—her dreams had known no limits. Doing this again now was bittersweet. It felt as though Rowan was trying to live a lifetime's worth of dreams in the small pocket of time she had left.

"Are you hungry?" Alice asked, already knowing the answer.

Rowan shook her head. "Not really."

"How about some juice, at least? A little sugar to wake you up?"

This had become the real morning routine now—Alice coaxing Rowan to eat anything at all. She knew her daughter wasn't trying to be difficult, that she truly had no appetite, but Alice was a mother. And mothers feed their children.

Rowan sighed but relented. "Okay, maybe some OJ. But not from the cafeteria—their juice tastes watered down."

"You got it. One vending machine orange juice, coming right up!" Alice kissed her on the forehead, grabbed her purse, and stepped out of the room.

The hospital was eerily quiet this early in the morning. Most patients were still asleep. Alice took in the soft sea-green walls, the plush chairs lining the hallways, and the little couches placed here and there. This hospital had gone to great lengths to create a calming atmosphere for parents who rarely left their child's side. They allowed food to be brought in, understanding that most families couldn't afford cafeteria meals every day.

By the time Alice returned, juice in hand, Rowan had already drifted back to sleep. She placed a gentle kiss on her forehead and whispered, "Hold on, punkins. Not much longer now."

Alice walked back to the lounge and placed the juice in the small refrigerator on the shelf labeled with their room number. Rowan would want it cold when she woke up. She poured herself a cup of coffee and turned to leave just as the lounge door opened.

Karen walked in, her head down, but when she looked up and saw Alice, her expression hardened instantly.

Alice gripped the door handle, resisting the overwhelming urge to pounce like a cat cornering its prey. Instead, she simply sidestepped Karen, her movements controlled and purposeful. But she felt Karen's eyes burning into her back. Alice turned, meeting her glare with one of her own.

Karen said nothing. She didn't have to. Her face radiated pure loathing.

Alice, however, didn't flinch. She held her gaze letting a slow, knowing smirk curl the corner of her lips—just enough to say, *I know something you don't.*

Karen's expression flickered—first confusion, then surprise, then, for just a moment, fear.

But oddly enough, the satisfaction Alice expected never came.

Lunch had just been served, and for the first time in days, Rowan ate a decent amount. It seemed to give her more energy, and when Jonathan arrived, he was pleasantly surprised to find her awake.

He walked over, kissed her cheek, and said, "Hi, beautiful."

Rowan grinned. "Yep. I take after my dad."

Alice feigned an insulted look, then smiled.

The morning passed without incident. When Rowan fell back asleep around two o'clock, Alice left her a note, telling her she was going to Ian's soccer game but would be back for dinner. wasn't necessary—Jonathan was staying with her—but it comforted Alice, nonetheless.

The night before, Rowan had voiced her frustration over Ian missing his games.

"I get it, Momma," she had said. "I really do. But I'm not the only child. Ian deserves parents, too. He deserves someone on the sidelines cheering for him, just like you sit here every day cheering for me. It doesn't matter why the support is needed—only that you give it in equal measure."

Alice had simply smiled, knowing Rowan was right.

Before leaving, she pulled Jonathan aside into the lounge. It was sometimes used for private meetings between doctors and parents, so when the door was locked, people understood. Though technically, she wasn't supposed to lock it now—there was no doctor present—what she had to say was private.

As soon as they were alone, she rose on her toes and kissed Jonathan softly. Then again.

He looked at her, surprised.

For a moment, Alice realized she couldn't remember the last time she had *really* kissed him—not a quick peck on the cheek in passing, but a real, meaningful kiss. He studied her with a slight look of confusion that quickly turned into that boyish grin—the same grin that had made her fall in love with him all those years ago.

"To what do I owe the honor?" he asked playfully.

She smiled, but inside, her thoughts turned dark. *What will this do to him? Will he still love me after?*

There were no answers to those questions. Only time will tell.

"No special reason," she said, forcing lightness into her voice. "I'm sorry we fought the other day. I wasn't sure you still knew that I love you. Because I do, Jonathan. I really do. I know I pour all my energy into Rowan, and I feel bad about that—not just with you, but with Ian, too."

Jonathan wrapped her in his arms, pulling her close. "I know you love me, Alice. It's obvious. I mean, how could you not? I'm *smoking hot.*"

He grinned, licking the tip of his finger and pressing it to his hip with a mock sizzle sound.

Alice rolled her eyes, laughing.

Then she sobered. "All joking aside, I love you. Just so you know."

But the fear crept in again. *Would he still want to say those words to me after today? After what I'm about to do? Would he ever condone my actions? It didn't matter- Rowan came first.*

She pushed the thought away. She had a soccer game to get to.

***

Alice parked and made her way to the field, choosing to sit in the visiting team's bleachers. She wanted to focus on Ian, not field fifty questions about Rowan. It was already halftime—leaving her daughter's side was getting harder and harder—so when Ian spotted her and ran over, she immediately noticed the alarm on his face.

"Is something wrong with Rowan? Why are you here?"

She smiled at her son. "She's fine, honey. I just wanted to see you play, even if I could only slip out for half the game. I keep hearing about all these impressive plays you make, and I want to see if they're true or just small fish talked up to be whales."

He grinned. "No fish stories here. Just watch and see." With that, he ran back to the field.

Alice watched as Ian moved up and down the field. He was exceptionally good—though she had known that long before today. Still, he wasn't cocky about it. If he scored a goal or an assist, he would simply accept the high five with a shy nod and move on.

When the game ended, he ran back to her, beaming and carrying his gear. "Two goals and three assists!"

Alice smiled. "I guess you weren't telling fish tales after all."

"Pretty awesome, right? Not too shabby, huh?" he said, still grinning.

She ruffled his hair, knowing full well he hated it because, in his words, he was "not a little boy anymore." Still, she did it anyway.

"Nope, not too shabby at all," she said, pulling him into a quick side hug as they walked.

Well, kind of a half hug—because stopping in front of "the guys" for a full embrace just wasn't going to happen. But that was okay. When you're the mother of a teenage boy, you take what you can get.

271

Even though she was enjoying the moment, Alice couldn't shake the growing anxiety pressing against her chest. She was eager to get back to Rowan. Pastor Carl was visiting, and Rowan had once again requested to be alone with him.

She called Jonathan. "I'm on my way back to the hospital."

"I'm heading home," he replied. "Rowan needed a few things, and she's actually a little hungry—which is a good thing, obviously—so I'm going to go through the mountain of donated food and put something together."

"Sounds good," Alice said before hanging up.

She and Ian made their way back to the hospital. When they reached Rowan's room, Alice knocked softly, not wanting to interrupt.

"Come on in, guys. Rowan and I were just wrapping up our talk," Pastor Carl said, glancing at Rowan for confirmation.

"Yep, all done," Rowan said. "How did the game go? Did you win? Do you have any videos?"

Ian nodded. "Yes to both questions."

"I'm going to grab a coffee in the lounge. I saw the game, so I'll leave you two to it," Alice said, stepping back. As she walked out, she only had to take one look at Rowan to know how exhausted she was—but she also knew Rowan would watch every second of those game videos, no matter how tired she felt.

It was as if she was trying to cram ten pounds of memories into a five-pound bag.

And that broke Alice's heart, but she told herself.

Soon, Rowan. Soon.

Chapter 44

Alice walked into the lounge and hefted her bag up on the table. She carried it around with her constantly now, not being able to take the chance for anyone to see what was inside for obvious reasons. After she had made her coffee, she sat down, grabbed a journal, and began to write. Feeling the instant relief she got whenever she had to express her emotions, even if it was only to herself.

A little later, Jonathan came in. Alice, startled, quickly closed her journal.

This act was not lost on Jonathan. "Must be a pretty top-secret book scene you got going on there. You about jumped out of your skin."

"You just startled me, is all, but yes, it's top secret," she said with what she hoped appeared to be a genuine smile. Alice noticed that he had a packed duffle bag with him and gave him a questioning look.

"I need to be there. I'm going to be there all day and night from here on out. If we don't get a heart..." He trailed off for a few seconds before continuing, "Well, you know. I'm going to be there when it happens."

Alice knew she should be comforting, supportive, and caring. But all she saw in that moment was an unexpected obstacle. She hadn't factored in Jonathan staying at the hospital tonight, but she understood his thought process. The clock continued to tick.

When they walked to the room together, Ian was sitting in a chair, focused on his phone, while Rowan lay asleep.

Ian looked up and said, "Rowan told me she wanted to nap before you got back so she could stay awake for dinner and a movie. She asked me to wake her up when you got here."

He started to get up, but Alice raised a hand. "Let's let her sleep."

Ian was having none of it. "Mom, she said she wanted to be woken up, so I'm waking her up. At this point, I think we should let her do whatever she wants."

Alice nodded her approval, and Ian gently shook Rowan's shoulder.

It seemed to Alice that Rowan had told Ian things weren't looking good. No one had explicitly said it to her, but Alice knew her daughter understood exactly what was happening.

She glanced at Rowan's vitals—her heart rate at 56, her oxygen level at 92%. She was fading fast. That meant it was time for dinner and a movie, and then Alice needed to get Ian out of there. Jonathan had arranged for him to stay at his friend Nate's house for a sleepover, but he did not yet feel comfortable with Ian staying alone at the house overnight. Nate's dad had told Jonathan that if anything bad *went down*, he would have Ian here within fifteen minutes. She assumed Jonathan had made those plans because he knew he would be staying at the hospital that night.

Rowan did manage to stay awake through the entire movie. Alice was pleasantly surprised by how much pizza she ate, but within minutes of the movie being over, she was beginning to drift off.

Ian said goodbye, promising to come back the next day. Alice and Jonathan walked him to the elevator.

When they reached the doors, Ian turned to Alice and said, "She didn't look so good, Mom."

It wasn't a question. It was a statement.

"Just a rough patch," Alice replied. "You'll see— tomorrow, she'll be better. She does this sometimes. It's temporary."

But it wasn't temporary.

Alice knew it. Ian knew it. Jonathan knew it.

Still, they kept up the charade because the alternative—acceptance—was not an option.

She hugged Ian longer than usual. And for once, he didn't pull away, didn't roll his eyes, didn't seem embarrassed. Instead, he held on just as tightly.

Jonathan cleared his throat. "I'll drop him off and then come back. Do you need me to stop and get anything?"

Alice shook her head.

Jonathan gave her a quick kiss, pairing it with a wink and a smile. As the elevator doors slid shut, Alice's eyes welled with tears.

When will I get to hug Ian again?

The odds were next to nothing, obviously. But even if she had the chance, would either of them even want her to?

She forced herself to shut her thoughts down. There was no point in wondering. The answer wouldn't change the outcome.

Turning away, she walked back to Rowan's room, hoping—just this once—that her daughter was still asleep.

Alice sat beside her, gently stroking her hand, her mind looping through the same tormenting thought: *How much time do we have left?*

She thought of Kelsey.

And of Karen.

She glanced at Rowan's vitals again and steeled her resolve.

When Rowan was awake, Alice tried not to check the monitors too much. It was easier to ignore the numbers when Rowan was moving, talking—when she *felt* okay or as okay as she could be. But when she was asleep, all Alice had was the cold, hard data flashing across the screen, a numerical countdown to the inevitable.

What must that be like for Karen?

Constantly staring at a screen that never changed— watching the paper scroll endlessly roll out of the brain monitor, waiting for a flicker of activity that would never come.

If that were *her*, would she ever be able to give up?

Would she ever be able to let go?

She had told Jonathan she would do it—that she would make the call if it came to that. That she would give up Rowan's life to save another if it were her daughter in Kelsey's condition.

But was that the truth?

The previous night, Alice had read the same things Karen had—three separate doctors confirming Kelsey was brain dead. And yet, there were stories—miracles, really—of people in comas for years who suddenly, inexplicably, woke up.

Was that what Karen was waiting for?

Was she prepared to sit there, day after day, year after year, praying that Kelsey would be one of *those* people?

And if there was even the smallest chance, even a fraction of a possibility, that she *could* wake up…

Would Alice ever be able to forgive herself?

She looked at her beautiful daughter and knew the answer.

Yes. I would wait forever if it meant she might wake up.

This was an obstacle she hadn't expected.

But she would deal with it.

She had no choice.

"The answer will present itself" Alice thought again as her mind circled back.

Alice reached for her journal, knowing it would be another sleepless night. She tore out all the other pages written on and shoved them in her satchel.

Kelsey wouldn't be helping Rowan.

But Kelsey's *mother* would.

She's been the obstacle all along.

And she brought this on herself.

Chapter 45

When Jonathan returned to the room; he found Alice sitting in the window seat, furiously writing in her journal. She glanced up briefly, gave him a small smile, then returned her focus to the page, her pen moving in quick, deliberate strokes.

"Got something you need to work out, do you?" Jonathan asked.

Alice looked up and smiled. "Yes, I guess you could say that."

She never had to worry about her journal with Jonathan. He would never betray her privacy. Instead, he walked over to Rowan's bedside, picked up her hand with one of his, and gently brushed her cheek with the other. He looked at Alice and nodded his head towards the door. She got up and followed him into the lounge.

They sat together, and he took hold of Alice's hand and said, "Remember when we brought her home? God, we were so clueless. I mean, we barely even got her home."

Alice remembered it clearly. It was December, and though they lived in the South, that day had been unseasonably cold. Nothing extreme, but when you lived in the South, fifty degrees felt like winter. She had dressed Rowan in a pink fleece jumper and then swaddled her in a fleece baby blanket. Jonathan had gone downstairs ahead of her to install the car seat in the SUV. They had kept it in the trunk, ready to go, but Rowan had arrived nine days early, and they hadn't actually set it up yet.

"How hard can it be?" Jonathan had said confidently as he left the hospital room.

Not long after, a nurse arrived with a wheelchair to escort Alice and Rowan down to the lobby.

Then came the real challenge—getting Rowan into the car seat. Through the glass hospital doors, Alice could see Jonathan, all six foot three of him, hunched over in the back of the SUV, fighting with the car seat.

At first, the nurse chuckled at the sight, but as ten more minutes passed, she stopped laughing and started checking her watch. Alice, still seated in the wheelchair, felt frustration building. She wanted to scream at Jonathan to *hurry up*.

Finally, the nurse sighed. "Those things can be tricky. Technically, we're not supposed to help install them—hospital liability and all that—but maybe I could just stand *close enough* to offer some direction."

Alice, utterly embarrassed, nodded gratefully. Three minutes later, after Jonathan had struggled with it for twenty, the car seat was finally secured.

Alice buckled Rowan in and climbed into the front seat. Jonathan, still uneasy, checked all five buckles, then tugged at the base of the seat to make sure it was latched properly. They had barely driven twenty feet before Jonathan abruptly pulled over, jumped out, and climbed into the backseat.

"Jonathan, what are you doing?" Alice asked, exasperated.

"I just need to check something." He yanked at the top of the car seat, testing its stability.

Alice sighed. "I already checked everything when I put her in."

Jonathan looked sheepish. "I just think, for now, we should double-check everything. I *swear* the top of that seat moved when I made that turn."

Alice smiled. That was the moment she knew—they would figure it out together.

She came back to the present and said, "Yes, I remember. But we did get her home. From there, we figured things out through trial and error, and it worked out fine. With Ian, though, we basically let him juggle knives."

Jonathan laughed. "Yep. Apples to oranges."

Jonathan, still holding Alice's hand, spoke in a broken whisper. "You don't think this was something we did? Something we *didn't* do? Some defect we missed?"

Alice moved beside him, leaning her head against his arm. "No. This wasn't something we did or didn't do. We can't let ourselves think that way. It's just... the luck of the draw."

Jonathan's shoulders shook as he began to cry—softly at first, then with quiet, gut-wrenching sobs. "I can't do this, Alice. I *can't*. I won't survive this. This isn't how it's supposed to go. Parents go first, not their children."

He seemed to shrink further into the chair, burying his face in his hands. "I don't know what to do. I try to picture life without her, and I *can't*. And then I feel like a terrible dad because Ian is still here, but it doesn't feel like he's enough to fill that void. How can I feel that way about my own son?"

Alice wrapped her arms around him. "It's going to be fine. It's going to work out."

She knew he thought she meant *they* would survive losing Rowan. But that wasn't what she meant at all. For a fleeting moment, she considered telling him everything. But she *couldn't*. She couldn't risk him trying to stop her. She couldn't see what her own future held, but she *could* see what Jonathan and Ian's would be—and she refused to let it be a future without Rowan.

"Ok, pity party over. I'm going back to Rowan. Get it together before you head back, okay?"

All Jonathan could muster up was a nod of agreement.

When Alice entered the room, she saw that Rowan was still sleeping. She looked at her daughter, so beautiful and so full of light. A light that Alice was determined would not go out.

It's time.

Chapter 46

While Rowan lay sleeping, Alice carefully slipped out of the bed and returned to her perch by the window. She picked up her journal, flipping to a fresh page, and began writing. About an hour later, she finished, a strange sense of accomplishment washing over her.

The door opened, and Genny entered to change Rowan's IV bag. She glanced at Jonathan, who was fast asleep on the cot, then gave Alice a small smile.

"I knew when he came in this morning that he hadn't slept much, if at all, last night," Alice said softly. "Given the situation, it's hard for either of us to leave."

Genny gave a knowing nod. "I've been doing this for over ten years, and it never gets easier. They tell us to be clinical and avoid getting attached, but that's easier said than done. This one here—" she gestured toward Rowan "—won my heart the minute I met her. She's one brave young lady."

Having settled Rowan, Genny turned back to Alice with a wink. "I'll find an extra cot for you, too, if you want."

Alice shook her head. "No need." It wouldn't be the first time Genny had come in and found Alice curled up next to Rowan in bed. She never reprimanded her for it, though.

"Alright, but if you change your mind, I'm here until nine," Genny said. "I take all the overtime they throw my way."

Alice smiled and nodded. As Genny walked to the door, Alice called after her. "Can you leave it open? It's a little stuffy in here."

"You got it." Genny smiled before disappearing down the hall.

Instead of sitting by Rowan's head, Alice repositioned her chair at the foot of the bed—this spot gave her a clear view of Kelsey's room. It had been a few hours, and Stephen was still inside. Alice knew he usually left by eight; he had no choice but to keep working to support his family. It was a race now—to see if he would leave before Rowan woke up again.

Fifteen minutes later, she had her answer. Stephen kissed Karen at the door and then made his way toward the elevators.

Alice turned back to her daughter, checking her heart rate and her oxygen levels. She steeled herself. Then, leaning down, she kissed Rowan's forehead and whispered, "I love you, punkins. Momma's going to make it better."

She stood, barely feeling the weight of the gun in her pocket. It was so light she instinctively checked to make sure it was still there.

The nurse's station was quiet, with only two nurses on duty. They moved between rooms, focused on their rounds. Alice walked past them without a single glance in her direction. Genny had just stepped away, a tray of small medication cups in hand, ready to make her next set of rounds.

Alice slipped into Kelsey's room and quietly shut the door behind her.

Karen looked up immediately, her expression shifting from confusion to alarm as Alice pulled out the gun. She didn't scream. She didn't move. She simply stared at it, still holding Kelsey's hand, her mind working to make sense of what she was seeing.

"Why are you in here?" Karen asked, her voice tight, her eyes locked on the gun.

Alice squared her shoulders, stepping further into the room. "Because you've left me no choice," she said evenly. "I told you I wouldn't let my daughter die, and I meant it."

Karen's confusion gave way to panic. She understood now.

"Please don't do this," Karen pleaded. "Just—please."

Alice's voice remained steady. "As I said, you've left me no choice. My daughter has days at most. Since you won't see reason, this is the way it has to be. Your daughter has been dead for—"

"She is *not* dead!" Karen interrupted, her voice desperate.

Alice's tone hardened. "She *is*," she countered. "For over two months, she has languished on these machines— machines that only keep her heart beating. A heart my daughter *needs*."

Karen's hands trembled, but her voice was defiant. "You can't possibly think you'll get away with this."

Alice gave a small, chilling smile. "I know exactly how this plays out. But in the end, my daughter will be *alive*. I don't care what happens to me."

286

And that was the truth. Alice had no idea what her fate would be. What her family would think, or even how God would judge her. It didn't matter.

Karen's eyes darted toward the call button, and Alice caught the movement immediately.

"Don't," Alice warned. "Back away from the bed."

Karen hesitated, her body half-turned toward the nurse's station.

Tears welled in Karen's eyes. Please don't take her from me. I don't care what they say," she pleaded. "They don't *know* my daughter. I do. People have woken up from comas before. I've read about it. It happens."

"I get it," Alice said, her voice eerily calm. "You love her. You're her mother. You're supposed to *fight* for her. But this—" she lifted the gun slightly "—this is *me* fighting for *my* daughter. I have no intention of shooting Kelsey. I did, at one time, but I changed my mind. You have already lost your child, as I have said before, and I hold fast to that opinion. However, as you say some people, albeit a very small percentage of people, do mysteriously come out of comas. I did some research as well. Therefore, I will not take away even a miniscule of that chance, and I will not make you watch her die twice. I would imagine watching someone die would be very traumatic. Something a person would have to live with forever. However, Kelsey *sees* and *hears* nothing. You brought this on yourself. With that being said, Alice motioned with the gun for Karen to back away from Kelsey.

Then, Karen's breath hitched, her eyes widening as realization set in.

"Why *now*?" Karen whispered. "And why *here*?"

"Because of the *golden hour*," Alice replied.

Karen frowned. "The *what*?"

"The golden hour is a medical term," Alice explained. "Once a heart is harvested, it needs to be implanted within four to six hours. But the odds of a successful transplant are highest if implantation begins within sixty minutes." She took another step forward. "The donor and recipient are already here, in the *same* hospital. A heart, that of a woman, is just the right size and the blood types are compatible. That's what makes this the perfect time. The perfect place. That's why *now*. That's why *here*. The answer has presented itself. Kelsey will not help save Rowan, but you will. It's all about the golden hour." Alice waved the gun again. "This will effectively start the clock. Do you understand?"

Karen's shoulders sagged, her body trembling. She looked down at Kelsey, then back at Alice and nodded her head.

"Say it." Alice commanded.

Her voice was barely above a whisper. "Yes, the golden hour. I understand. Can I at least call Stephen?"

"No time," Alice said firmly. "Move away from Kelsey, back against the wall. Now."

Karen didn't move. She was still *trying*—still clinging to hope, still searching for an escape.

Alice's own thoughts went to Rowan..*always* to Rowan…

Hiking up Travers Trail.

Racing Ian down the slopes.

Cheering under the Friday night lights.

Graduating college.

Falling in love.

Getting married.

Having children...

A whole lifetime stolen.

Alice clenched the gun tighter, bracing herself.

Karen opened her mouth—to argue, to plead, to beg. A look of pure terror on her face.

Alice raised the gun higher and pulled the trigger.

Chapter 47

T he shot rang out, deafening in the small hospital room. Almost instantly, Genny burst through the door, her face a mask of pure horror. She screamed—once, twice—before the sound of rushing footsteps filled the hallway as more staff arrived. Dr. Mason and Rebecca, the other nurse on duty, heard the commotion and ran toward the room. Amidst the chaos, urgent words cut through the air:

"Sixty minutes! The golden hour! Please, hurry— hurry now!"

Dr. Mason pushed through the crowd, scanning the room, his brain struggling to process what he was seeing. And then, the physician in him took over.

He pulled out his pocket watch. "Ok, everyone, it is now 8:57 pm, the clock is ticking. Genny, call down to the OR—get two surgical suites ready, one for the harvest, the other for transplant—stat!"

Genny's eyes darted around the scene once more before she turned and sprinted out of the room.

He grabbed Rebecca. "Call security. They need to cordon off this room and notify the police. Other than the orderlies coming in with a gurney, this is a crime scene—no one goes in or out."

Rebecca, momentarily frozen in shock, blinked, then nodded before rushing off to carry out his orders. Within minutes, security officers arrived, securing the room as police were told.

Down the hall, Jonathan came running, his face pale with panic. But before he could get far, two security guards blocked his path.

"Sir, you need to stand back," one of them, the larger of the two, instructed firmly.

Jonathan's heart pounded. "What's going on? I heard a gunshot!"

The guard's expression remained impassive. "I'm not at liberty to say, but this is a crime scene. Please return to your room."

Dr. Mason spotted Jonathan and rushed toward him. "Go back to Rowan's room. We're coming to get her now—we have a donor. But we need to move fast."

Jonathan's breath caught in his throat. "You're taking her *now*?" His eyes darted wildly. "But Alice—she's not in the room. I don't know where she is, but she'll want to see Rowan before surgery. And Rowan will want to see *her*."

Dr. Mason hesitated. He understood. He really did. But there wasn't time.

"We don't have time to get into it right now," he said, his voice tight.

Jonathan's pleading gaze locked onto his, desperate for answers. Dr. Mason exhaled sharply and made a decision. He took Jonathan by the arm and pulled him toward the door of the hospital room.

"Look inside," he said.

Jonathan turned, peering into the room. His face drained of all color.

"Oh my God..." His voice was barely a whisper. He stared at the scene before him, eyes flitting from the people in the room to the chaos unfolding. Then, the realization hit.

His knees nearly buckled. "Alice... what have you done?"

Several orderlies rushed into the room with a gurney, their voices rapid, overlapping. Nurses barked urgent orders. Over the din, Jonathan heard a faint, trembling voice from inside.

"Oh, Jonathan... I'm so sorry. I am *so* sorry. But I couldn't let her go. I couldn't let her die. I *couldn't*."

Jonathan instinctively moved toward the room, but Dr. Mason grabbed his arm, stopping him.

"No," Dr. Mason said firmly. "You *can't* go in there. As I said, it's a crime scene, and we need to harvest the heart now. You need to be with Rowan."

Jonathan's head whipped toward him. "But Alice— please—"

Dr. Mason tightened his grip on Jonathan's shoulders, forcing him to focus. "What's done is done," he said, his voice steady but urgent. He motioned toward the room. "*That— this*—is now a matter for the authorities. *My* concern is Rowan. Regardless of how it came about, we have a heart for her, and we need to move *now*."

Jonathan just stood there, paralyzed.

Dr. Mason's voice softened only slightly. "Go be with your daughter. You only have about five minutes before she's taken down for surgery. It's going to take five to seven hours to complete. The police are already on their way. You can deal with all of this *after*." He gestured toward the room once more.

Jonathan hesitated for only a moment longer before turning and running back toward Rowan's room. He arrived just as nurses and orderlies worked quickly to untangle the wires and lead from her machines, preparing her for transport.

Rowan looked up at him, blinking sleepily. He forced a smile, though he felt like he might collapse at any moment.

"I guess today's the day my baby girl gets her new heart," he said, his voice shaking despite his best effort.

Rowan gave him a small, tired smile. "There was a loud noise. It woke me up. What was it?"

Jonathan's breath hitched. "It was nothing," he lied. "Some big piece of equipment fell over or something—I'm not sure."

She studied his face for a moment but didn't press the issue. Instead, her brows knit together in concern. "Where's Momma? Does she know this is happening?"

Jonathan swallowed hard.

Rowan turned toward the nurses. "I don't want to go until I see my momma."

Genny knelt beside her, forcing a reassuring smile. "I know you do, honey," she said gently, glancing at Jonathan before continuing. "But… she's not here right now, and we *can't* wait. This surgery needs to happen *now*."

Rowan's lip quivered. "But—"

Genny squeezed her hand. "Sweetheart, your mom and dad come and go from this hospital. How upset would your mom be if you delayed this surgery just because she wasn't here?"

Rowan turned to Jonathan, searching his face. "You'll find her? She'll be here when I wake up, right?"

Jonathan's throat felt like it was closing. He took her hand and squeezed.

"I *promise* she'll be here when you wake up," he said, forcing every ounce of conviction he could muster into those words.

Rowan nodded, her trust in him unwavering.

As they wheeled her toward the door, he leaned down, kissed her forehead, and whispered, "It's all going to be okay now. Everything's going to work out. I love you."

She smiled weakly, squeezing his hand once more before they pushed her out into the hallway.

Jonathan turned away, his body trembling. The tears came slowly at first, but soon, they wracked his entire body, gut-wrenching sobs that echoed through the quiet hospital room. He didn't even attempt to go back to Kelsey's room. He knew they would not let him in and most definitely not to see Alice.

After several minutes, he pulled himself together, wiping his face roughly with the back of his hand. He moved toward the chair by Rowan's bed, ready to collapse. That's when he saw it.

Alice's tote bag.

It sat on the chair, exactly where she had left it. He reached for it, intending to move it aside, but as he lifted it, something slipped out.

A white envelope. Then another. And another.

Jonathan's fingers trembled as he picked up the envelope with his name on it.

His emotions, already raw, threatened to split him open completely.

He knew what this was. *Justification.* Alice's reasoning. Her *explanation* for what she had done.

He wasn't sure if he could bear to read it.

How could she even *try* to justify something like this? How do you make sense of the *unthinkable*?

His hands clenched around the envelope.

Because she knew I would have stopped her.

Jonathan exhaled shakily. He knew he needed to call Ian and get him to the hospital. He knew the police would want to speak with him soon. And more than anything, he knew that Rowan was in surgery, undergoing a life-or-death operation that could go either way.

But the longer he held the letter, the heavier it felt.

Jonathan walked to the window, staring out into the night. Then, taking a deep breath, he tore open the envelope and began to read.

Chapter 48

Rowan was in surgery for a little over seven hours. Now, she was back in her hospital room, slowly emerging from the anesthesia. Her eyes fluttered before opening fully. The first thing she saw was Jonathan, who gave her a warm smile. "Hey, punkins... they must have really knocked you out. You've been asleep for hours since the surgery."

Rowan rubbed her eyes, letting out a long yawn before reaching for the button to raise the hospital bed. She turned her head toward her father.

"Where's Momma? Where's Ian?"

Jonathan's smile remained, but there was something weighted behind it. "Ian just ran down to the cafeteria. He's such a weirdo; he actually *likes* the food here.

Rowan chuckled and noticed he did not smile at his own joke, which he usually did. "So where's Momma?"

Jonathan took a deep breath, exhaling slowly. "That's... something we need to talk about, honey."

A crease of confusion appeared on Rowan's face. "Talk about what? Why isn't she here?"

Jonathan lowered his gaze, his fingers steepled together as he tried to find the right words. But there was no easy way to say it. No way to soften the blow.

"Rowan, your mom did something, and... it's not good." He hesitated, struggling against the lump rising in his throat. "I mean, something good came from it, but—"

Rowan's brows furrowed further. "What do you mean something bad? I don't understand. Why isn't she here? Where is she? You promised she would be here when I got out of surgery."

Jonathan lifted his head, his tear-filled eyes locking onto hers. His hands trembled as he reached for hers, pressing a soft kiss on her fingers. Then, with infinite tenderness, he guided her hand to rest over her heart.

"She's here," he whispered. "Just like I promised. She's right here with you... always."

My Dearest Rowan,

You are angry. That's not a question—it's a statement. And it's okay to be mad. But please, hear me out. I need you to understand.

You know I didn't become your momma when I gave birth to you. No, it was long before that. The moment that second little pink line appeared, I loved you. It's strange, isn't it? How can you love something so much when you've never even seen it, never held it? But I did. I knew. I don't know how, but I knew you were a girl. My baby girl.

I called your daddy at work to tell him; then I called everyone we knew. He cautioned me to wait for the blood test to be sure, but men—they don't get it. I already knew.

That same day, I went straight to the mall. I stopped at the bookstore (you know, the one that gives out lollipops to the kids) and headed straight for the family health section. I grabbed *What to Expect When You're Expecting*, a baby name book, and a guide on making homemade organic baby food. I sat right there on the floor, flipping through *What to Expect* for at least fifteen minutes until an employee came over. She tried to be polite, but I could tell she wanted me to buy the books or leave.

I must have spent over a hundred dollars that day, but I didn't care. Afterward, I went to the food court for a coffee— then immediately threw it away when I read that caffeine wasn't good for you. (I had gotten that far in the book while still at the bookstore.) So, I bought a bottle of water instead.

I remember standing in the crowded line, and someone bumped into me. Without thinking, my arm flew to my stomach, shielding you. You weren't much bigger than a grain of rice, but instinct took over—Momma Bear protecting her cub.

I watched everything I ate. I exercised—not too much, but not too little. I took every vitamin the doctor recommended. I even started moving the seat back in the car, worried that if I got into an accident, you'd hit the steering wheel. (Your daddy got a big laugh out of that one.)

After my baby shower, I washed all your tiny clothes in baby detergent and neatly folded them away in your nursery. Everything was in its place—everything but you. At night, when I couldn't sleep, I sat in the rocking chair and read bedtime stories aloud because I had learned you could hear me from the womb. (Maybe that's why you love to read so much?)

I thought about you every second of every day.

I was nervous about the delivery, and it wasn't easy, believe me. But when they placed you in my arms, all the pain, all the sleepless nights, all the fear of *How am I going to do this?*—it all disappeared.

It was just you and me.

Your daddy later told me he had asked to hold you, but I just pulled you closer. The nurse told me he laughed and said, "Well, okay... maybe later then." I knew I should have let him hold you, but what if he dropped you? What if he bumped your head or breathed on you wrong? I had to protect you. It sounds silly now, but at the time, nothing else in the world mattered.

The nurse told him most new mothers are like that.

But I wasn't a *new* mother. I had been your mother for nine months already.

And Punkins, that never changes. That fierce instinctual pull.. that never stops, Rowan. That never goes away. Whether you are two, twenty-two, or fifty-two, it never goes away.

No matter how old you get, no matter how independent you become, that feeling only grows stronger. I *could not* let you die. Please try to understand that. If I had let you go, half of me would have died with you anyway.

As selfish as it sounds, for Daddy and Ian, I would have never been the same. The wife and mother they knew would have been gone. I know Ian is angry—he has every right to be—but in time, he will understand. He will know I would have done the same for him without hesitation.

Sixteen years was *not* enough.

I pictured your future—your graduations, your first kiss, your prom, your wedding, and yes, your first child. I saw all of it... and then I pictured *nothing*. And my heart, already breaking, shattered completely.

I could not reconcile your *existence* with *nonexistence.*

Forty-three years had to be enough for me. And when I truly thought about it... it *was* enough.

When I envisioned your life, there was too much left for you to live. You had to stay.

This choice—it wasn't new for me. It was me placing a protective hand over my stomach. It was me straining organic apricots for your baby food. It was me putting

301

bumpers on every sharp corner in the house. It was me throwing that coffee away.

You might not see it that way, but to me, it was the same.

There is no *me* without *you.*

One day, you'll be a momma too. None of this will make sense to you now, but just wait.

I ask only one thing—live your life. Don't let my absence weigh you down. That would defeat the whole purpose.

This is what *I* wanted.

I am at *peace*.

I am *happy* with my decision.

And I will still be with you. I will be the cool breeze on your face when the sun is too hot. I will be the butterfly that lands on your knee as you lace up your hiking boots. I will be the bird that lingers longer and a bit closer than it should.

I will be there on your wedding day. I will be there when you have children of your own.

And when you must take your own walk through the valley—seventy or so years from now, God willing—I will be waiting for you.

God blessed me with the greatest gift when He made me your momma. And I am still your momma.

Keep your faith, Rowan. Never lose sight of it.

I will see you again someday, and that's a promise. If you ever feel alone, if you ever need me, just reach up and touch your heart—because I am with you. I'll never be more than a heartbeat away, always.

Love,

Momma

***

Six Months Later

T he sky was clear, not a cloud in sight. The sun blazed overhead, making it hotter and more humid than expected. As Jonathan and the kids hiked up Travers Trail, he kept a watchful eye on Rowan, though he tried to do so discreetly. She had been adamant about taking her recovery seriously, promising to follow every directive from her doctors, and so far, Jonathan had been impressed with her commitment.

Losing Alice had been hard on all of them, but he knew it had hit Rowan the hardest. Many nights, Jonathan would pass by her room and hear her softly crying. He never intervened, understanding that she needed to process her grief in her own way, on her own terms. He had learned that grief had no rulebook—no checklist to complete that would allow you to simply *wrap it up* and move on. Grief was deeply personal and unique to each individual. It was a living thing that had to be acknowledged before it could fade. You couldn't ignore it or shove it aside; you had to let yourself *feel* it— whenever, wherever, and for however long it demanded.

The hole left behind by loss never truly disappeared. At best, over time, it would be filled—not completely, but enough—with memories that brought more smiles than tears. Mourning would eventually transform into remembrance, the kind that allowed for laughter instead of pain. One day, moments that once hurt too much to recall would become cherished memories they could embrace.

Rowan had started grief counselling, which seemed to help her open up. The loss of her mother was overwhelming, but she also struggled with survivor's guilt—an understandable weight given that

Alice had taken her own life *for* Rowan. Jonathan's grief was profound, but he couldn't begin to fathom the burden his daughter carried. The best he could do was hope that, in time, she would understand that Alice had done what she believed was necessary.

Talking to someone outside of the family had been good for her, and if Jonathan was honest with himself, he was relieved. He had his own struggles, and he often became too emotional to be the steady support Rowan needed. Ian, on the other hand, had processed things differently. Surprisingly, he hadn't been as angry as Jonathan had expected. He had always been a practical kid, and the "*Mom-o-Gram*, as he called it, helped him make peace with it. The few times Jonathan had tried to get him to open up, Ian simply smiled and shook his head.

"I'm okay, Dad. I mean, yeah, it's hard, and sometimes I get angry... but only at the situation. That it had to happen this way. But when I really thought about it, it wasn't that shocking. It was just... "*Mom being Mom*."

As the months passed, life continued. They did their best to move forward, just as Alice had asked them to. They spent time together, and slowly, laughter and playful banter began to creep back into their days. Each chuckle, each light-hearted moment, strengthened their resolve to honor Alice's last wish: *to live their lives fully, even without her.*

As winter gave way to spring and spring turned to summer, they worked on keeping that promise. This weekend, they were hiking to Travers Lake for a camping trip—their first without Alice. That made it all the more important. They were determined not just to live *without* her but to live *for* her.

As they reached the bend at the top of the trail, Rowan stopped and slid her pack off her shoulders.

"Whew! I need a quick breather," she said, exhaling deeply.

Jonathan let out an exaggerated sigh, dramatically wiping his brow with his sleeve. "Oh, thank God. Yes, a break, please. I know I *look* like a buff Adonis, but I'll let you in on a little secret—" he leaned in conspiratorially, "I have the stamina of an eighty-year-old woman. But that's just between you and me."

Rowan laughed. "Don't worry, *Adonis*, your secret's safe with me."

They both sank onto a couple of boulders, pulling out their canteens. Jonathan had packed extra water for Rowan. Although she had a new heart, she hadn't completely outgrown her POTS, and she might never. Fortunately, it has been downgraded to mild, causing only occasional lightheadedness that never lasted long. Most importantly, it no longer sent her heart into dangerous rhythms. With a low dose of blood pressure medication, continued hydration, and salt intake, Dr. Mason assured them she could live a normal life.

Ian, who had been far ahead of them on the trail, turned back when he heard them laughing. "What the hell are you two *grandmas* doing back there? It's hotter than hell, and I am *balls-deep* in sweat up here."

Rowan doubled over, roaring with laughter. Jonathan *should* have reprimanded the foul language and crude anatomy reference—Alice certainly would have. A lecture about inappropriate humor followed by the ever-present threat of a *stern talking-to* from Pastor.

Carl usually did the trick, at least temporarily. But Jonathan had seen Alice turn away more than once, barely suppressing a smile after Ian's antics. *The bottom line—he made everyone laugh, appropriate or not. And in Alice's eyes, her baby boy could do no wrong.*

"Rowan needs a break, Ian, so your *balls* will have to wait."

Another burst of laughter from Rowan. It was music to Jonathan's ears.

Ian threw up his hands in mock exasperation before turning back around. Jonathan knew it was his way of saying *I got you* without actually saying the words.

Rowan took another sip of water, watching as Ian began snapping selfies. No doubt, he was already planning to post them on Snapchat and Instagram—angled just right to make it seem as if he were conquering Mount Everest rather than a modest Georgia hiking trail.

She smirked and took another sip. "Have you noticed that most of his jokes involve his *balls*?"

Jonathan nearly spit out his water, laughing. "I have. I wonder if he'd even be *capable* of telling jokes if he didn't have *balls*."

Rowan burst into another fit of laughter. Then, for a while, they simply sat in comfortable silence, sipping their water.

"So... you doing okay?" Jonathan asked. "We don't *have* to stay the whole weekend if you get tired. Ian's going camping next weekend with Nate and his family at Amicalola Falls, so..."

Rowan shook her head. "No, I'm fine. It's just hotter than we expected. I want to stay the whole weekend. I *can* if I listen to my body—just like Dr. Mason said."

Jonathan nodded, swelling with pride at her growing maturity.

Rowan rummaged through her pack and popped a salt tablet from its blister pack. As she put it away, Jonathan caught sight of the waterproof bag tucked inside. The corner of an envelope peeked out—the letter from Alice. He knew she carried it *everywhere*. To school. To cheer practice. It had a permanent place on her nightstand. Sometimes, he'd find it open as if she had fallen asleep reading it.

Sometimes, the sight of it made him smile. Other times, it made him ache.

He no longer tried to control those emotions. He just let them come.

"Alright, people, let's *move*!" Ian called from up ahead. "It's still hotter than hell, and by the time we get to the lake, it's gonna be as dried up as Aunt Laura's Thanksgiving turkey and about as useful as tits on a teddy bear."

Jonathan and Rowan exchanged glances before dissolving into laughter.

"Well," Rowan said, wiping tears of mirth from her eyes, "I guess he *can* tell jokes that don't involve his *balls*."

Jonathan shook his head. "Yeah. *Barely.* But it's good—those ball jokes were getting stale. A comedian of his caliber can *do better*."

Rowan stood, shouldering her pack. "He's right, though. It's *so* hot. That lake is going to feel amazing."

As she adjusted her second strap, a sudden cool breeze swept over her. It came out of nowhere, rolling over her from head to toe, lifting strands of her hair. She closed her eyes, tilting her face into it, a peaceful smile spreading across her lips.

"Thanks, Momma," she whispered. "I love you too."

Epilogue

Alice arrived at the doctor's office about twenty minutes early. Truth be told, she was feeling anxious about what the doctor would say regarding all the tests she had ordered. The doctor had insisted on being thorough, given Alice's persistent symptoms, and had assured her it was best to evaluate every possible angle.

Jonathan had wanted to come with her, but she had convinced him otherwise.

"We're just going over the results," she had told him. "Dr. Wyngarden thinks the migraines are all stress-related— honestly, with everything going on, it makes perfect sense. Besides, we agreed that one of us should always be with Rowan."

He had been reluctant but eventually relented, though she could tell he wasn't happy about it.

Sitting in the waiting room, Alice tried to distract herself. First, she picked up the book she had brought, but she couldn't focus. Then she mindlessly scrolled through Facebook, not really reading any posts—just keeping her hands busy, anything to keep the gnawing anxiety at bay.

Thirty minutes later, a nurse called her name. She followed her into the exam room, where the usual routine unfolded—vitals taken, chart updated. The room smelled of disinfectant, and its walls were covered with colorful diagrams of the human anatomy. Various pamphlets sat in holders, detailing an array of medical conditions.

After the nurse left, Alice lay back on the exam table and closed her eyes. She was exhausted—not just physically but emotionally and mentally drained. This wasn't the kind of exhaustion a nap could fix. It was the kind that settled deep in the bones, the kind that no amount of rest could shake.

Before she had much time to think, the door opened, and the doctor walked in, a warm smile on her face.

"Good morning, Mrs. Miller. How are you feeling today?"

Alice sat up, smoothing down her blouse. "Actually, I feel great. I haven't had any issues this past week. Maybe it really was just stress, like you said. How did all my tests look? There were quite a few."

She rolled her stool closer and then glanced at Alice's chart on the computer screen. "Yes, I ordered quite a few tests, given the severity and frequency of your symptoms, especially considering how suddenly they appeared."

Alice nodded, waiting for her to continue.

"Well, the good news is that everything came back completely normal. Your scans were clear, and the lab work all came back within normal limits. Based on these results, I believe your symptoms were brought on by stress—understandable, given your daughter's health scare and the writer's block you mentioned."

Alice straightened slightly, forcing a bright smile. "Yes, everything seems to be settling down now. Rowan is doing much better. It turned out to be a really nasty infection, so she needed hospitalization, but she's..fine now and recovering. I feel like I can finally breathe again. And with that weight lifted, I've actually been writing again—several chapters, in fact. My editor is thrilled since I was pushing my deadline extensions a bit too far."

The doctor smiled. "That's great to hear. I also don't think it's a coincidence that since I put you on a low dose of Klonopin for anxiety, your symptoms have improved. If it's been working, you might consider keeping it on an as-needed basis, just to help when things get overwhelming."

Alice thought about the bottle of pills she never picked up from the pharmacy.

Alice hesitated before nodding. "Maybe. We'll see."

The doctor gave her a reassuring look. "Of course. Just know it's an option. However, being a cardiologist, I would have to refer you back to Dr. Wyngarden if you wanted to stay on the Klonopin. So, medically speaking, though, I don't see anything wrong with your heart at all. You're in excellent health."

Alice exhaled, relief washing over her. "That's great to hear. And my blood type?"

Dr. Osborn glanced back at the screen. "You're type O-negative, just as you thought, which is great if you're a blood donor for someone else, as it is known as the universal blood type and can be transfused into anyone. However, not so great for you if you were to ever need a transfusion yourself as it is hard to come by. We have wallet-sized blood-type cards at the front desk. I recommend taking one and keeping it in your wallet in case, well, God forbid, you would need that.

"Yes, God forbid..." Alice said.

Dr. Osborn continued, "Given the severity of your symptoms and how suddenly they appeared, I'd like to schedule a follow-up in six months just to check-in. But if anything starts up again before then, please don't hesitate to make an appointment."

Alice slid off the exam table, reaching for her bag. "I appreciate it, Dr. Osborn, but that won't be necessary."

Dr. Osborn tilted her head. "Oh? Why's that?"

Alice smiled, adjusting the strap on her shoulder. "I'll be leaving the area."

Surprise flickered across Dr. Osborn's face. "Oh, so you are not originally from here?"

Alice's smile deepened, though there was a hint of something unreadable in her expression. "No, not originally. My time here was always meant to be temporary. And soon... it may be time for me to go home."

Acknowledgments

First and foremost, yes, this book was based on a true story, my true story, and Rowan's true story, up to the ending anyway, obviously!

I want to thank you, the reader. Writing this book has been an incredible journey, and the fact that you've taken the time to read it means the world to me. As this is my first book, your support and feedback are invaluable.

If you enjoyed the book, I would truly appreciate it if you could take a moment to leave a review. Your words not only help other readers discover the book but also encourage and inspire me as I continue writing. You can leave a review on Amazon, Goodreads, or your favorite book retailer's website.

I'd also love to hear from you! Feel free to reach out to me at tghjmiller@gmail.com—whether it's to share your thoughts, ask questions, or just to say hello. visit my website at www.authorjannamiller.com for announcements on upcoming books and blogs. Your support makes all the difference!

With gratitude,

Janna Miller.

About the Author

J anna Miller was born and raised in Baltimore, Maryland, but has called West Virginia home for the past twenty-five years. She and her husband have built a life there, raising their two children together.

As a writer, Janna gravitates toward literary fiction, using storytelling as a way to explore deep, meaningful themes. This book, based on a true story, was inspired by her unwavering belief in the power of parental advocacy. She hopes to illustrate the importance of trusting your instincts—especially when it comes to your children. No one knows a child better than a parent, and sometimes, even those with extensive experience can get it wrong. Janna's message is clear: It is okay to question, to push for answers, and to stand firm when you feel unheard.

Beyond writing, Janna enjoys quilting, crocheting, gardening, and spending time with her family, finding joy and creativity in both her craft and her loved ones.

www.ingramcontent.com/pod-product-compliance
Lightning Source LLC
Chambersburg PA
CBHW032148190626
46814CB00005BA/1889